FREEZER BURN

A Novel

by
Gayle Carline

Published in the USA by Dancing Corgi Press

This is a work of fiction. All characters, organizations, places, and events portrayed in this novel are either products of the author's imagination or are used fictitiously.

Cover art by Joe Felipe of Market Me (www.marketme.us).

ISBN: 0985506008
ISBN-13: 978-0-9855060-0-1

ACKNOWLEDGMENTS

First of all I want to thank the Southern California Writer's Conference. Michael Steven Gregory and Wes Albers run a real working conference two weekends each year, and I learn something new every time I attend. It was at the Palms Springs event that I first invented Benny Needles and his ice cube tray. I specifically need to thank Jean Jenkins for her valuable editing advice, Judy Reeves for her constant reminders to bring the reader into each scene, and Marla Miller for her marketing wisdom.

My next group of people to thank helped me with this particular story. My friend, Robin Reichelt and I used to joke about a detective for our times - Peri Menopause, Private Eye, who solves every case by crying, eating chocolate, and bitch-slapping people until they confess. Who knew I could make her a real character? Then there's Mark Tieslau, bartender extraordinaire at the Gray Eagle Lodge, a resort in the Sierra Nevada Mountains. I was looking for a signature drink for Peri, and Mark makes killer cocktails. He introduced me to the dirty martini, a perfect contrast for the woman who used to clean houses. Also, thanks to Rhonda Carpenter, a writer/private investigator I met in San Diego, who gave me great insights into being a P.I.

Finally, there are three people in my life who I swore I'd thank when I either got published or won the Pulitzer. One is my grandmother, Myrtle Wetherholt Pike, who is with me in spirit. She taught me how to tell a story people would want to hear. The second is my friend, Kip Mistral, who kicked my butt until I started writing. Lastly, my husband, Dale, who simply assumed that I could write a book because I told him I would. If I ever win a Pulitzer, I'll just have to repeat myself, because I can't thank these people enough.

Also by this author:

Hit or Missus (A Peri Minneopa Mystery)
The Hot Mess (A Peri Minneopa Mystery)
Clean Sweep (A Peri Minneopa Short Story)

What Would Erma Do? Confessions of a First Time
Humor Columnist
Are You There, Erma? It's Me Gayle

From the Horse's Mouth: One Lucky Memoir

Murder on the Hoof

To Dale and Marcus.

CHAPTER 1

Such exquisite hands. What a pity to waste them.

Long, tapered fingers balanced the size of the palms perfectly. Half moons shone in the nails, which were strong and rounded, and extended the line of the hand. The porcelain skin blushed the slightest pink, although it seemed to be fading quickly.

The shadow knelt in the darkness, eyes glowing.

I'd better use the electric knife. No, the hacksaw.

Under the sliver of moonlight, deft hands opened the toolkit and went to work.

CHAPTER 2

"Miss Menopause?"

"Benny, it's Minn-ee-OH-pa," Peri corrected him as she sat behind her desk, reading the Private Investigators Legal Manual.

Benny Needles stood in the doorway. He was the kind of man who made most people want to disinfect their eyeballs when they looked at him. Short and swarthy, he considered himself Dean Martin's twin. Although he plucked his overgrown uni-brow and curled his thinning hair, he failed to convince anyone. The slim dark suits that had made Martin look like a pencil made Benny look more like a wide-tip marker. Benny might resemble Dino, but it would require either squinting, or heavy drinking, both from a great distance.

"Ah, Miss Minnie—oh, you know I can't pronounce that," he said.

He slunk into her office and plopped his weight onto a chair, the smell of Aqua Velva rushing to fill every corner. Sitting across from Peri, he picked up a mesh pencil holder from her large wooden desk and rolled the pencils around.

"Just stop calling me *Menopause*," she told him. "How did you even find me?"

"Aunt Esmy came over last Thursday. She said she saw you in Albertson's and you told her about this place." Benny looked around the tiny office. "Nice digs. You keep it real clean."

Peri looked up from her studying and sighed. "What do you want?"

"I got a job for you."

"I'm not cleaning your house, Benny. I'm a private investigator now."

"But you used to clean houses, Miss Meno-Miss Peri." He fidgeted. "No kidding, I really did lose something. I'd pay you to find it for me."

Peri leaned back, and studied the white speckled ceiling, fluffing her blonde hair through her fingers. "What is it?" She dreaded his answer.

"It's my ice cube tray."

At least he didn't disappoint her.

"You want me to find a freakin' ice cube tray?"

"It's not just any tray." His voice reached a high, nasal whine. "It's my Dean Martin ice cube tray. It was used to make Dino's drinks on the set of Ocean's Eleven. He autographed it."

"Someone actually conned you into buying that?"

Benny rose up from his chair, pounding a chubby fist on the desk. "It's been authenticated." He eased back down. "I paid five hundred bucks for it on eBay."

"Okay, okay," Peri said. "But I gotta charge full rate, two hundred fifty an hour plus expenses."

"No problem."

Reaching into her desk organizer, she pulled out a notebook and opened it to write. "Where'd you see it last?"

Benny stared at the ground, sheepish. "In my freezer."

Peri frowned. "Benny—"

"Don't yell at me. I know it was wrong, but I just wanted one scotch on the rocks with Dino's ice cubes."

"Benny, you don't even drink scotch. You hate alcohol."

"I just wanted to try it, and now my freezer's all snowed in and I can't find the tray and I'm afraid that Dino's signature will get rubbed off or something."

Peri looked at her potential client. She needed the money, but she knew he didn't want her sleuthing services. He wanted her to clean his house, the way she had cleaned it for his mother. Not only had she left that career behind, she didn't want to get sucked into dusting and organizing his ever-increasing collection of souvenirs.

Maybe she didn't need the money that badly.

"So hire a housecleaning service. They'd be a lot cheaper."

Benny's hands wrung together as if each finger tried to strangle the others. "I know Miss Peri, but what if they use too much heat or dig too hard and ruin my tray? I used to watch you clean Mama's good china. You're the only one I can trust to be gentle, to get it out of my freezer in one piece."

His plea tugged at her. She couldn't say she actually liked him, but she felt a kind of loyalty to the little guy. His mother was her first housecleaning client, and Peri had watched Benny grow from geeky boy to awkward man.

"Okay." Peri reached into the bottom drawer and pulled out her travel hairdryer. "I was about to go get some lunch anyway. I'll meet you at the house in thirty minutes."

"Oh, good, I'll go straighten the place up," he said, and scampered out.

"Yeah, you do that," she told the closing door.

Peri glanced around the room while she dug into her bag, searching for her car keys. She thought about Benny's assessment. A twelve by fifteen cubbyhole, it contained exactly one desk, two chairs, and a small file cabinet. She liked it because it had a window overlooking the building's atrium. She had leased it because, at three hundred dollars a month, she could work it into her monthly budget and still afford beer.

Someday, she hoped to be able to afford Grey Goose vodka.

She looked at the name on the door: *Peri Minneopa, Private Investigator*. Cleaning Benny's freezer didn't quite fit the job description, even if she was looking for a lost object.

"What the hell," she said, sticking her hairdryer in her oversized, leopard-print tote. "It's a paycheck."

After filling up at the corner Arco Station, Peri pointed her blue Honda sedan east on Yorba Linda Boulevard and headed toward a little side street behind the post office. The sun had finally burned off the June gloom, a morning haze typical of early summer in southern California. She turned off the wide avenue, divided by palm trees and colorful flowers, onto the quiet, residential street. The temperature was supposed to hit the 70s by mid-afternoon, just another perfect day in Orange County.

She pulled up in front of Benny's place, a small, older bungalow that served as a buffer between a tract of cookie-cutter stucco homes and the parking lot of Our Redeemer Lutheran Church. The house had originally belonged to Benny's mom and was well-known for its quirky charm by everyone in the neighborhood.

While Mrs. Needles lived there, the salmon pink house with cobalt blue trim had been meticulously maintained, down to the waist-high white picket fence around the front yard. Plaster gnomes sat in the immaculate flower garden, and wind chimes played a cheery, if incessant, tune from the porch.

After his mom's death, Benny lived there alone. It didn't take long for the neighborhood curiosity to become the neighborhood eyesore. Large strips of paint peeled away from the house, the fence was missing pickets, and weeds had strangled the gnomes.

"Come on in, Miss Peri." Benny played with the doorknob as he held the door open.

Once inside, she paused, taking in the chaos he called home.

"Wow, Benny, you got a lot more...stuff...than the last time I was here."

Peri knew Benny had turned the house into a shrine to Dean Martin, but she didn't realize how much memorabilia he had amassed in the year since his mother had died. The living room, wallpapered in Dino, had posters from all of Martin's movies, plus autographed pictures of the Rat Pack at their peak.

The space, crammed with mismatched furniture Benny had collected from various Dean Martin movie sets, looked like a warehouse. Peri counted two couches, five chairs, a set of bar stools, and at least six accent tables in the small room. Every table contained a bookend or ashtray or other piece of flotsam that had been *authenticated* as belonging to his idol, and all of it needed serious dusting.

As Peri surveyed the mess, she thought she could hear the sound of Mrs. Needles spinning in her grave.

"This way, Miss Peri," Benny said, as he cleared a path to the kitchen.

Peri entered the room and inhaled. The smell that had greeted her at the door became full-bodied in the kitchen. Most people shut their noses down at bad odors, but she found them fascinating. She detected peanut butter, rancid chicken, and mildew, among other things, and noted the bad sock smell actually decreased here.

"Fridge is in the corner," Benny told her.

"I know." Peri walked over to the ancient, white General Electric. "I've always wondered, how old is this thing?"

"I dunno, Mama got it the year Daddy went to work for GE—maybe 1956."

7

"Wow, fifty years old and still ticking," she said. "Just like me."

She looked around for someplace to set her bag, but the counter, the table, and even the chairs were covered in dirty dishes. Finally, she hung it on the back of a chair and opened the freezer, bending her tall frame slightly to look inside.

"Geepers, Benny, how long did it take to get this way?"

"The seal's broken," he replied. "It gets frozen over real quick."

"Pardon me for saying so, but, if you've got enough money to buy all of that Dino crap, why can't you splurge on a new fridge?"

Benny looked as though she had asked him to burn his Matt Helm posters. "Miss Peri, I don't use the freezer that much. I have to have my memories."

Peri went through the kitchen drawers, looking for something to scrape ice. There were a couple of knives, but they looked too narrow to be of much use. Finally she settled on a metal spatula that might have been used to turn hamburger patties on the grill.

She plugged in her dryer and began melting the crystalline layers of ice, scraping them off into a trash can. The condensation had frozen and re-frozen so much that, below the crystals, it was like trying to melt concrete. As she worked, she pulled plastic bags out of the freezer, filled with shriveled unknowns. She tossed those into the trash can, too.

"Find anything yet?" Benny asked after a half hour.

Peri growled, wiping the sweat off her temples. "Yeah, I found out you're a bigger slob than I thought possible."

"No, I mean the tray," he replied. "Did you find the tray yet?"

"Benny—" She reminded herself that he was a paying client. "Could you open a window or something? It's like an oven in here."

As she slid her hand further into the freezer, it felt as though someone grabbed her back, gliding their fingers along her wrist and settling their palm against hers. Surprised, but curious, she grasped the object and pulled it out.

"What the hell—"

Sealed tightly in a plastic bag, wrapped in gauze, was the shape of a human hand, each finger distinct, curved slightly in an eternal handshake.

"Um, Benny?" Peri held the bag up to the light.

He moved a little closer, stretching his neck upward to get a better look. "What is it?"

"Offhand? I'd say it's…a hand." She placed her hand around the back of the palm, stretching her fingers to match the ones in the bag. "A right hand. What's a hand doing in your freezer, Ben?"

Benny shook his head, his face pale. "Not mine," he told her. "It's not mine."

"What do you mean, not yours? How did it get in there?"

"I don't know. I didn't put it there." He stared at the bag, his eyes bulging from his ashen face.

"Are you telling me a stranger walked into your house and left a severed hand in your freezer? What, for fun?"

"No…I don't know…no." Beads of sweat formed at his hairline. "I'm telling you it's not mine. I haven't put anything in there since I put the ice cube tray in. That was two weeks ago."

Peri thought for a moment. "Well, let's unwrap it and see what it really is. Maybe it's some weird leftover you just forgot." She looked around the room. "Do you have *any* surface in this place that *might* be clean?"

"Sure," he said. "I never use the patio table."

Benny opened the sliding glass door. A small concrete slab took up half of the miniscule yard, shaded by a patio cover of narrow wood slats. In the center of the slab sat a round metal table with a glass top and four chairs. It surprised Peri to see it all so spotless.

"Geez, Benny, your backyard is cleaner than your whole house."

"Oh, I hose this part down every night," he told her, then shuddered. "Bird poop."

Peri laid papers down on the table and went to work. She put on disposable gloves and removed the object from the bag. The faint smell of cold decay greeted her immediately. She used tweezers to unwrap the gauze, trying to preserve all of the evidence for a forensic examiner, just in case. As she peeled back each layer, she noted a large bulge on the ring finger. The last of the material removed, Peri sat down and looked at the object in front of her.

"So?" Bennie asked from his position of safety in the kitchen. "What is it?"

"Well, it ain't meatloaf. Stay back, Benny, it's kind of gruesome."

She turned the hand around, engrossed and repelled at the sight. Two bones peeked out from the wrist, rough and jagged from being hacked off. Muscles, tendons, flesh also looked ragged, as if cut by a dull knife.

The skin had a yellowish tinge, and was slightly wrinkled. It reminded Peri of a chicken's foot. A really big chicken's foot, with pink fingernail polish, and an enormous ring.

A ring like no other she had ever seen. Diamond shaped, it stretched between the knuckle and the first joint of the ring finger. The outer edge was a vine of clear stones, cut in the shape of leaves, punctuated by large round jewels at the corners. Inside, another layer of green, jeweled leaves overlapped the outer row. At the center perched a remarkable stone, the size of a marble, with the facets cut so that when she looked down, it resembled a rose.

"Wow," Benny said, behind her.

Peri jumped. "God, Benny, don't sneak up on me like that."

She saw his eyes fixed on the ring, moist and glowing with desire. "How much do you think it's worth?"

Putting the hand and the gauze back into the bag, Peri stood up.

"I don't know," she said, "but it's time to call the cops."

CHAPTER 3

"Oh, no, no police," Benny protested.

Peri stared at him. "Are you insane? You have a frozen hand in your possession with a big freakin' ring on it. You claim you don't know where it came from, and you don't think we should call the authorities?"

Hands up, palms forward in supplication, he said, "Miss Peri, please. Calling the police means they'll be in my house, going through my things. My *memories*."

"I know, but the police need to find out where this came from." She shook the bag at him. "This isn't right, Ben. This shouldn't be in your freezer, whether you put it there or not."

"No, no, I don't want them in here. I don't want them touching my stuff."

Peri fished her cell phone out of her purse. "I'm sorry, Ben, but we need to report this."

"You don't even know if it's human for sure," he told her. "We don't know, right? We don't know for certain?"

"Oh, Benny, look at it. It's the real deal." Peri's finger was poised over the Send button. She had to admit, she had never actually seen a dead body, much less a severed hand. It smelled real enough, but it would be a great trick to play on a brand new P.I. She had a lot of friends who'd love to tease her. They might even pay Benny for his help. "You're not trying to pull a prank on me, are you, Ben?"

"No, no, I wouldn't do that to you, Miss Peri."

He lurched forward suddenly, grabbing her free hand. "Oh, puh-lease, Miss Peri, don't call the police, at least not yet."

Peri pulled her hand away from the chubby little man and looked down at him. She could see his scalp shining through the strands of black hair.

"Oh, all right," she said. "I'll call Blanche first."

Blanche Debussy worked in the Forensic Science Facility of the Orange County Sheriff's Department, and she happened to be Peri's best friend since high school. Married, with two teenagers, she had encouraged Peri to change careers, pointing out how her friend's eye for detail and penchant for mysteries could be parlayed into investigative work.

"Beebs, it's me," Peri said into the phone. "I've got something I'd like you to look at."

"Brochure of a day spa, or a list of college scholarships for kids who hate school?" Blanche asked in a husky voice.

"Close. A human hand...I think."

"What the hell, Peri?"

"I can't tell you where I found it," Peri said, looking at Benny, "yet. But I need you to tell me whether it's a real hand, or a really good fake."

"Sure, bring it down, I'll give it a look."

"Umm, could we do the first look unofficially?"

"Think my gang'll tease you if it's a Hollywood prop?"

"It's not the kind of reputation I want at the coroner's office."

"Come by the house at seven and bring some limes. I've got the tequila."

Peri stuck her phone back in her bag and dug out her camera. She took several pictures of the freezer, and of the room.

"Hey, wait," Benny said. "What about my ice cube tray?"

Peri reached over his head and picked an object up from the top of the old refrigerator. She dumped the old water out in the sink and handed it to him.

"I only wish I'd spotted it before I started digging through the ice age," she said.

"My ice cube tray." Benny turned it upside-down and ran his fingers, delicately, over the signature.

There, on the silver bottom, something had been scribbled in black marker. Peri couldn't tell whether it said *Dean Martin* or *Dim Mutton*, but her client was happy, so nothing else mattered.

Peri held out her hand. "That'll be two hundred and fifty bucks, Ben."

Heading toward Blanche's house later that evening, Peri thought about the money in her purse. Most of her rent covered for the month, earned in only an hour. It sure beat scrubbing toilets all day.

She hadn't planned on being a housekeeper for twenty-five years, but a degree in English Literature didn't translate to anything in the "Help Wanted" section of the local newspaper, at least, nothing she wanted. Writing ad copy or articles on twenty things to make with paper plates did not excite her.

Cleaning houses may not have been a thrilling job, but it bought her a home, kept her supplied with the basics, and left plenty of hours for reading books and watching old movies, so she couldn't complain.

As her late forties turned the inevitable corner, however, Peri thought of the manual labor involved in scrubbing and mopping five days a week, and wondered if her body could keep doing it for many more years. When Blanche suggested the private investigation business, it sounded like a great transition. After all, Peri could tell, when she cleaned a house, which client had secrets. Most of the time, she could figure out what they were.

She pulled into the driveway of a two-story house in the rolling hills of Yorba Linda. The Debussy home sprawled across an enormous piece of land, a large white house with brick accents. The luxury of the estate seemed to reinforce the license plate frame on Blanche's minivan: "Yorba Linda, Land of Gracious Living."

"Land of spacious living," Peri said as she walked to the front door. "And deep pockets."

She gave the doorbell an obligatory ring before turning the latch and letting herself in.

"Hey, Beebs, anybody home?" she called out. "I'm here with limes and—" She looked down at the small cooler that contained her ghoulish discovery. "Stuff."

"In the kitchen, Peri." Blanche's voice came from the recesses of the expansive home.

Peri walked around the corner just in time to see a petite brunette open the refrigerator and remove a gallon of milk.

"Mom, is this still good?" the teen asked, opening the cap and sniffing.

"Don't ask me, Danielle, you know I can't smell a thing," Blanche told her. "See what Aunt Peri thinks."

"What's your Super Smeller say?" Danielle held the container under Peri's nose.

"Hmm..." Peri inhaled, her eyes closed, analyzing the bouquet. "Fresh in the middle, with dead opossum on the edges. I'd say you're a day away from expiration."

Blanche's daughter put the cap on and returned the milk to the fridge. "Nick can have it. I'm going over to Janet's house."

Blanche pulled a pitcher out of the cupboard while Peri chopped limes and squeezed their juice into a cup.

"Should we do the autopsy before or after the Cuervo?" Blanche asked.

"How about during?"

"Bring your glass into my office." Blanche picked up her own salt-rimmed cup of green lightning and, tucking Peri's cooler under her arm, walked to her study.

The assistant coroner's study did not fit the conventional description of a home office. The obligatory desk and bookshelves of rich, golden oak lined the dark green walls. A computer sat on the desk corner, framed in candid photos of Debussy family life.

In the middle of the room, however, stood a small, stainless steel table, a souvenir from Blanche's university days of autopsying cats, rats and other four-legged critters.

"Let's see what we got here," Blanche said, lifting the bag out of the cooler.

Peri watched her friend work. Petite like her daughter, Blanche's mahogany hair had become lightly dusted with silver. Half-glasses sat below large dark eyes. Wearing gloves, she removed the hand, placed it on the table, and turned it around, stretching the fingers out, and poking at the insides with tweezers.

Finally, she rolled the hand back and looked at the ring. "Where'd you get this?"

"Is it a real hand?"

"Oh, yeah, it's real. I'd have to run tests, but from the elasticity of the skin, I'd say it's a young person's hand. The delicacy of the fingers and the manicure makes me think it's female, but I could be wrong. And that ring…" Blanche whistled. "That's some major bling."

"You think it's real, too?"

"Oh, yeah, Baby." Blanche took a sip of her margarita, and licked the salt from her lips. "So, where did you get this?"

"Housecleaning."

"I'd say it's time to call Skip."

Peri looked at the hand, now showing the effects of thawing, both in sight and smell.

"Oh, yeah, Baby," Peri repeated, and downed her drink.

CHAPTER 4

"Hey, Dollface."

The sound of Skip Carlton's deep, melodic voice always sent shivers through Peri.

"Do they have phone sex numbers for women? You could earn some big bucks," she told him.

He laughed. "Call me at home tonight and we'll discuss it. What's up?"

"I found something you should see."

"Dead body?"

"Well, maybe part of one." Peri knew that, as a detective in the Placentia Police Department, Skip handled mostly robberies, and a little vice. In the quiet little community of 50,000 residents, he didn't often get to work on murders.

"Any bodies turn up missing a hand recently?" she asked. "Young, probably female?"

"Mmm, I love it when you talk gruesome. Where are you? I'll be right over."

Peri prepared for a lecture. "Okay, don't get mad, but I'm not at the scene. I took the hand to Blanche's house to be verified, but I took lots of photos, and I can take you to where I found it."

"Doll, didn't P.I. school teach you anything?"

She bristled. "I got the highest grades in my class and yes, I know I wasn't supposed to move the evidence, but—oh, hell, just get here and I'll explain."

Once at Blanche's, the tall, pepper-haired detective calmed down as Peri explained her discovery.

"Oh. Benny," he said, rolling his eyes. Everyone knew Benny for his Dean Martin fanaticism, and the local police knew him for his irrational fear of law enforcement. The officers still talked about how a routine traffic stop once sent him to the hospital with heart palpitations.

"Are you going to arrest him?"

"Not right now. Body parts are never a good discovery, but believe it or not, a crime may not have been committed. We'll just ask Benny a few questions, then watch him for awhile."

"I told him that if the hand is real, the police had to come in," she said. "Be gentle with him, okay?"

Skip pulled out his notebook and turned to Blanche. "Take the hand down to your office, Beebs. I want fingerprints, DNA, the works. Have the guys get forensic evidence from the ring. Oh, and could you call the other counties to see if anyone has a body with no hand? I can call them, but they don't always get back to me."

He scribbled a few notes, then turned to Peri. "Email me those pictures tonight, along with a write-up. I'll get the search warrant and have Jason come with us to Benny's first thing tomorrow."

"How early is *first thing*?"

Skip shrugged. "I dunno. I can probably get the warrant by seven, so eight? Nine?"

"Here's the thing," Peri told him. "Benny doesn't get up before noon. If we come in there at eight in the morning, banging on his door, he's going to be less than enthused about letting us in."

"I think he should be happy we're not dragging his ass off to jail."

"If he's got any info at all, he's not going to cough it up if you force yourself on him. You know, you draw more flies with honey…"

"That may be, but I want some answers about that thing and how it ended up in his freezer."

"Skip, you know how odd Benny is. He lives on *Dino time*—staying up late, sleeping through the morning, pretending to be a smooth-talking, hard-drinking man about town. But on the inside, he's an obsessive-compulsive wreck. If you push him at the beginning, you'll get nothing, except maybe a trip to the hospital."

Skip growled something unintelligible.

"There may not even be any useful forensic evidence in his place. It's so filthy, I don't know how you'd find it," Peri said. "Trust me, he won't have cleaned anything up by tomorrow afternoon."

She poured another round into her glass. "He's still waiting for *me* to come over and do that."

Skip conceded. "All right. We'll start out your way, but after you give me the initial report, you're off this thing, right?"

"Why?"

"Well, first of all, this isn't your expertise, is it? You didn't get into the P.I. business to investigate murders."

"No, but—"

"You don't even carry a gun, do you?"

"No, but I'm still—"

"You only want to do surveillance, background checks, low risk assignments, right?"

"Right, but, Skipper, this is so interesting."

The detective leaned forward and kissed her on the nose. "No," he said. "We still on for Friday?"

"You buying the martinis?"

"Grey Goose, just the way you like 'em."

"Then it's a date." Peri licked at the salt on her glass. "Besides, after I pour alcohol down you, I plan to pump you for information."

"Would this be a good time for a margarita, Skip?" Blanche pointed toward the pitcher.

He smiled. "It's no use trying to get me drunk until I've got information to spill. Besides, I'm still on duty for another hour."

After he left, Blanche put the hand, along with the bag and gauze, into a large plastic envelope with a red police label on it. She wrote her name across the seal and put it in her office freezer.

"I'll take it down to the Coroner's in the morning." She picked up her glass. "Bring the pitcher and I'll get out the chips and salsa."

The two women sat on the patio, watching the daylight melt away into evening.

"I should have brought my suit," Peri said. "Your Jacuzzi looks so inviting."

"You could borrow one of mine."

Peri laughed. "Thanks, but exactly which hip would I put into it?"

"Don't say that. You're not any bigger than me, you're just taller." The small brunette rose from her chair. "Come on, the hot tub sounds great, and I have some really stretchy suits."

Ten minutes later, the two friends rested their backs against bubbles, relaxed and sunken in the hot water.

"So, how's business?" Blanche asked. "I mean, apart from finding frozen hands."

"Pretty steady. I've done four insurance frauds, some background checks, and I'm meeting a new client next week who wants me to tail her husband."

"Great. Sounds like you're building a reputation."

"I don't know, Beebs," Peri said. "I worked on those insurance frauds for several weeks and didn't find proof of any wrongdoing each time. Maybe I'm not good at this."

"Did you convince the insurance company there wasn't any fraud?"

"Sure, I had photos, videos, everything to show the person wasn't doing anything they claimed they couldn't do." She sighed. "I guess I thought I'd catch at least one out of four people trying to beat the system."

"Sounds like you're just too cynical about human nature."

They heard the slide of the screen door, and an adolescent male voice, soft and high with crackling edges. "What's for dinner?"

Blanche turned and looked at her son. "Hey, sweetie. You can either nuke the leftover chicken or order a pizza."

"Where's Dani?" He scratched his dark curls with long, knobby fingers.

"At Janet's," Blanche replied.

Nick gave his mother a quizzical look, then disappeared to graze in the refrigerator.

"Do you know Janet?" Peri asked.

"Not very well. I met her once, but she wasn't particularly memorable. Dani's been going over to her house to study at least one night during the week."

Peri's eyebrows lifted.

"What?" Blanche asked.

"Nothing."

"Tell me."

"It's none of my business," Peri said. "I don't know anything about having kids."

"Believe it or not, I don't either. Just because I'm their mom doesn't make me an expert at raising teenagers. What's on your mind?"

"Well, it's just that, you've only met this Janet once, and Dani spends at least one night a week with her. The way she was dressed when she left looked less like a study night and more like a date. And Nick looked surprised when you told him where she was."

Blanche considered her friend's analysis. Her daughter had been wearing a silky camisole with a short denim skirt. She looked cute, too cute for a trip to a girlfriend's house to do homework, and school would be getting out in less than a week. What kind of studying did she need to do?

"I'm just saying," Peri said. "I don't know anything about being a mom, but I remember plenty about being a teenager."

Blanche picked up the phone to call her daughter. "Damn your suspicious mind."

CHAPTER 5

Peri arrived at the Placentia Police Station by eleven thirty, in order to stall her boyfriend sufficiently until she knew Benny would be receiving visitors.

The sun already blazed, brightening the Placentia Civic Center courtyard. Earthy bricks decorated the walkways in a complex pattern of rectangles and diamonds, leading up to the large, arched fountain of ocean blue tiles, outlined with smooth stones.

Peri paused to check her reflection in the dark glass of the door, then straightened her beige skirt and fluffed her Nordic blonde hair away from her scalp before entering the station. She stopped at the coffee pot to fill a Styrofoam cup on her way to Skip's office. He held the receiver in one hand and waved her in with the other.

"Hey, Doll," he said when he had completed his phone call. "Is it time to wake His Highness?"

"Aw, Skipper, be nice."

"I don't get it," Skip said. "Why do you care if we step on this guy's toes? He had to be lying to you about knowing whose hand that is."

"You didn't see him when I pulled it out of the freezer. Benny's not an actor, unless he's stressed. Trust me, he wasn't channeling his inner Dino."

Peri took a sip of coffee and grimaced. "Who made the coffee today?"

"Ed. I think he used to work in waste management. So, back to Benny, you got a little crush on him or something?"

She laughed. "Oh, yeah. He's quite the ladies man, all that Dino aura. Obsessive, compulsive, delusional... not exactly endearing qualities. But I guess, after cleaning house for his mom all those years, I feel a little protective of him. After all, his momma loved him."

Skip looked at his watch. "Well, come on, Miz P.I., it's noon. Time to go interview the Mini-Martin."

They walked down the hall past Jason Bonham's office. "Hey, youngster," Skip called. "Grab your kit and come with us."

"Cool."

In the parking lot, Peri turned to see Jason loping toward them, long and gangly legs pumping to catch up. He had pulled an Angels baseball cap over his short, blond hair, and swung his tool case as he ran.

"God, Jason, are you even old enough to drive?"

He smiled, his freckles crinkling into laugh lines. "Legal, single, and ready to rock."

It took ten minutes to reach Benny's door. Skip and Jason stood at the gate while Peri knocked.

"Benny? It's me, Peri. Are you home?"

There was no answer for a few minutes, and then Peri saw a crop of thinning curls in the lower window of the door, followed by a bloodshot blue eye.

"Miss Peri," he said, opening the door, then saw Detective Carlton and Officer Bonham, behind her on the sidewalk.

"Who's that?" he asked, scowling.

"That's Detective Carlton of the PPD," Peri told him, gesturing toward the two men at the bottom of the stairs. "And his associate, Officer Bonham. Detective Carlton needs to talk to you about the hand we found, and Officer Bonham is going to look through your kitchen to see if that hand left any evidence."

"No police," he shouted, and tried to shut the door, but Peri stepped in to block him.

"Benny, calm down." Peri adopted her most soothing, maternal voice. "It's all right. Detective Carlton doesn't want to mess up your things. He just wants to ask you about your freezer, and if you've had any visitors."

Benny's body still held firm against the door, so Peri tried again.

"He heard you have a picture of Frank and Dino at the Flamingo. He'd love to see it."

The door gave way, just a bit.

"He likes Dean Martin?"

"My favorite movie of all time is *Some Came Running*," Skip said from his position at the front gate. "I even visited the town in Indiana where it was made."

Benny opened the door, a black umbrella with a curved cane handle in his right hand.

"No kidding?" he asked. "Did you take any pictures?"

"Sure did." Skip stepped up to the porch. "I'd be happy to show them to you."

"We okay, Ben?" Peri asked, pointing to his weapon.

"Yeah." He giggled a little, and leaned the umbrella against the wall.

"Benny," Skip said, handing him a piece of paper. "This is a warrant, signed by a judge. It says it's okay if I look around in your house. I know you don't like it, but we'll be very careful."

Benny read the paper, nervous sweat beading around his hairline. "I guess it's okay." He looked at the detective. "Bama Dillert was my favorite character, ever. I have an end table from the house they stayed in...and an ashtray."

As the trio made their way to the kitchen, Peri looked over her shoulder to see Jason lingering in the front room, eyeing the incredible piles of memorabilia.

"Wow, get a load of this stuff," he said. "It's, like, ancient."

"It's only fifty years old, Jason," she told him. "You're such a pup."

Benny hovered around his things, watching his visitors as if they might each grab a handful of loot and run.

"I'm going to show them your freezer while you find the ashtray," Peri said.

Skip and Jason looked around the room before opening the refrigerator. The freezer, showing the effects of Peri's cleaning, was almost empty.

"Oh, I saved the bucket of water I scraped out, and the baggies of shriveled up food, just in case," she told them.

"I'll take it back with me," Jason said, poking around the freezer. "You're right, I don't know how we'd find evidence in this room. It'd take us months to process it all."

Suddenly he leaned in and looked at the freezer door. "Except maybe this. Hand me a baggie and a scraper of some sort."

Peri did as he requested.

"See this pinkish coloring?" He pointed to a small sliver of red against the silver door. "That might be blood from someone's hand as they touched the freezer."

"Freezer burn?"

"No, a regular freezer's not cold enough, but I'm guessing that someone cut themselves, then touched the sides. It's probably Benny's, but I'll have the lab analyze it, just in case."

Benny came into the kitchen, his eyes bright with excitement. "I found it."

He held the ashtray up proudly to Skip. "It's nice glass, isn't it? And if you look in the corners, there's still leftover stains from the cigarettes."

The slight man admired his trophy. He saw a smudge on the clear glass and licked his fingers to rub it off.

Skip took the ashtray, felt the weight of it and tried to act suitably impressed. "Wow, Benny, this is nice."

"Of course, I don't know if the stains are from Dean's cigarettes." Benny sighed, then looked up at Skip. "Do you think the police lab could run a DNA test on the stains? I see them do that kind of thing all the time on TV."

Skip opened his mouth to tell Benny that the Orange County Forensics Lab would not waste its money trying to authenticate useless relics, but shut it again and looked at the ashtray.

"Well, Benny, if you wouldn't mind me taking it to the lab, we could find out."

He frowned. "Oh…. I don't know…"

"I understand you wouldn't want it to leave your house," Skip told him. "But Jason could put it in an evidence bag and log it into our system so it wouldn't get lost."

"Wow, an evidence bag?" This piqued Benny's interest. "Could I see it?"

Jason looked up from dusting the refrigerator for fingerprints. Reaching into his kit, he produced an official bag, red label across the top.

"See, I put the ashtray in, then I seal it," Jason told him. "Now, I write on the bag, *Property of Benny Needles. DNA Typing requested.* And I'll return it to you—what's today—Wednesday? I'll have it back to you by next Wednesday."

Benny shifted his weight from one stout leg to the other. "I don't know, I don't know," he said, then finally asked, "Next Wednesday?"

"For you, Benny," Peri said, "Detective Carlton will put a rush on it."

Skip frowned a bit, but backed her up. "Sure thing, Ben. Maybe we can have it back by Monday."

"Monday would be better."

"We'll do our best," Skip told him. "Now, why don't we sit down on your porch and talk about that hand?" He ushered Benny toward the front door. Removing him from the house would allow Jason to work undisturbed.

"I don't know anything about a hand," Benny said. "I don't know how it got in my freezer."

"When's the last time you looked in your freezer?"

"Two weeks ago, like I told Miss Peri. There was no hand in my freezer two weeks ago, I swear." Benny's brows folded in the middle as he pouted. "I wouldn't be caught dead touching it."

His mood brightened. "Dead touching it—get it? Hey, Detective, did you see the ring? That was amazing."

"It's a nice ring, Ben," Peri said. "Had you seen it before?"

"No." He looked back at Skip. "If no one claims it, can I have it?"

"We're not in charge of that, Benny. Right now, we're trying to figure out how it got in your freezer, attached to a hand."

The mention of the hand made Benny shudder.

"Has anyone else been in your house lately?" Skip asked.

He nodded. "Yes."

"Who?"

"Miss Peri was here yesterday."

She rolled her eyes. "Anyone else, Ben?"

"Not while I was here, but maybe when I was out."

"Why would someone be here when you were out?" Skip wrote in his notebook as he spoke.

"I don't know. But sometimes, when I come home, my stuff has been rearranged."

"Has anything been taken?" Peri asked.

"No, just moved." Benny looked around, as if imparting a secret. "I sometimes think it's Dino's ghost, looking for something he can't find. Maybe if I get more of his stuff, he'll find what he's looking for."

Peri could feel Skip's stare burning into her head, but she didn't dare look at him, for fear she'd laugh out loud.

Jason came out of the house, carrying his kit, a bag of evidence, and a bucket of dirty water. He nodded to Skip, then walked to the SUV.

"Okay, Benny," Skip said. "We're going to take your ashtray down to the lab. You're not going on any vacations, are you?"

"No, Detective. I only take one trip a year, to Vegas for Dino's birthday, on June seventh."

Skip and Peri managed to get in the car with Jason, and drive halfway down the street before bursting into laughter.

"Poor Benny," she said. "I feel so sorry for him."

"Especially if Dino's ghost is messing with him."

"By the way, what was that all about?" Peri asked, pointing to the ashtray. "Are you really going to test that for Dean Martin's DNA?"

"Not Dino's, Benny's. This way I can find out if it's Benny's blood on the freezer."

"Oh, smart cookie," Peri said as they drove back to the station. "By the way, was that true, what you told Benny? About visiting the town where that movie was made?"

"Of course it is." Skip smiled. "There's a lot to learn about me."

"Right, Skipper. It's nice to know that, after all these years, you're still a man of mystery."

At the police station, Skip slid his hand down Peri's arm. "Thanks for your help with Needles. The police will take it from here, right?"

Peri smiled at him. "Well—"

"Right, Peri?"

"Oh, all right. But will you at least keep me informed? It's all so fascinating."

"You know I'm not supposed to share information about an active case."

"Not even if I ply you with drinks and sex?"

Skip laughed. "Not a chance, Mata Hari."

"We'll see," she told him. "You sure you want to take me out this Friday?"

CHAPTER 6

"Case number…" Peri leafed through papers as she sat in her office. "Where's that case number?"

She knew any job involved some mundane tasks, but filling out insurance forms always sucked the joy from the room. In addition to case numbers, she had to use insurance lingo to describe the work she performed. Boring, boring, boring.

"Claimant was observed on porch at 160 Cardinal Way on May 25th, 2:55 P.M," she typed. She sat back and looked at the computer screen, the morning sun warming her back. "How do I describe something that didn't happen?"

She looked at the photograph and thought about the day. The man had claimed a permanent and disabling back injury. Peri watched him for a week. All she discovered was that he was a colossal jerk who treated everyone in his family like his personal slaves. When he walked out onto his porch that afternoon, and stood looking at a new television that had been delivered, Peri thought she had him at last.

Instead, he howled at his son and wife, "Get out here and carry this damn thing in the house. The game starts in an hour."

"Claimant is guilty of being an asshole, but not a fraudulent asshole," she typed, then erased it and entered a more appropriate description.

While Peri struggled to complete the report, she kept thinking about the hand and the ring, and wondering how much Benny knew. Reminding herself that a finished report equaled a paycheck, she managed to focus long enough to get the job done and the envelope stamped.

She continued to think about Benny as she meandered through the grocery store later, a gray basket hanging on her arm. There were brightly colored fruits and vegetables available in the produce section, but she headed toward the freezers. Strawberries sounded better when they were in a pint of Ben & Jerry's Strawberry Cheesecake ice cream. She grabbed a six-pack of Diet Coke to go with the dessert, paid and went home.

The steady ring of the phone greeted Peri as she walked through her back door. After setting her purchases on the counter, she picked up the cordless and answered.

"Miss Meno—?"

She recognized the voice at once. "Benny, please call me Peri. How did you get my home number?"

"You didn't answer your other phone."

"I didn't hear it. Who gave you my home number, Benny?"

"Aunt Esmy. She said you left it at the church, so I looked it up."

"You broke into the church office to get my private information?" Peri asked, irritated.

She could almost hear the mental back-peddling as Benny defended his actions. "No, no, I-I-I just happened to be in the office—it was an accident—well, here's the thing." His voice turned hard. "Sometimes I just ask myself, what would Dino do?"

Walking over to the refrigerator, Peri asked, "What can I do for you?"

"I'd like to hire you again."

"First of all, Ben," Peri said as she stuck the ice cream in the freezer and the soda in the fridge. "My office hours are Monday through Friday. Second, I'm still not cleaning your house."

"No, no, it's nothing like that. I want to hire you to investigate, you know, what you found in my house."

"What's to investigate? I found the hand. I turned it over to the police."

"I know, Miss Peri, I know. It's not like you have to investigate anything. I just want to keep tabs on it, on what they're doing."

"They?"

"You know...the police."

She fished a bottle of cold cranberry juice from the back of the fridge. "Why?"

"Because I don't like surprises." Benny's voice rose half an octave. "I don't want them back in my house. I don't want to be accused of anything. I need to know if they think I did something, if they are coming back here."

"Okay, okay, calm down." Peri took a swig of juice. "I'll do it, although I think you should hire an attorney instead. Come by my office on Monday and we'll sign a contract."

"But I want you to start now. Can't you start now?"

Peri sighed. Cleaning houses may have been hard work, but at least the hours were better.

"Can you get to my office in about an hour?"

"Um, probably not, Miss Peri. I promised Aunt Esmy I'd help her at the church."

"God, Benny, if you want to hire me, why can't you get your ass to my office?" Peri stopped and took a breath. "Sorry, Benny, I guess I'm a little cranky. Of course, I'll meet you at the church in about an hour."

She looked at the clock. Benny usually didn't get up before noon, but it was only eleven. Clearly, finding a hand in his freezer had shaken him. After a quick shower, she slipped into a more professional outfit, pulled her hair into a ponytail, and left.

Peri drove into the parking lot of Our Redeemer Lutheran Church, next to Benny's house. Sunday services had ended and a constant flow of well dressed people exited the large, open doors. Some groups moved directly to their cars, no doubt trying to beat the Sunday brunch crowd at El Torito's. Others formed small clumps on the walkways, where they stood like crows, bobbing and squawking.

A dark blue Toyota sat in the corner of the church lot, with a shadowed figure behind the wheel. Peri recognized him immediately as Benny's personal bodyguard, assigned by Skip to watch his comings and goings.

After getting out of her car, she smoothed her khakis and polo shirt. She went in to the sanctuary, moving past the pews, to the door behind the choir loft.

Esmeralda Bean was gathering up large plastic toys and putting them in a basket. A short, hefty woman, her coppery bouffant hairdo stood as a monument to her years as a stylist, even though it did not match the roadmap of lines now gracing her 70-something face.

Peri was always struck by the resemblance between Esmy and her late sister, Benny's mother. They were fraternal twins, but they looked identical.

"Why, Peri, how nice to see you," she said. "Too bad you're not here to pick up a wee one."

"Yeah." Peri looked around the nursery, aware of the smell of diapers sweetened by baby powder and anti-bacterial wipes. The alarm on her biological clock had been set to snooze long ago. "How are you, Esmy? I'm supposed to meet Benny here."

"He's downstairs in the kitchen, dear. I needed some help unloading the food for the women's dinner this Wednesday."

"Benny told me you work at the shelter, too. You sound busy."

The older woman straightened the belt of her polyester pantsuit. "Two days here and two days at the shelter. Then I host my book club on Thursday nights."

"Wow, that's a lot of work for you."

"It's just volunteer work, so it's a labor of love."

Benny appeared at the door. "Auntie, where did you want the big jar of pickles? Oh, hi, Miss Peri. I got money for you."

"Good, Ben." Peri dug a paper out of her tote and handed it to him. "Sign here."

As Benny read over the contract, Peri looked around the room. Dancing sheep on the walls watched over the cribs, and baskets of soft-edged, hypo-allergenic, God-approved toys. A small shepherd boy, standing amid the sheep, smiled as if he approved of the merriment. It looked cute, but it still didn't make Peri want children.

"Here's two thousand." Benny handed Peri a stack of neatly folded bills. "Let me know when you need more."

Peri stuffed the money in her bag. "I'll check in with you regularly, and give you a written report at the end."

"Regularly?" he asked. "What time?"

"I don't know, Ben," she replied. "Possibly not until the evening. I've got a couple of other cases."

"Other cases? But you're working for me."

"Yes, Benny, I am, and I can assure you, I like your case best. But it's impossible to work your case actively eight hours a day. Lab analysis takes time, and we may not find the leads we're looking for. I've got to have something to do in the meantime."

Her explanation seemed to placate him. "All right, Miss Peri."

"With any luck," she told him, "The police will get this solved quickly."

Back at home, Peri sat in front of her television, her laptop perched on her legs. She read through her email messages while Basil Rathbone stood in the middle of her TV screen, brilliant and logical, solving a crime as Sherlock Holmes. The dialogue seeped into Peri's brain as she worked, the characters discussing the Star of Rhodesia diamond.

"It's as big as a duck's egg," she heard Dr. Watson say.

Suddenly, Peri looked up at the scene. "A big diamond always seems to have a name. I wonder if a big ring would have one, too."

Turning back to her computer, she typed in "diamond emerald ring" and pressed Enter. The search results were a jungle of jewelers, offering diamonds, emeralds, and rings. What would be a more specific description of the ring? The center stone was the most unusual aspect. She had never seen a diamond with the facets cut to look like rose petals.

She tried "diamond ring rose" next. This time, the results were a little more diverse: discount stores luring her with promises of "Bargain Prices on Diamond Ring Rose," and a blogspot for a high priestess named Lil Rose Diamond.

At the bottom of the page Peri saw a news article about a ring named "Forever Roses." She clicked on the link and was taken to the homepage for Christie's auction house. As soon as she saw the photo, she dialed Blanche's number.

"Beebs, I found the ring."

"What ring?"

"The ring on the hand. There's a story on the Internet about it."

"What did Skip say about it?"

"I haven't told him yet. You know I tell you everything first. Listen to this."

She began to read, "In September, Christie's will auction the estate of Elizabeth Marquette and Melvin Conway, the famed actor-actress couple of many 1940s melodramas. Included in the sale are autographed scripts, yadda, yadda, and the famous *Forever Roses* ring, a magnificent, custom-made piece of diamonds and emeralds set in platinum. According to Kevin Conway, grandson of the couple, the ring was last appraised at $1.4 million."

"Holy crap," Blanche said.

"Are you sure the thing is real?"

"I don't know, I sent it to trace to be analyzed. But if the real one's being auctioned off at Christie's—"

"Either the one on that hand isn't real," Peri said. "Or that one-of-a-kind ring isn't so very one of a kind."

"Or Christie's is in for a big surprise."

"What have you found out about the hand?"

"Cut off post-mortem," Blanche's voice assumed a professional air. "Young female. I sent fingerprints and DNA results to Skip. Trace still has the ring and fingernail scrapings."

"Any handless bodies turn up?"

"Nothing yet. I've checked L.A., Riverside, and San Bernadino counties."

"Maybe if we find out who she is, we'll have a better idea of where to look," Peri told her.

"We? I thought Skip said you weren't on this case."

"I'm not...exactly. Talk to you later, Beebs."

Peri hung up and called Skip.

"How far have you gotten with that hand?"

"There's a charge for phone sex," he said.

She laughed. "Not your hand, the hand from the freezer. Have you identified it yet?"

"Maybe. Come over and we'll talk about it."

"Hmm," she purred. "Is that all you want to do?"

"Hey, you said you'd ply me with alcohol and sex."

"Give me half an hour. And get the martinis ready."

CHAPTER 7

Skip met her at the door with a dirty martini and a mischievous smile. He pressed the stemmed glass into her fingers.

"Four olives," Peri said, then took a sip. "Mmm, just the way I like it."

"I know how you like a lot of things," he told her.

She put her drink down and wrapped her arms around his waist. "Yes, you do."

They made it as far as the den, where Peri pulled him down to the rug in front of the fireplace. Laughing, stripping each other, stripping themselves, they made effervescent, enthusiastic love. At last satiated, they lay back on the pillows, propped against the fireplace bricks.

Skip groaned. "Man, we're too old for this."

Peri traced his jaw line with her fingers. "Speak for yourself, buddy. When you can't stand to look at my wrinkles, we'll just do it in the dark."

He laughed. "Why don't you marry me?"

"Because, we can't even live together, remember? Besides, I've already tried marriage. Three times."

"Just because you married three louses in a row. You know what they say, fourth time's a charm."

"I don't think so. Besides, they weren't all louses. Number one was a druggie, two was a psycho, and three was a nice guy who I turned into a louse."

"A nice guy who was gay."

"Hey, nobody's perfect," she told him. "Besides, you're still paying for college tuition. What would we live on?"

"The last one's almost out of the ex's nest. She graduates in January and is getting married in June."

"Graduation, then a wedding," Peri said. "Like I said, what would we live on?"

"Fine, I give up. We'll just hop back and forth, between houses, having a series of random, emotionless sexual encounters."

"Oh, Skipper, they're not emotionless." She wiped an imaginary tear from her eye. "Hey, where's my drink?"

Peri threw on his t-shirt and went to the kitchen.

"What am I supposed to wear?" he asked.

"Nothin' but a smile, baby."

The dusk seeped through the windows and made everything in the kitchen glow soft reds and golds. Peri grabbed both glasses and stuck a box of Triscuits under her arm before returning.

Handing him his martini, she slid down to the pillows and took a sip of her own. "Now, about that hand…"

"You are as relentless as a bulldog," he said. "Stubborn as a mule."

"But am I pretty as a picture?"

Skip kissed her nose. "Definitely."

She stared at him until he relented.

"Okay, we got an ID from the prints. Her name was Marnie Russell, in the system for petty theft, a little prostitution, nothing big time. Her last known address was HIS House."

The Homeless Intervention Shelter House, run by the Presbyterian Church next to it, assisted homeless people in finding jobs, homes, and new lives.

"I'm going over there tomorrow to see if anyone remembers her," he told her.

"Any report on the ring or any trace yet?"

Skip looked at her and paused. "Yes."

"Well?" Peri asked. "Here, have some more alcohol. Or do I have to ply you with sex again?"

He smiled. "The ring is the real deal, diamonds, emeralds, set in platinum. Appraiser put it at roughly one and a half mil. We found a strand of hair and fibers in the prongs. I'm still waiting on trace for that."

"Know anything else about the ring?"

"Not yet."

"I do." Peri grinned and reached for her shorts. She pulled a piece of paper out of the pocket. "Read this," she said, handing it to him.

Skip read the news article. "I think I'd better go talk to this Kevin Conway guy, find out if he's missing a ring."

Peri sipped her martini, thinking. "You know, if Marnie's last address was HIS House, she was probably local. Which means—"

"Which means her body should be around here somewhere. We're calling in a cadaver dog to help us."

"Who knew a body could be so easy to hide in Placentia?"

Peri ran her hand down Skip's chest. "Skipper," she said as her hand traveled farther south. "Can I go with you to HIS House tomorrow?"

He laughed and rolled her onto her back, kissing her, hard. "Damn, you are conniving."

They made love again, slower this time, more languid and sensual. At last, they lay together quietly, as if they barely had enough energy to breathe.

"Mmm, that was lovely," she said.

"Yes it was," he replied, then paused. "And yes, you can go with me tomorrow."

Peri laughed. "Oh, Skipper, you're so good to me."

"But here's the rule, Doll: You don't talk to anyone about what you see and hear on this case. No matter what."

"Not even Blanche?"

"Blanche is part of this case, so she's allowed. But no one else."

"How about my reports to Benny? He hired me to keep him informed."

"I'd rather you didn't. Does he have to have details?"

"Not necessarily. He just wants to know if he's on the short list of suspects."

"And when do you plan to tell him that?"

"Hopefully, one step ahead of the handcuffs," Peri said, and popped a cracker into her mouth.

CHAPTER 8

Peri stood in the parking lot of the Homeless Intervention Shelter House, waiting for Skip. While she waited, she took pictures of the pale blue farmhouse with its white picket fence. She wondered how many people drove past without even seeing it from the road, much like they passed the homeless people who stayed there, without seeing them. The day shone brightly but not hot. Still, no one took advantage of the large, green backyard.

I guess the occupants have spent enough time outside, she thought. *They probably savor each moment being under a roof.*

Finally, Skip's black SUV pulled into the lot. Peri smiled as he got out, noting his gold polo shirt and navy chinos, his short, peppery hair impervious to the breeze. *Damn, he's a handsome guy.*

"Golf day?" she asked him.

Skip looked down at his shirt. "Why, yes, Miss Eagle Eye, this is my golf league shirt. We tee off at three."

Karen Anderson met them at the door. A tall, lithe woman in her 30s, she smiled at Skip and Peri with her mouth, but the rest of her face did not share the enthusiasm. Although her body looked fit, and her light brown hair styled, there were stress lines around her eyes, particularly between her eyebrows.

Peri had met her type before, usually in the grocery store. Muscles as firm as the expression on their faces, these tightly wound gals used their shopping carts as ramming devices in an attempt to meet their schedules. Peri could see at a glance she and Skip were ruining Mrs. Anderson's timetable, and they weren't appreciated.

"Oh, yes," Karen told Skip, looking at Marnie's last arrest photo. "I remember Marnie. She stayed with us for about six months."

Skip and Peri sat down in the tidy living room while Karen quickly dug through a blue folder.

"Here it is," she said at last, handing Skip a piece of paper and sitting down. "Marnie was a helpful girl, pretty quiet, though. She kept her room clean, helped with the household chores, always came in before curfew. I thought she was making progress here. She had a job at McDonald's, up on Yorba Linda Boulevard."

The shelter manager shifted her weight in the chair, perching forward as if she wanted to leave. "Then David came along."

"David?" Skip replied, scribbling notes.

"I don't remember his last name. He worked at the drugstore across from McDonald's. Marnie started spending a lot of time with him. I didn't like him, and I'm not even sure Marnie did. She was just so needy. I thought he was opportunistic, self-absorbed, and maybe violent."

Peri looked at Skip, who was reading the shelter report on Marnie and writing notes in his own book. He didn't say anything, so Peri asked, "What makes you think he was violent?"

"After Marnie hooked up with him, we were in the kitchen and she accidentally dropped a mug. It broke. It wasn't a big deal, she'd dropped things before, but her reaction was so different. She cringed and started crying, as if she thought I might do something to punish her." Karen tapped her hand on the table. "A week later, she was gone. That was two weeks ago."

Skip looked up from his notes. "Could you describe this *David*?"

"I only saw him a couple of times." Karen swung her crossed leg back and forth, jiggling her foot. "Really tall, over six feet. Beefy. His hair is dirty blond, down to his shoulders. I think he's got a beard, a scraggly one."

"Could we see Marnie's room?" Skip asked.

"Certainly." Karen rose from her chair and led them up the stairs to a room on the left. She opened the door and stood aside for them to enter. "We usually don't keep the room available for more than a week. The homeless don't always give us notice, or a forwarding address. But no one has requested the space, so it should be like Marnie left it."

Skip and Peri looked around the ten by twelve-foot room. Skip noted the white walls and spare furnishings. Peri noticed the smell of lemon-scented cleanser and the emptiness of the built-in shelves. There were three books standing on the middle shelf, a tattered romance novel, *Tom Sawyer*, and the Bible. A small music box sat against them as a bookend.

Peri opened the music box. The Blue Danube Waltz, high and tinny, played at a frenetic pace.

Skip had kneeled down to look under the bed. He looked up at the box. "What's that white thing under the lid?" he asked.

She picked up the box and removed a piece of white cardboard.

"It's a business card." Turning it over, she read the print. "Maria Castillo, Bradford Square."

"Bradford Square's that assisted living facility down the street, right? Maybe they know something about Marnie, or this David guy."

They returned down the stairs. "Well, thank you, Mrs. Anderson," Skip said. "If we need any more information, we'll be in touch."

"Karen? I brought some new colors." Benny's Aunt Esmy bustled into the room, her arms loaded with bags and cases. "I'm sorry, did I interrupt something?"

"No, Esmy," Karen said. "Detective Carlton and Miz Minny—what exactly was your name? Minnyplease? Anyway, they just stopped by to talk about Marnie."

"Did you know her?" Peri asked. "Marnie Russell."

"Oh, my yes," Esmy said. "I used to do her hair and nails all the time here. She is such a beautiful girl, with that thick, dark hair and those pretty hands. Even with the life she lived, orphaned, fostered, homeless, she never chews her nails. I haven't seen her around for awhile, maybe a week or two."

"Esmy, we have reason to believe she's dead," Peri told her.

The older woman's hands fluttered at her throat. "Oh, dear. Oh, dear that isn't good."

"I'm sorry," Peri said. "If you can think of anyone who might have hurt her, or remember anything she might have said before she left, would you give me a call?"

Skip cleared his throat, so she added, "Me or Detective Carlton here."

He and Peri walked to their cars.

"So, what do we do first, try to find David, or go talk to Kevin Conway?" she asked.

"We?"

"Wait, I've got an idea. We can split up. I can search for David while you go talk to Conway."

The detective took her by the arm. "What is it about *you're not with the police* you don't understand?"

"Well, if you're such a law enforcement demigod, why was I asking all of the questions in there?"

"Because you wouldn't let me ask them."

"Because you were too slow."

"I was trying to pace out the interview, keep it calm and draw out the information."

"Oh, Skipper, I'm too old to wait for all that," Peri told him. "I'm gonna start looking for David. Let me know what you find out about the trace on that ring."

Skip sighed and stared at her over his sunglasses. "Okay, Miss Minny-Please."

"Ha ha. Anyway, I'm sure your pacing will work better on the rich and famous."

The sun had peaked over the shopping center by the time Peri eased her car into a parking space. She dashed around other drivers in their normal lunch hour panic, then strolled into the local drugstore.

"Excuse me," she said to the woman at the counter. "May I speak with the manager?"

"Are you looking for a job, honey?" the older lady asked.

"Oh, no, I—" Peri didn't want to explain, but didn't want to appear rude. She took out her license to show the woman as she introduced herself.

"I'm a private investigator, working with the Placentia Police Department, and I need to talk to the manager about an employee."

For a moment, the woman's face didn't change, frozen in an open-mouthed, wide-eyed look of shock so Peri told her, "Oh, it's not you."

The woman laughed. "Lord, child, I couldn't imagine what you'd want with me. Let me call Max up to the front."

Peri introduced herself to Max the manager. "I'm looking for either a current or former employee," she said, and gave him the description Karen had supplied.

Max, a round, dark man of about forty, nodded. "It sounds like David Waters. He stocked shelves for two, perhaps three, months." His soft voice had the precise clip of an Indian accent. "I caught him trying to break into the pharmacy two weeks ago, so I fired him."

"Did you file a police report?"

"No," he told her. "I probably should have, but nothing was broken, so I simply told him to leave."

He shook his head, looking down at the floor. "He was a disagreeable young man. Quite disagreeable."

"We're looking for him in connection with a disappearance." Without an actual body, Peri found it difficult to say the word *homicide*. "Would it be possible to get his last known address?"

"Oh, yes. Come with me to the office, and I'll get it for you."

Armed with information, Peri drove to the police station. She saw Skip's SUV in the parking lot, so she went in and helped herself to the chair in his office.

"His name is David Waters. Here's his last known address, we can look him up and see if he's got a record," she said. "Have you talked to Kevin Conway yet?"

Skip looked up from his paperwork. "Hey, Doll, nice to see you, but I've got other cases, you know."

"But they're probably boring, Skipper."

"True, but I get paid, just the same. And right now, we don't even have a body."

Peri leaned over the desk. "Oh, Skip, let me work this one. I can gather all the information and give it to you for the arrest."

He laughed. "Arrest? Aren't you a little ahead of yourself? We may never find Marnie's body. The killer might have even dumped it off Ortega Highway."

Highway 74, or Ortega Highway, named for a local don, wound over one hundred and ten miles of mountainous wilderness between San Juan Capistrano on the coast and the inland Lake Elsinore. Dead bodies had a habit of turning up there, if the wildlife didn't claim them first.

"All the more reason to let me handle the legwork."

"Here's the thing, Peri—you've just gotten your license and you don't even carry a gun." Skip looked at her, his face serious. "I know it sounds like a typical background check, but it's not. You're asking strangers a lot of questions, and one of those strangers just might be a murderer. Murderers don't want to answer questions, and one more body doesn't usually bother them."

"Don't worry, I know I can do this. That I'm new to the job just means I still remember the rules of the road, so I'm not going to put myself in harm's way. No, I don't like guns so I don't carry one, but I think you're making a tremendous leap from a severed hand to gun-toting killers. Plus, I've got a good instinct for bad people. If a situation feels wrong, I'm outta there."

"Okay," he told her. "On one condition. You tell me where you're going and who you're going to see *every step of the way*."

"Yes, sir," Peri said with a salute and a smile. She walked to the door, then turned to Skip. "Can I go to Kevin Conway's house, now, Dad?"

Skip put his papers down and stared at her. "Go on. But be careful, Doll."

CHAPTER 9

The drive to Kevin Conway's house felt like steering through a maze. Peri wound her car back and forth along Mulholland Drive until she came to the turnoff specified by Mapquest, after which she began a mind-numbing series of twists down tiny, crowded streets, to the left, then right, then left. Even where there were no vehicles stacked against the curbs, each street seemed to be the width of only one car. Old trees extended their branches across the sky, forming canopies, making her feel claustrophobic.

One hand on the steering wheel and the other clutching directions, she finally arrived at the address. The house stood in the middle of the hill, the driveway slanting down while the walkway slanted up. She perched the Honda in the drive, wishing her parking brake could be set to Extra Strength.

As she approached the front door, Peri noted the casual elegance of the house. The long walkway to the craftsman-style home held little mini-gardens to surprise the visitor. A fountain here, a koi pond there, a sitting bench surrounded by lush greens.

It certainly impressed Peri, who lived in a two-bedroom bungalow with dead miniature roses and an overgrown bougainvillea. The sun dappled the leaves, moist from the sprinklers, and created a reservoir of cool air around the home.

Peri pressed the doorbell and heard a low, dulcet tone in response. After a few moments, the door opened.

"Miss Minneopa? Come in," Kevin Conway said. He extended his hand to shake and smiled politely through his sultry eyes. His hand felt firm but unenthusiastic.

"Mr. Conway, so nice to meet you." She took stock of her host as they walked across the earthy Mexican tile into the living room. A slender man in his thirties, his entire presence suggested the preening Hollywood lifestyle. Wool pants and a V-neck cashmere sweater, both in soft butter cream, accentuated the evenly tanned, polished skin. His hair looked as though each strand had been individually cut, to showcase its beauty. She had never seen a man so stunningly groomed.

They entered a large room of eclectic décor. The clean lines of Shaker-style tables balanced the softness of a leather couch and chair. Saturated teal and peach colors played against the rich, golden tones, in accent pillows, an upholstered rocking chair, and a thick, beautiful area rug.

Kevin eased into the leather chair with the grace of a Siamese cat. "How can I help you, Miss Minneopa?"

"First of all, I'd like to thank you for pronouncing my name correctly," Peri told him, sitting at the edge of the sofa. "I've come to ask you about your grandparents' estate. I understand you're auctioning off a major portion of it in a few months."

"Well, there's not much left of it to sell. Their house was taken over by creditors in the late 80s. Most of what's left are portraits, signed scripts, a few paintings and some jewelry."

"You're not keeping anything for sentimental reasons?"

Kevin smiled. "I'm afraid you're looking at the last of the line. And I'm not very sentimental."

"I'm no one to talk, but maybe you shouldn't shut the door completely on having your own family."

"Miss Minneopa, I have a family. It consists of a life partner and two cats, none of whom care about Nana's old tiara."

"Still, I'm surprised you're selling the *Forever Roses* ring."

He shook his head. "It was less of a family memento and more of a showpiece. To the world, my grandfather personally created this magnificent ring as a proclamation of love for my grandmother. In reality, their relationship was plagued by his carousing and her ruthlessness. For them, the ring was an enormous symbol for *Forever a Heel*. Would you care for a drink? I've got some great single malt scotch."

Peri glanced at her watch. "It's a little early for me, thanks. Besides, I'll need a clear head to find my way back to the freeway, if the birds haven't eaten my trail of breadcrumbs."

Kevin stretched out of the chair and moved to the bar, where he assembled something clear and bubbly with a wedge of lime. "So, what would you like to know about the ring? Forgive me, but you don't appear to be a buyer."

"No, I'm afraid it's not my color," Peri said. "Do you actually have the ring?"

His eyebrows arched slightly. "Why, of course. Not here, but we have it stored in the family vault."

"When's the last time you saw it?"

"I visited the vault a few months ago," he said. "Rick and I went through everything and decided what to keep and what to sell."

"And the ring was there?"

"Certainly." Kevin's voice took a hard edge. "Why?"

Peri took a deep breath. "Is it possible that there was a second ring made?"

"I doubt it. The original was quite expensive and unique. Why do you ask?"

"When's the last time you had it appraised?"

"Well, I personally haven't had it appraised yet," he said. "And I can't find any paperwork on the previous appraisal, although my grandparents' records weren't very thorough. We're taking it to the dealer on Monday. Miss Minneopa, these questions are becoming tiresome. Why do you want to know about my grandmother's ring?"

"Because, we found a ring in Placentia recently, diamond and emerald leaves surrounding a diamond with facets shaped like a rose. Our analysts estimate it's worth $1.5 million. Sound familiar?" She handed him a photo.

Kevin's face slackened as he processed the information. "This certainly looks like Grandma's ring."

"Do you know Marnie Russell?"

"Who?"

Peri took another picture out of her tote and handed it to him. He looked it over carefully.

"She doesn't look familiar. Why do you ask?"

"Did your family ever spend any time in Orange County? North O.C., to be exact."

"Is this Marnie woman the one who has the ring?"

"Sort of."

"Well, obviously, if it's the real ring, it belongs to my family, although I don't know how she could have stolen it. Where do I go to claim it?"

"That I don't know," Peri told him. "You may have to file a motion or something in court to establish ownership. Even so, you won't be able to get it back right away."

"Why not?"

"We found it on Marnie's hand. We haven't found the rest of her yet."

His bedroom eyes opened at last.

Peri rose from her seat and gave him a business card. "Here's my card. I've written the number for Detective Carlton of the Placentia Police Department on the back. When you've verified your ring, give us a call. We're interested in figuring out why these rings look so much alike."

As Peri returned to her car, she glanced up at the second story window of the house. She saw Kevin, looking down at the street, a phone against his ear.

Holding her directions, Peri carefully retraced her steps back to the 101 and pointed her Honda south. She thought about the puzzle pieces while she drove. A homeless girl's hand found in Benny's freezer, wearing an old movie star's ring. What the hell did any of it mean? She glanced at the clock.

"Two," she said aloud, braking hard. Rush hour started early in Los Angeles. Traffic on the 101 had gone from a smooth pace to a stop-and-go stutter. She'd be on the road for at least another hour and a half. "By the time I hit Placentia, it'll be time for that drink."

CHAPTER 10

By ten o'clock the next morning, Skip had written three reports about the men they had arrested for fighting over on Santa Fe Avenue. He would have handed them over to the Gangs Unit, but the men were from the same gang, knifing each other over a parking space in one of the nearby duplexes on the street. It didn't count as *gang activity* so Skip got stuck with the paperwork. As he typed, he became aware of someone at his doorway.

"I'm looking for Detective Carlton," the man said.

Skip kept staring at his computer screen, typing. He hated when people stood at his doorway, with 'Skip Carlton, Crimes Persons Detective' clearly visible on the window, and asked if he was Detective Carlton. Who else would he be?

"You found him," he said at last.

The stranger walked forward and extended his hand. "My name is Kevin Conway."

Skip looked up. He stood briefly and shook Kevin's hand, then sat back down as he watched the slight frame glide into the gray plastic and metal chair across from the desk.

"How can I help you, Mr. Conway?"

"I've come about my grandmother's ring."

Skip leaned back in his chair. He knew what Conway wanted to talk about, but he didn't feel like making it easy for him. "What about your grandmother's ring?"

"A woman came to see me, a private investigator named Minneopa." Kevin smoothed his black cotton shirt, picking a stray hair from the sleeve. "She showed me the picture of a ring you have in evidence. Something to do with a murder."

He paused there, waiting for Skip.

"And?"

"According to Miss Minneopa, the ring you have has been appraised at $1.5 million. I think there's been some mix-up."

"What kind of mix-up would that be?"

"Let's not be coy, Detective Carlton," Kevin said.

"The one thing you'll never find me is coy," Skip told him. "I know who you are, and I know about the Forever Roses ring. Now, why don't you tell me why you're here."

Kevin smiled. "You see, Detective, the ring in my family vault should have been the one worth millions, not the one on a dead woman's hand."

"Do you have a ring in your vault, one that's not worth millions?"

Kevin's smile faded. "There's been a mix-up."

"What do you expect me to do?"

"Detective Carlton, my family believed the ring in our vault was the real Forever Roses. The one I found in there yesterday afternoon was a very nice, much less expensive replica. Now that I'm trying to auction the rest of the Conway/Marquette estate, I need the real ring. It's the showpiece of the collection."

Skip scratched his head, frowning. "You expect me to give you the ring we found?"

"Not give, exactly," Kevin told him. "Trade. I've brought the replica with me today. I thought we could just trade it for the real one."

Skip laughed. "First of all, Mr. Conway, the ring we have in evidence is just that: evidence, in a murder investigation. We won't be releasing it to anyone, anytime soon. Second, once we do release the ring, it will be up to the court to decide who is the rightful owner."

"Of course I'm the rightful owner," Kevin said, his words clipped in anger. "My grandfather had that ring made. It was all over the papers when he gave it to my grandmother."

"Maybe, but it looks to me like your grandfather had two rings made," Skip said. "One ring went to your grandmother and the other went somewhere else."

Kevin Conway glared at the detective. "Now you're just being ludicrous. It's obvious someone else had a replica made and swapped it for the real one."

Skip had reached his nice guy quota for the day. "Nothing seems obvious to me, Mr. Conway, except that you're wasting my time. The ring we have in evidence is going to stay in evidence until we're finished with it. I suggest you consult with an attorney."

The phone interrupted their argument. Skip answered it, turning his back on Kevin.

"Hey, Doll," he said. "Guess who's in my office?"

"If it's George Clooney," Peri replied. "I'll be right over."

"He's too young for you. Actually, Kevin Conway's in here, demanding his ring back."

"No joke. Where's his?"

"He says the one that's been lying in the vault for years is a fake."

Skip could hear Kevin's voice over his shoulder, restating his case, or perhaps, threatening legal action. He put his hand against his ear to block out the noise.

"I told Mr. Conway the ring is still part of an ongoing investigation, and we can't release it to anyone."

Kevin's voice grew louder at this point.

"I just called to see if I could talk to you about the case today," Peri said.

"Sure," Skip told her. "Come by this afternoon." He glanced over his shoulder to see Kevin Conway storming out of the office. "And thanks so much for sending Conway to see me."

"Sorry. Let me clean up, and I'll be right there."

After her shower, Peri stood at her closet door, considering her clothing options and trying to avoid the full-length mirror to her right. She liked the way her curves looked in a skirt and blouse, but fifty years of gravity could be seen clearly in her panties and bra. At last, she pulled out a denim skirt and a fitted top with a sweetheart neckline. Maybe Skip wouldn't be quite as angry with her if she wore his favorite outfit.

She drove down to the station and swept into his office.

"Wearing your *don't be mad* clothes isn't going to work," Skip said.

"Not even if we follow it with some make-up sex after work?"

"I don't know," he replied. "I didn't like being ambushed this morning by that snooty, Hell-Lay boy. What a presumptuous asshole."

"I told him to call when he knew anything about his ring," Peri said. "And I gave him both our numbers, just to let him know the police were involved. I had no idea he'd come down here."

"After you left, he made a beeline to the family vault. I guess, once he met with his appraiser, he couldn't be bothered with a phone call."

She sat down. "So, what did he say about his ring?"

"Oh, there's still a ring in the family vault," Skip told her. "But it's a fake. A good, high quality fake, which was no consolation to him. He actually brought his ring down here and expected me to just swap him for the one in our evidence locker."

"How could Marnie have gotten hold of the real thing?"

"That's the question of the day. According to Conway, no one's been in that vault since last February, when he catalogued the contents. And the ring hasn't left the vault since the '60s."

Peri glanced at Skip's notes on the desk, trying to read the upside-down scribbles. "How would Conway know that?"

"He told me there was a big brouhaha when Grandma died in 1964. His granddad tried to have her buried with the ring, but the son threw a fit. Told him his mom only kept it in case she needed to hock it for living expenses. If it hadn't been so valuable, she'd have tossed it in the ocean. It made for quite a family story around the table every Thanksgiving."

"So what happens now? Can Kevin claim the one I found?"

Skip waved his hands. "I don't know. After this morning, I don't care. That's for the court to decide."

He tossed a folder across the desk. "In the meantime, I pulled David Waters' sheet. He's been floating around the system for quite a while, all over the county. Assault, theft, a lot of dangerous activities."

Peri looked at the rap sheet. "The assault charge is interesting. Says he used a knife."

Skip nodded. "That's what I figured, too. Want to go with me?"

She jumped out of the chair. "Don't have to ask me twice."

Nutwood Apartments mostly served the students who attended California State University in Fullerton, but with its month-to-month rent, less ambitious tenants often found a temporary home as well. Skip and Peri walked down the faded stucco hallway, the walls scarred by years of traffic, toward Apartment 132. Two doors from their destination, the apartment manager met them with the keys. Skip put his hand out to stop Peri's forward motion.

"You stay here," he told her.

As she watched him step up to the door and knock, it occurred to Peri that a ground floor apartment might make a back door escape easy. She retreated down the hall and around to the outside of the building. There were no back doors, but she tried to count windows to determine where Waters might be.

As she scanned the building, Peri saw glass sliding open and hands fiddling with a screen. She ran over to the window to see a shaggy blond head pop out from the opening.

"Hey," she shouted.

The young man looked up at her, then kept scooting out the window.

"Stop," Peri told him.

Ignoring her, he turned sideways to fit his shoulders through the opening. Peri had never had to restrain anyone physically. Unsure of whether she could hold him, she did the only thing she could think of to prevent his escape. She swung her tote bag. The large, leopard-print satchel made contact, knocking him back inside as she heard the apartment door open and Skip's voice.

"David Waters?"

"Ow, somebody hit me with a brick," the young man said.

Skip looked out the window and saw Peri, feet squarely planted in the wet grass, holding her tote in both hands. "You do this?" he asked her.

She shrugged. "He was climbing out the window. I had to do something."

"Get in here." His words clipped in irritation.

Peri went back down the hall and into the apartment. In the living room, she looked around at the spare furnishings, then at the pale, doughy man sitting on the couch, holding his head. The room smelled of pizza, body odor and unwashed hair.

"What have you got in that thing?" Skip asked her, pointing to her bag.

"Bricks."

He rolled his eyes, then turned his attention back to the young man. "Mr. Waters, we need to ask you some questions about Marnie Russell. We can either do this here, or we can go down to the station."

"What about Marnie," Waters said, his raspy voice belligerent. "She file a complaint or something?"

"When did you last see her?"

"I dunno. She dumped me, like, two, three weeks ago." He rubbed his temples. "Bitch actually said she could do better. Homeless, strung-out loser, could do better than me? Hah."

He huffed. "Stupid bitch." Looking up at Peri, he said, "You the one who hit me? I oughta—"

"You oughta what?" Peri asked. "Hit me back, like you used to hit Marnie?"

He sat back, his voice softened. "Nah, it's okay, I'm not mad."

"Did Marnie make you mad, David?" Skip pulled out his notepad and pen.

"Mad? No, I pitied her. Poor, stupid bitch, didn't know when she'd hit the gravy train."

"Dating you was such a step up for her?"

"Well, sure. I had a decent job, this place, I was moving up. She was staying at the shelter, for God's sake. She coulda lived with me."

"From what I hear," Peri told him, "You don't have a decent job lately."

"Ah, that stupid manager," Waters said. "He's a nutcase. Thought I was trying to steal from him. Like they keep anything interesting in that drug case."

"From your record, I'd say he had a good reason to be suspicious," Skip told him.

"David," Peri said. "Did Marnie tell you why she was living at the shelter?"

He chuckled. "Cause McDonald's don't pay a living wage. She couldn't afford no place else."

"Tell us about the last time you saw Marnie," Skip said.

"We was having lunch at Mickey-D's. She told me she thought her luck had turned. Said she was getting outa the shelter, moving up, way up." He looked down at the worn carpet. "Then she said we was done, that I was some kinda brute or something. Brute. I didn't even hit her that hard."

"Yeah, the nerve," Peri said.

"That's the last time?" Skip asked.

"Yeah. I stopped by the shelter once after that, but they told me she was gone."

"Mrs. Anderson told you that?"

"No, the old bag," he said. "The one cutting hair."

Peri looked up from her notes. "Do you mean Ms. Bean?"

"Is that the old lady? I seen her around, sure."

"How about Benny?"

The unkempt man looked up at Peri, his face a big question mark. "Who?"

"Benny Needles," Skip said. "You know him?"

"Needles?" Waters laughed. "Sounds like a drug dealer." His laughter died away as he looked up at the detective's scowl. "Not that I would know about drug dealers, Officer."

Skip's cell phone rang. Peri watched him step out into the hallway to answer, then return to the apartment after a few moments.

"Thank you for your time, Mr. Waters," he said. "Stay close by. We'll be in touch."

Skip turned and left the apartment, subtly pushing Peri in front of him. Once they reached the car, he took her by the arm. "What the hell's wrong with you, hitting Waters in the head like that?"

She pulled out of his grasp, surprised. "He was escaping."

"So let him go. We can always catch him later." Skip held the door for her. "You'll be lucky if he doesn't press assault charges. And I'll be lucky if the department stays out of it."

"This would've never happened to Philip Marlowe."

"Because the rules for cops and private dicks were different in the 30s, and, oh yeah, Marlowe was *fictional*."

"Fine." Peri fastened her seatbelt. "By the way, who was on the phone?"

"Blanche. She's at Kraemer Park. Someone just found a body there, with no hands."

CHAPTER 11

The red lights from the squad cars were barely visible in the midday sun. Peri saw Skip dig his way through the crowd as they swarmed around the yellow police tape barricading the corner of the Backs Building. She took her time getting out of the car, excited about investigating a murder, but anxious about the scene.

Peri wound through the curious onlookers and slipped under the tape, stopping on a rise of grass, where she could watch Skip and Blanche work. She couldn't see the body clearly, but could only discern a tangle of dark hair and a golden covering, either a blanket or a coat. Blanch knelt beside the body, pointing and speaking into a digital recorder. Skip stood to the side, looking down at Blanche and taking notes.

After a few minutes, Skip waved Peri over. She hesitated, having never seen a dead body, except for relatives in their caskets. Even from a distance, she could tell this one needed brighter lipstick. As she moved closer, she saw the skin looked dark and pocked, decomposed from daily watering. Although it fascinated her, Peri did not want to showcase her inexperience by suddenly fainting or throwing up.

"What's it look like, Beebs?" Skip asked.

"I'll know more when I get her back to the office, but it's definitely a young female, dead at least a day, or two."

Peri had finally joined them, looking over Blanche's shoulder at the corpse. Still tucked against the building, the body looked as if she had laid down for a nap, a rich, golden coat buttoned and smoothed over her legs, her arms crossed in front, modestly hiding the fact they had no hands. Peri could smell a combination of rotting meat, wet dirt, and general compost, not as horrible as she had feared. Neither was the sight of the darkened skin, patchy from deterioration. Even the face, missing lips, and most of the nose, didn't creep her out as much as she had imagined. Peri relaxed and listened to the conversation.

"My first guess is blunt force trauma," Blanche said, pointing to a dark spot in the victim's forehead. "I'll get you results as soon as I can. By the way, Peri, thanks for your insights about Dani the other night. Turns out, she's been seeing a Goth saxophonist who dropped out of college. We're having him over for dinner on Tuesday. Wanna come?"

Peri laughed. "Wouldn't miss it for the world. Maybe I should try to corner the 'moms with teenagers' market. I'll bet they could use an investigator sometimes."

Skip and Peri watched as the coroner's technicians loaded the body into the dark wagon.

"What are your thoughts?" he asked.

She turned to answer when a familiar voice shouted from beyond the yellow tape.

"Miss Menopause."

Skip erupted in laughter while Peri shushed her client. "Benny, we've talked about the name thing. What are you doing here?"

Benny leaned across the tape. "I heard about the body, Miss Peri. I thought maybe you'd be here, you could tell me something." He peered at the bag being rolled into the coroner's van.

"She probably could tell you a few things, Benny," Skip said. "But first, I think there are some things you'll tell me."

Benny's widened eyes amused the detective, but Peri jumped in to save the deer from the headlights.

"We just need a little more information," she told him. "Could we take you to lunch? We'll all have a nice little talk."

"I dunno," Benny replied.

"My treat," Peri said. "Capone's?"

The mention of the local Italian restaurant changed everything. Skip held the door of his SUV open for Peri while Benny scrambled to climb into the back.

"I should've brought a booster seat," the detective whispered into her ear.

The small storefront in the Placentia Towne Shopping Center hid a cavernous room with tables and booths, a small bar in the front of the house and a large kitchen in the back. Over calzones and minestrone, Skip and Peri began the long process of dragging information out of Benny.

"So, Ben, do you visit HIS House often?" Skip asked.

"Not very."

"Perhaps when Aunt Esmy's there?" Peri said.

"Yeah, sometimes she asks me to drive her. I think she's trying to save gas, fixed income and all that."

"So you've maybe seen Marnie Russell at the shelter?" she asked.

"Who?"

"Marnie Russell," Skip said. "The dead girl."

"No, no," Benny replied. "I mean, I don't know, I might have seen her. I don't know anyone by name there, except Mrs. Anderson."

Skip put Marnie's picture on the table and shoved it forward. Benny looked at it in fleeting increments, peeking at the photo and then gazing at the wall.

"Maybe," he said at last. "I might have seen her there."

"Do you remember the last time you saw her?" Peri asked him. "What she was doing, who she was talking to?"

Benny said nothing for awhile, concentrating on his food, shoveling each bite into his mouth with ferocity. Skip looked at Peri and sighed, his eyebrows a stern line of displeasure.

"Think, Benny," she said. "It's important. Unless you want the police to come back and search your house."

"Okay, okay, I kinda remember her getting her nails done. Aunt Esmy was painting them bright pink, going on and on about how pretty they looked. Then some big guy came in and started yelling. I don't like yelling, so I left."

"Some big guy? Did he look like this?" Skip shoved David Waters' picture at him.

Benny identified him at once.

"What day was that?" Skip asked.

"Aw, geez, I don't know."

"Well it had to be Monday or Tuesday," Peri said. "Those are the only days Esmy is at the shelter."

"It was Tuesday." Benny spoke with sudden certainty. "Aunt Esmy needed a ride and I didn't want to give her one, cause I was waiting for the UPS guy to deliver my ashtray. It was a week before Dino's birthday, and I missed the UPS truck and had to go all the way to their facility to pick up my package."

He stared down at his meal. "They were closing, but I made them open the door. I opened it right there, I didn't even wait, I was so excited. Imagine, Bama Dillert's ashtray."

"The big guy was yelling at Marnie?" Skip tried to get Benny back to the subject.

"Yeah, yeah, he was making a fuss. I think she dumped him. He kept saying she'd be sorry."

Skip and Peri looked at one another.

"Thanks for the info, Benny," Peri told him. "Want some tiramisu?"

After dropping Benny off at his car, Skip drove Peri to the station. They walked in together, pausing for coffee before heading to his office.

"Wonder if Waters has an alibi," Peri said.

"We don't even know time of death," Skip told her.

"I know, but I'd like to hear his schedule for the past week or so. It sure sounds like he had a motive." She sat down in the visitor's chair. "Still, maybe David Waters didn't kill her."

"Why not?"

"First of all, he acted from the beginning like he was God's gift to Marnie. He's the one with the great job, the great future, she's the ungrateful witch who turned it all down."

"So?"

"So I don't think he knew about the ring."

"The ring doesn't have to be motive, Peri," Skip told her. "It could have just been a crime of passion."

"Except that, if he'd gotten mad and accidentally killed her, he had to have seen the ring on her finger. Why didn't he take it for himself?"

"Maybe he couldn't get it off. He cut off the hands, then—"

"Then hid it in Benny's freezer, a man he doesn't know?" Peri shook her head. "It's not like Benny lives close to the park. He's at least half a mile away. And why cut off both hands to get to the ring, when you could just cut off a finger?"

"To keep the police from identifying the body."

"You think Waters would think like that?"

Skip smiled. "No, he's a petty crook. I see him as the type who'd cut and run if he killed someone. The trace report should be done by now. Let's see if anything turned up on that ring, Miss Menopause."

He had only a moment to laugh before Peri slugged him in the arm.

A few moments later, he returned with a stack of paper from the fax machine, the results of the trace analysis, prepared by the county forensics team. He sat down and leafed through the papers.

Peri watched him read for a few minutes before impatience overwhelmed her. "So, what's it say?"

He continued to flip through pages. "Sorry, sometimes it's hard to digest these things. They found a few partial prints on the bag, but no hits in the system."

"I'm assuming that means Benny, too?"

"Nope, they're not Benny's." Skip read further. "Partials seem to match full prints on the freezer door. Oh, and Jason wanted to thank you for wearing gloves when you were cleaning the freezer. Made the printing so much easier."

"It had nothing to do with processing a crime scene," Peri said. "It was so filthy in there, I'd have wrapped my body in Saran Wrap if I could have."

Skip looked over at her, raising his eyebrows suggestively. "Maybe you could show me that look sometime."

"I don't think so. Too sweaty." She pointed to the report. "What about the ring?"

"On the ring, there's DNA from two donors, a hair sample that matches one of the donors, and a wool fiber. Donor one is our victim, Donor two is unknown."

"Didn't they run the DNA through CODIS?"

"It's not like CODIS has everyone's DNA." His eyes scanned down the page, looking for results. "No hits."

Peri sat back in her chair and put her feet up on the desk. "So, Marnie is wearing a famous ring, one that should have been in a family vault, of an actor who was an infamous wolf." She looked at Skip. "Is it possible he gave the ring to one of his conquests?"

"It's possible." He sat up, following her thread. "For that kind of bling, she'd have to be quite a gal."

"I guess we could go through the gossip columns of that era," Peri said. "It'll be excruciating."

Skip smiled. "You said you wanted to help."

"Do you know how many years' worth of newspapers and gossip rags I'll have to read through?"

"Poor, poor baby," he told her. "But think of the gratification when you find the link."

Peri stared at him, scowling. "Maybe there's another way. Conway gave that ring to his wife in, what, '47? If he gave a duplicate to someone else, it would have been after that...and she'd be pretty old by now."

"If she's still alive." Skip rubbed the back of his neck. "If Marnie came by the ring locally—"

"There's that assisted living facility right down the street from HIS House," Peri told him. "Bradford Square."

Skip nodded. "Looks like we need the list of residents."

CHAPTER 12

Bradford Square stood like a large and stately vessel amid the plain, boxy apartments lining the street. The blue clapboard building, trimmed in white, invited visitors to sit on the large front porch and rest before entering the double doors. Once inside, the atmosphere balanced the delicacies of assisted senior living, trying to maintain a peaceful and relaxed mood while extolling the virtues of exercise and vitality. This could be difficult for those residents with Alzheimer's, who sometimes became mired in restlessness, and whose exercise might consist of breathing in and breathing out, repeating as necessary.

Peri took a few snapshots before walking up to the porch with Skip.

"I admit, these places creep me out a little," she told him.

"This is one of the nicer ones, Doll. I only hope I can afford something this nice when I need assistance."

"I know." She stood at the door, waiting for Skip to open it. "I just don't want to think about losing control, you know, of my life…or my mind."

"Too late."

Peri pinched his arm as she walked past him. "Ha ha."

Skip and Peri greeted the director of the facility and showed her their IDs. A small, fair-skinned woman, the director's warm smile and inviting gestures made her the perfect person for a job dealing with the public. Peri could picture her as the hostess of a fundraising luncheon, or the nurse coaxing her patient to take his medicine. Maybe even the high-priced madam of an old West bordello, she thought with a smile.

"I'm Maria Castillo, how may I help you today?"

"Ms. Castillo, first of all, we were wondering if you knew Marnie Russell," Skip said, showing her the picture.

"No." She shook her head. "I don't believe so."

"She had one of your business cards," Peri told her. "She was a resident at HIS House."

Ms. Castillo looked at the picture again. "No, I'm sorry. Her face is not familiar to me. You know, I do leave my business cards around town."

"We're trying to find out who this girl knew," Skip said. "She was murdered."

"Ah, this is the one in the news." Ms. Castillo traced the girl in the photo with her fingertip. "A pretty girl, so young."

"Okay, then, would it be possible to get a list of names of your female residents?" he asked.

"Certainly, Detective. If you'll have a seat in our lobby, I'll get it for you."

As she turned to go, Peri told her, "We're interested in any of your female residents who talked about being actresses or working in the movies, especially in the 40s, if that helps."

Ms. Castillo stopped and faced them, her eyes a little too wide for her smile. "Why, that would be Miss Banks."

"Who?" Skip asked.

"Sylvia Banks. She was so sweet, always sharing stories of being in the movies and old Hollywood."

"You said 'she *was* so sweet'," Peri said.

"Yes, she passed away about three weeks ago. She lived here for about a month. We were all very sad when she passed."

"Had she been ill?" Peri asked.

"Not particularly, but she was in her 80s and frail, just tiny. One night she wandered away, which she'd never done before. We found her the next morning behind Ralph's, nearly frozen, a little cotton jacket over her nightclothes. She only lasted a week after that."

"Was it from the exposure?" Skip said.

The director shook her head. "No, it was more like the life went out of her. I can't explain it, except that her mood suddenly changed. She was depressed, didn't want to eat, and actually became incoherent."

"Incoherent how?" Peri asked. "Did she track your conversations, understand what you were telling her?"

"Oh, yes, she'd answer questions," Ms. Castillo said. "But mostly she kept saying, 'I've lost him in my coat'. By the end, it almost sounded like a chant."

"I've lost him in my coat," Skip repeated as he wrote. "Any idea what she meant?"

Ms. Castillo shook her head.

"Did she have any particularly close friends here?" Peri asked. "Or did anyone visit regularly?"

"Her daughter came every day, from Palm Springs. She was so devoted. You could tell by watching them how close they were."

"Could we get the daughter's name and address?" Skip asked.

"And how about any nurse or attendant who regularly took care of her," Peri added.

"Certainly, let me get Mrs. Lopez." Ms. Castillo and Skip went into the office, where the director made a phone call, then searched for Sylvia Banks' information on the computer at her desk.

As she waited at the office door, Peri felt a bump on her calves. She turned to see a wheelchair trying to push her legs out of the way. A lean, angular woman sat tall in the chair, her purple floral dress high on her neck and low on her ankles. Her thin lips drew a red line across her face as one eyebrow lifted in expectation.

"Halls are to remain clear of obstructions," she said as if reciting.

"Yes, of course," Peri replied, "Terribly sorry." As the woman wheeled past, Peri asked, "Excuse me, but did you know Sylvia Banks?"

The wheelchair stopped. An ancient, manicured hand reached down and turned the right wheel until the woman faced Peri, her expression stern.

"I should say not. Parading around like she belonged in polite society—she was nothing more than a Hollywood tart. And that coat, ugh." The woman wrinkled her nose. "She claimed it was cashmere, but I saw the label. It was nothing more than Australian Merino."

Giving one more disdainful glare, she wheeled her back to Peri and continued down the hall, passing a short, slender woman in the facility's uniform of blue cotton top and white pants. The woman wore her long dark hair pulled into a ponytail, revealing a wide face, high cheekbones and sparkling eyes.

"Mrs. Lopez," Ms. Castillo said. "This is Detective Carlton and his associate, Miss Men—"

"Just call me Peri."

"They'd like to ask you a few questions about Miss Banks." She pointed toward her office. "Please, sit in here. You'll be more comfortable."

"Mrs. Lopez, could you give us an idea of Miss Banks' routine?" Skip asked, as they all found chairs and sat down in the cluttered room. "Specifically, anyone she visited with, and any places she went outside of the facility."

"Miss Banks is a lovely woman," Mrs. Lopez told them in a lilting Mexican accent. "So easy to take care of. Every day, I brush her hair and help her with her make-up. She never leave her room without her make-up, and we go to breakfast."

She stopped and looked at the ceiling. "Two pieces of toast, lightly buttered, and hot tea, the same every day. Then I take her to the sunroom, and she sits by the window and enjoys the heat. She say to me, 'Claudia, I wish it wasn't so cold, I'd like to sit on the patio.'"

"She was probably so used to the Palm Springs heat," Peri said. "Orange County must have felt like the North Pole to her."

"Si, yes. She read for awhile, I think. When I come to get her, there are always people around, asking her about the movies."

Peri eased back into her chair. "Ms. Castillo said her stories were very popular."

"Very. She is a quiet woman, but when you ask her about playing a part in a movie, and the stars, she tell wonderful stories."

"We heard that her daughter visited every day," Skip said.

"At lunch time," Mrs. Lopez told him. "They have lunch together every day, then spend the afternoon talking, watching TV. Her daughter, Mrs. Ressler, is very pleasant, always tip the servers at lunch."

"Tell us about the night Miss Banks wandered off," Peri said.

Mrs. Lopez frowned. "I am not on duty that night, or it would not have happened."

"Who was on duty?" Skip asked.

"Rory," she spat the name out. "Rory Green. He does not work here now."

"Can you tell us what you do know?" Peri said.

The small woman leaned forward. "I take Miss Banks to her room after dinner and help her into her nightgown. I make certain she has her pitcher of water next to the bed, and her book. We say our goodnights, and I leave. When I come in the next morning, everything is in such a state. People are running around, and the police are asking questions, and suddenly, Mrs. Castillo want to see me. The policeman asks, do I know where Miss Banks is, and I say I don't know, that I put her to bed last night. The policeman, his name is Officer Monroe, I don't think he believe me. Then he get a call. Miss Banks is in the hospital. Someone find her behind Ralph's." She stopped and looked at Skip.

"Behind Ralph's," she repeated. "Like a homeless person."

"Mrs. Lopez, did you ever see Miss Banks wear any jewelry?" Peri asked.

The nurse smiled. "Ah, yes, the pretty ring. She wear it all the time. I even help her to clean it, every morning."

"Every morning?"

"Poor thing, she is so thin that her ring is too big for her. It fall off, so it is always in her pocket by the end of the day. There is lint in the corners."

"Did you notice anyone who might have wanted her ring?" Skip asked.

"Oh, no, everyone know it is not real," Mrs. Lopez told him. "She say, 'This trinket? It not worth a dime.' She say it is from an admirer, that it is for the memories she keep it."

Skip leaned forward. "Mrs. Lopez, did she tell you anything about that night? Did she say how she got to Ralph's?"

Gayle Carline

"And did she still have her ring?" Peri asked.

"No, and no," she replied. "She come back a different woman. She does not put on her make-up, or tell her stories, or go out to meals. She doesn't ask me to brush her hair or clean her ring. She keep saying, 'I lost him in my coat.' And when her daughter come to see her, she just lay in her bed and cry."

Tears misted in Mrs. Lopez's eyes. "I'm sorry," she said, dabbing at the moistness. "We see death here many times, we are used to it, and the ones who are confused. But seeing someone's heart break, that is hard."

"Thank you very much for the information," Skip told her and handed her his card. "Please call me if you think of anything else."

He and Peri walked back to the car. Before she got into the seat, she turned and took several photos of the facility for her records.

"It's six o'clock," he said as they got in. "I'm off duty. Is it Miller time?"

"If you're offering pizza with that, I'm there," Peri said.

"Sure. We can go over our notes."

Peri reached over and ran her fingers across his cheek to his ear, and down his neck. He turned to her, a sly smile playing on his mouth.

"Or not," he said.

CHAPTER 13

Peri's new client was late. A wealthy, neurotic-sounding woman, she had insisted on meeting at eight in the morning to discuss surveillance on her husband. Peri sat at her desk, staring at the clock as the numbers morphed into eight thirty. Tapping her pencil against her coffee cup, she fanned the pages of a procedural manual, and fumed.

She remembered the woman from Bradford Square trying to push her out of the way with the wheelchair, as if she were an errant piece of furniture. The blood throbbed in her ears, her heart pumping fast and hard. The rich are so disrespectful, she thought.

Suddenly, her stomach felt like a concrete mixer, rolling and tossing her breakfast around. Surprised, she grabbed the trash can and leaned over it, holding her hair back in her fist. Trembling, sweating, she leaned her body against the desk. The nausea slowly passed, leaving heat that spread through her limbs and up to her head, where it swirled through each hair, every pore. She grabbed a tissue and began dabbing at the sweat.

The phone rang. Peri grabbed it, snapping into the receiver, "What?"

A high, breathy voice faltered. "Miss Menniepenny?"

"That's Minneopa."

"S-S-Sorry. It's Mrs. Cheavers. I'm sorry I'm late."
The voice sounded mortified. "My mother's had a stroke.
I thought I could get her settled in the hospital and make
it to our meeting, but she's just so—I'm so afraid that....
I can't leave her."

Now Peri felt guilty. "Of course, Mrs. Cheavers, I
understand. Why don't you call me later, and we'll make
another appointment?"

Peri drove home and threw her shorts on. Maybe a run
would make her feel better. The momentary nausea had
not returned, but she still felt a little shaky, and a little
annoyed that her new client's emergency wasted her
morning, even if it was justifiable.

Her path, from Bradford Street, to Yorba Linda
Boulevard and around, measured three miles, give or take
a step. June gloom still claimed the morning, with gray
skies and cool air smelling of the ocean, a mere thirty
miles to the west. Adjusting her earpieces, she began at a
quick walk, stretching out until her muscles felt warm.
She made note of the colorful flower beds of her
neighbors' houses as she strode, breathing deeper and
quickening her step. By the time Peri reached Ralph's
shopping center, she ran at an easy pace.

She could feel her lungs working, her throat and nose
opening to let in as much oxygen as possible. Her heart
had begun at a slow rhythm, then pounded vigorously,
before leveling off to a steady beat. Eric Clapton sang in
her ear, his guitar crisp and soaring.

Ah, Slowhand, after all these years, you're still tasty.

At the corner of Chapman and Bradford, Peri felt a familiar warmth gushing between her legs that every woman recognizes.

"Eew," she said aloud and picked up the pace back home. Running to the bathroom, she prepared to clean up a mess, but found nothing. No embarrassing stain awaited her. Looking at the calendar, Peri counted the days. Then she called Blanche.

"I'm late," she said. "Almost two weeks, Beebs."

"I thought you were being careful."

"I am, dammit. Skip and I always use protection."

"*Always?*"

"Shut up and be supportive. What if I'm pregnant?"

She heard Blanche laugh. "Sorry, Peri, it wouldn't be funny. But I'll bet Skip would love to be a dad again."

"Skip is almost finished paying for his youngest daughter's college, I don't think he'd be anxious to dip into his retirement account for one more. Besides, I'm fifty. I can't be raising a baby at my age."

"Sure you could. But before you get all excited, go buy a test kit and pee on the stick."

"You're right. No sense getting my panties in a knot over nothing."

"Right," Blanche said, "And call me when you find out."

Peri walked into her bedroom and hung up the phone. She selected an outfit from her closet, and then started the shower. The hot water felt good as it beat down on her skin. After she had scrubbed herself thoroughly, she stepped out of the shower and grabbed a towel. The phone rang, so she wrapped the towel around her body and answered.

"Can you come by the office?" Skip asked. "I got reports back on the body."

"Sure, how about this afternoon?" Peri wanted enough time to get a kit from the store, wanted to know for certain, before she saw him.

"Sorry, Doll, I got a training session this afternoon. I thought you'd jump down here just to read over my shoulder."

"Yeah, of course," she told him. "I'll be right over."

Damn, Peri thought as she wiggled into a pair of capris, I'll have to go to the drugstore after the police station. Sucking her stomach in, she pulled the zipper up, and then looked into the mirror. Was that a baby bump, or last night's Ben & Jerry's? She grabbed her keys and left, hoping she wouldn't babble to Skip prematurely.

"Looks like there's a baby on the way," he told her as she walked into his office.

"What?" Peri's mouth fell open.

Skip held up the report. "The body was definitely Marnie Russell. It says she was pregnant."

Relieved, Peri sat down before her knees buckled. "Oh, right. What else?"

"She was about eight weeks along," he said, leaning back in his chair. "We're having the amniotic fluid analyzed to see if we can narrow the list of donors. COD was blunt head trauma. Blanche is trying to model the indentation, see if we can match it up with an object."

"Any trace found on her?"

"Her clothes are still at the lab. They're hoping to have some info by tomorrow." Skip looked back at the report. "Beebs was able to narrow the time of death down to two days ago, either Saturday night or Sunday morning. I thought that, after my training class, you and I could go ask Waters what he was doing."

"Sounds like a plan."

He put the report on his desk. "Maybe after that, I could grab some dinner and take it back to my place. You could meet me there."

"No." The word blurted from her mouth.

"Okay, then your place."

"No, no, it's just that I can't tonight. I have to meet a client." She hated lying to Skip, but reasoned she would tell him the truth, eventually. At least after she knew what the truth was.

"How about tomorrow?"

Skip shook his head. "Can't tomorrow, I teach over at Fullerton College."

Peri smiled, rising from the chair. "Well, when we both have a free evening, then," she said. "Later, Skipper."

"Later, Doll."

Buying a pregnancy test kit sounded easy, but as Peri drove toward the local CVS, she realized she knew people there. What if she ran into Max the manager, or even that older woman who had helped her? That would be awkward. She kept driving, all the way into Fullerton, to an Albertson's grocery store, where no one would know her.

Peri stood in the aisle, looking at the family planning section and trying to figure out whether she should buy the generic brand for five dollars or spring for the designer version at ten bucks.

"Miss Moneypenny? Is that you?"

She looked up to see Karen Anderson from HIS House. Turning to face the lanky brunette, Peri curled the corners of her mouth up to approximate a smile.

"Hi, Mrs. Anderson," Peri said. "You know, you can call me Peri. My last name can be a mouthful."

"What a surprise to run into you. Do you live around here?"

"No, I'm just visiting a client," she told her.

"And you stopped at the grocery store? How odd."

Peri looked at the items on the next shelf. She saw bandages and cortisone cream. "I, um, had some extra time, so I thought I'd restock my first aid kit."

"Oh. I see," Karen said. "I heard about finding poor Marnie in the park. How awful. Are you going to arrest her boyfriend?"

"Well, I'm not a police officer, so I'm not arresting anybody. They're still looking at the evidence to try to figure out what happened."

"He was very jealous. I remember when she got a new coat, he accused her of having a sugar daddy." Karen shook her head. "It got pretty ugly in our front yard until I came out and threatened to call the police. And now the poor thing's dead. If you want my opinion, I think David Waters did it. I bet he bashed that poor girl's head."

Peri picked up a box of gauze and a bag of cotton balls. "Thank you, that's interesting information. I'll let Detective Carlton know."

After paying for her items, Peri got back in her car and drove. She knew of a Walgreens Pharmacy a little further toward Harbor Boulevard. Her cell phone rang just as she was maneuvering her car around a parked bus.

Benny's high yelp nearly deafened her. "Miss Peri, you gotta help me. They won't let me go."

"Who won't let you go, Benny?"

"They're in my house, they're touching my things."

"Benny, who are they? Where are you?"

She heard him squeal and a scuffling noise on the other end. "Benny—" she shouted.

A deep voice came on the line. "Who is this?"

"Peri Minneopa," she said. "I'm a private investigator. Who am I talking to?"

"Officer Tony Monroe."

"Where are you, Officer Monroe, and what are you doing to Benny Needles?"

The sound of Benny howling could be heard in the background. "We're at the Needles residence, ma'am," the officer told her. "We're here to bring Mr. Needles in for questioning, and to search the premises. Mr. Needles is being quite uncooperative."

"Officer, I think you can tell Mr. Needles is a little high strung. I'm about fifteen minutes from you. Would it be possible to wait until I get there? I know Benny, and can probably get him to cooperate."

"I have my orders, ma'am."

"I know, Officer Monroe, and I appreciate your situation," Peri told him. "I just think I could help you avoid a nasty struggle if you could wait for me to get there. If you want references, you can talk to Detective Carlton."

"Oh, are you the lady I see in the police station? Sure, Miss Mmm—I'm sorry, I didn't quite get your name."

"Just call me Peri. Can I speak to Benny?" Seconds later, she heard high, frantic panting. "Benny? I'm coming right over. I need you to wait with those officers. Can you do that for me?"

"Yes, Miss Peri."

After calming Benny down, Peri dialed Skip's number, which rolled over to his voicemail. She tried to keep the shrew from her voice, but snapped anyway. "What the hell are uniforms doing down at Benny's? He's all in a state, and now I've got to go take care of him. Frankly, I've got other things to do. Ugh. Call me."

She hung up and threw her phone back in her bag.

"Crap," she said. "I guess I'll get to the drugstore tonight, if they're open late."

CHAPTER 14

Benny stood on the porch, one hand in the pocket of his sharkskin suit and the other hand fingering an unlit cigarette, his head cocked slyly, to match the smile on his face. An officer stood with him, although they did not appear to be speaking to one another.

Great, Peri thought, *he's already retreated into his Dean Martin personae, complete with a cigarette, even though he doesn't smoke. After all, when in doubt, what would Dino do?*

"Miss Peri, good of you to join the party," he said.

"Believe me, Benny, I didn't have any clue they were coming, or I would have been here." She turned to the patrolman. "Are you Officer Monroe?"

Big and beefy, Tony Monroe looked like he had never missed a meal, although he had clearly forgotten to tell his clothes, which strained in every direction to contain him.

Peri introduced herself.

"Nice to finally meet you," Officer Monroe said. "We were told to bring Mr. Needles in for questioning."

"And what are you looking for inside?"

"We have a search warrant for any tools with a serrated blade, like a hacksaw or any large, serrated knife."

"I might be able to speed things up, Officer Monroe," Peri told him. "Do you mind if I go in?"

He nodded once, toward the house. "Knock yourself out."

Peri turned to Benny. "Sit tight, Ben. Let me take care of their search, first."

She took the stairs in one bound, then strode into the house. A young, trim officer with gloves on stood in the kitchen, looking around at the mess with an expression of disgust.

"Hi, I'm Peri Minneopa, and I've been working with Skip Carlton on the Russell case."

"Officer Kenneth Chou," the young man told her.

"I understand you're looking for a serrated weapon. I cleaned this house for years, although you'd never know it."

The officer smiled. "It's gonna take me all day to process this."

"Look, I know Benny. You can check the garage, but Benny's never even been in a Home Depot, so I doubt you'll find much more than a hammer. As for serrated knives, his mother had two, an electric carving knife, and a bread knife."

Peri opened a drawer to the right of the sink and pointed to a large blade with a black handle and a jagged edge. "Here's the bread knife." She opened the cabinet under the drawer and removed a long, narrow box. "And here's the carver."

Officer Chou took the items and looked around at the filth. "I'm surprised you didn't have to dig these out of the dirty dishes, too."

"Benny wouldn't use them," Peri said. "He wouldn't know what they were for. By the way, do you know why they want to question Benny again?"

The officer glanced around, as if revealing classified information. "I overheard the captain talking about a witness who saw the dead girl at Benny's place. Pretty coincidental that she visits him and part of her ends up in his freezer."

Peri smiled. "Yeah, pretty coincidental."

Back outside, Benny strained to see and hear what was happening in his house. When Peri appeared at the door with the other officer, he smiled.

She called Officer Monroe over. "If I could have a couple of minutes to explain to Benny, I can get him to come quietly. If you'd like, I could even drive him to the station myself."

The officer nodded, so Peri sat down with Benny on the porch. "Here's the thing, Ben," she said. "A witness saw Marnie at your house. I'm sure you can see how that looks, with her hand in your freezer and all."

"Miss Peri, I never killed her. I never killed no one. Okay, maybe she walked past my house and we talked, but she never came inside."

"Well, then we should go to the police station so you can tell Skip about it."

Benny pouted. "Why doesn't he come here like before?"

"Maybe because he's busy and can't take the time to drive over. Plus, maybe he's a little mad that you didn't tell him about Marnie being at your house." Peri's phone rang. She dug it out of her bag and answered. Hearing Skip's voice, she moved away from Benny for a more private conversation.

"He's a clear suspect, Peri, I can't baby him," he told her. "Especially not if he lied about knowing Marnie."

"I know, Skip, but I'm trying to get information out of him, too. He won't talk if he's frightened or flustered. He's already gone into Dino mode. You'll be lucky if you get more than the dialog of a Matt Helm movie from him now."

"Well, he'll just have to cool his heels in Interrogation until the real Benny returns."

"Don't be mean to him, Skip. If he killed her, it had to be some kind of accident." Peri was beginning to hate having to stick up for Benny. "Could you at least give him his ashtray back? Or show him your pictures of Al Diller?"

"It's Bama Dillert, and I have pictures of Madison, Indiana."

"Whatever. Just have something fun to show Benny when I get him there. He needs a reward."

"For what? Killing someone?" Skip said. "Look, I gotta get back to the session. Let me talk to Monroe."

Peri handed her phone to the officer and watched him nod and agree to what the detective was saying. He closed her phone and handed it back.

"The detective says you can bring Benny by the station in an hour. He'll be ready to talk to him then." He paused, then added, "Oh, and he said he'd have the ashtray, whatever that means."

Peri smiled and went back to her client. "Benny, we're going to visit Skip around four. He wants to give you your ashtray back."

Benny brightened. "Did he get the DNA back yet?"

"I don't know, but we'll find out when we get there."

CHAPTER 15

By the time Skip finally entered the interrogation room, Benny had asked the same question at least six times, and Peri had exhausted her limited list of topics they could both discuss. She didn't know whether she should be happy to see Skip or bitch slap him for getting her into this mess today.

"Here's your ashtray, Benny," he said. "Forensics is running the DNA tests, but I haven't gotten the report back yet."

Benny took his treasure and held it to the light, then smiled.

"Now, Benny, we need to talk about you and Marnie." Skip's voice became stern. "You lied to me about knowing her. That makes me mad."

"Ain't that a kick in the head," Benny asked.

"Dammit, Benny, cut the Dino act." Skip pounded the table. "I want to know how you knew Marnie and what she was doing in your house."

Benny sat up, eyes wide. "She was never in my house. She was in front, going through my trash cans. I yelled at her to leave my trash alone."

"Why would she be going through your trash?" Peri asked.

"She said she was looking for cans." Benny scoffed. "As if I drink anything from a can."

"And you got mad at her, right?" The detective leaned over him. "You got so mad you hit her, right?"

Benny closed his eyes and shrank away. "No. Yes, I got mad, but I let her go through my trash. There was nothing in there for her, anyway."

Skip's cell phone rang. He checked the caller ID and then took the call. Peri and Benny watched his face, listened to his grunts and one-word answers, trying to discern the other side of the discussion. After a few moments, he hung up and turned back to Benny.

"You can go for now," he told him. "But stay close by."

Benny leaped toward the door like a rabbit from a trap.

"Benny, go wait outside by my car and I'll drive you home," Peri said. After he left, she turned to Skip. "Okay, spill."

"That was the lab. Preliminary analysis of the knives from Benny's shows no blood of any kind. They're clean."

"Skip, I just can't imagine him hacking off anyone's hand."

"Well, who *can* you imagine doing that?"

Peri thought for a moment. "I guess David Waters has to go on my short list, even though it's still hard for me to believe. After that, I'm stumped."

The phone rang as Peri dropped Benny off at his house.

"What did you find out?" Blanche asked her.

"Skip let Benny go, since there still isn't any evidence he killed Marnie," Peri said.

"Not about the case, you goofball. Did you pee on the stick yet?"

"Oh, that." Peri had nearly forgotten about it. "Do you know how hard it is to buy one of those test kits?"

"What's so difficult? You grab it from the shelf, take it to the counter and, voila."

"But I don't want to buy it in front of anyone I know," Peri told her.

"Oh, for Pete's sake, Peri, you buy tampons and condoms all the time. Why would a pregnancy test be more embarrassing?"

"Because then more people will be waiting to know how the test came out." Peri sighed. "I'd rather stay below the radar, Beebs. If I'm not pregnant, no one will know about my recklessness."

"And if you are?"

"I'll burn that bridge when I come to it. If it's so easy, maybe you could buy a kit for me."

"I'm not buying a pregnancy test kit. What if my kids want to know why Mommy thinks she's pregnant? And Paul would jump all over it. He keeps hinting he'd like to have another one."

"So you *do* see how it is?" Peri grinned. "I'm going to Palm Springs tomorrow. I'll pick a kit up when I'm there."

"I don't know how you can afford to wait so long," Blanche said. "I'd be on pins and needles."

"It's easy. As long as I don't take the test, I'm not pregnant."

"By the time you take the test, the kid'll be in high school."

"Look, Beebs, I'm exhausted. I've been playing mommy to Benny all afternoon. I just want to go home and relax. I'll worry about the whole pregnancy thing tomorrow."

"Okay, Scarlett," Blanche told her. "I won't hold my breath waiting for the call."

CHAPTER 16

Back at home, Peri opened her refrigerator and took out a beer. Her left hand drifted down toward her stomach and lingered for a moment. Sighing, she put the beer back and reached for the cranberry juice.

Children had never been on Peri's list of things to do. Even when her failed marriages were thriving, she knew she didn't want to share a child with any of the men. Sometimes she worried that it made her a circus freak to be so uninterested in growing life, then she'd look around at her dying plants and empty fishbowl, and know she made the right choice.

She wandered through her house, imagining two extra legs toddling around. It had taken her years to perfect the little Spanish-style bungalow and create her own personal oasis. An étagère sat in the corner with her collection of moose figurines, a charming mix of ceramic and blown glass animals. Her shelves were full of older, hardbound books from used bookstores. A few were first editions, and although none were extremely valuable, all were fragile. A home theater system sat along the far wall, a modest splurge, for watching her old movies.

None of it would survive if she had to raise a child. Especially if her late mother's curse came true and she had a child like herself. While not a hellion, Peri had been precocious, often dismantling household appliances to see how things worked. This wouldn't have been so bad if she had known how to put them back together.

"Okay, I can't see it," she said, and walked to her bedroom.

Suddenly, that horrid feeling returned, of her stomach lurching wildly while her internal organs became blazing hot pokers, melting her from the inside out as her heart beat a staccato rhythm in her throat. Peri ran to the bathroom, preparing to throw up. She kneeled in front of the toilet, tempted to lay her sweaty brow against the bowl. Finally, the feeling subsided, so she returned to her bed, threw off her clothes and lay on top of the covers. Maybe I ate something bad, she thought, knowing that if she did, she'd already be locked in the bathroom, throwing her guts up.

After changing into a nightshirt, Peri sat in bed and finished a pint of Ben & Jerry's Vanilla Heath Bar Crunch while she watched *The Thin Man*. At midnight, she turned off the TV and spent the next two hours squeezing her eyes shut in an attempt to sleep. Finally, she surrendered to her insomnia and got out her notes. Spreading them around her quilt, Peri tried coupling Marnie's notes with David's, then David's with Benny's, and then all of her cast of characters with the ring.

None of it made sense. If David killed Marnie, why didn't he take the ring? Why would Benny ask her to clean out his freezer if he knew Marnie's hand was in there? Where was the other hand? She finally drifted off in the middle of questions with no answers.

Peri awoke as Dean Martin handed her an apron and asked her to be his BMF, Best Maid Forever. Sunlight filled her bedroom.

"Nine thirty?" She had planned to be on the road by eight. Grabbing her phone, she made a quick call to Sylvia Banks' daughter to apologize. Then she leaped into the shower, then into her clothes, and finally, into her car.

The drive to Palm Springs involved the fine art of negotiation. Peri had to traverse through three different freeways, all filled with ruthless semis, crazy drivers, and delivery trucks on schedules. In a world of SUVs and Hummers, her Honda sat low and invisible, and each lane change required her to be polite but firm. She made the last transition, to the I-10, with only a single use of her middle finger, at the driver careening sideways across four lanes to cut her off.

"Plan ahead, you moron," she said. "Why do I have to pay for your sins?"

As she drove further on the I-10, the scenery became less urban and more interesting. The city of Banning ended abruptly, leaving the San Bernardino Mountains to her left, and the San Jacinto Mountains to her right, with large expanses of dirt and scrubby plants on either side. Soon she saw the familiar rows of white-bladed fans, hundreds of them. The wind farm in the San Gorgonio Pass always amazed her. She wished she could pull over and admire them, but it was impossible on the freeway. After she passed the stark windmills, she turned right and entered the desert community of Palm Springs.

Jeanine Ressler lived in a low, sand-colored home that blended into the landscape, much like the other houses in the neighborhood. Only fools built tall homes with high ceilings in this desert, where the average temperature for four months of the year exceeded 100 degrees and the average air conditioning bill could easily quintuple that in dollars. From the natural landscaping to the solar panels on the roof, everything about the house said energy efficient.

Peri pulled up to the curb. A white-haired woman, curled over in age, glared at her as she walked her chubby dachshund down the sidewalk, so Peri moved her car, parking in the driveway instead. The air baked her skin as she got out and rang the doorbell.

"Hello," Jeanine said. "Won't you come in?"

"I apologize again for my tardiness, Mrs. Ressler," Peri told her. "Hopefully, I won't take up much of your time."

"Oh, it's all right, I have to wait for the repairman anyway. My dishwasher's broken, and you know how those service companies are. They were supposed to be here by eleven." She looked at her watch. "Eleven-thirty. I'm still waiting for the phone call to say they're late."

They walked into an expansive living room, the spare furnishings decorated in soft pastels. Peri noted exactly three photos on the mantel, all families, each one different, none of them featuring Jeanine. She regarded the slim woman who handed her a glass of iced tea as they sat on the L-shaped sofa. An ice-blue Capri pant set hung model-perfect on her bronze frame, her short brunette hair swept back from her face. Peri thought she looked like a fabulous representative for life after fifty.

"Now, what did you want to know about Mum?" Jeanine asked.

"I'm looking for answers about her last few months," Peri told her, "And maybe a little of her life as an actress."

Jeanine leaned back into the couch, her sleek, tanned hands caressing her drink. Her almond-shaped brown eyes closed briefly, then opened as she spoke.

"Mum moved in with me after my divorce," she said. "She was such a help, always looking at the positive side of things when I felt the worst. We shared a lot of laughs, and a lot of tears."

"When did she move into Bradford Square?"

"At the end of April." Jeanine shook her head. "I wanted to find a place closer, but assisted living facilities here are so expensive, and Mum needed a lot of help toward the end."

"Must have been quite a drive for you."

"It was hard in so many ways. I hated having her so far away from me, and I hate the relief I feel now that I don't have to make the drive every day."

Peri nodded. "How did you like the facility?"

"Oh, they took wonderful care of her, except for the night she ended up behind Ralph's. After that, let's just say my relationship with the facility became strained."

"The staff at the home said she was so frail, did it surprise you she'd been able to get that far away?"

"Definitely," Jeanine said. "She couldn't walk down the hallway, much less a block away. I had some words with the manager, but no one could ever figure out how it happened."

"Mrs. Lopez said your mom changed after that," Peri said. "That she kind of 'turned a corner' for the worse."

"Yes. I don't think being out in the night air in that little cotton nightgown helped at all. And someone stole her coat."

Peri leafed through her notes. "Is that what she could have meant when she was telling them, 'I've lost him in my coat'?"

Jeanine sat forward. "She said that?"

"Didn't they tell you? Ms. Castillo said she kept repeating it, like a chant."

"She never said it to me, and I was there every day. The staff never told me she said that." She gazed at her hands, her eyes filling with tears. "Now I understand. After the incident, she cried when I visited, couldn't stop crying. Now it makes sense."

"What do you think it could mean, other than someone taking her coat?"

Jeanine got up from the couch and disappeared down a hallway. She returned, carrying a photo album. Opening it to one of the pages, she laid it on the table and sat down next to Peri.

"That's what she lost," she said, pointing to a picture.

Peri looked at the photo. A beautiful young woman stood in front of Grauman's Chinese Theater, dressed to the nines in a silky black dress and fur stole, clutching a small sparkly bag. She smiled at the camera.

"Look at her hand," Jeanine said.

Even far away, in the grainy distortion, Peri recognized the ring at once. The Forever Roses ring.

"Maybe this is where we talk about your mom's life as an actress," Peri said.

Jeanine rose and refreshed their drinks. "Mom was never a big star. She had bit parts here and there, but she was kind of shy and insecure. What she wanted most of all was love. Being so attractive got her lots of attention on the sets, including Melvin Conway's."

"I hear Melvin Conway's eyes roved so much they should have fallen out of his head. No offense, but why would he give the Forever Roses ring to a starlet, even if she was pretty?"

A throaty laugh escaped Jeanine, her eyes twinkling. "Oh, no, she didn't have the real ring. He had a replica made for her. It was a nice fake, but not nearly as valuable as the real thing."

"Do you know if he had duplicates made for his other, um, girlfriends?"

"I don't know." Jeanine looked down at the album. "I always thought he only made one, for Mum."

Peri looked at another picture in the album. Sylvia stood on a movie set, fresh-faced and naïve, gazing at the great Melvin Conway. The handsome actor's dark eyes and full lips looked familiar.

"Why just for your mom, Jeanine?"

"Well, because she was so special, to everyone. Everyone loved her."

Peri let her hand rest next to the photo. "Oh. I thought maybe it was because he felt he owed her a little something."

Jeanine stared at the photo as well. "There is a resemblance, isn't there?"

"Did she tell you he was your father?"

"Not until last year, when we were going through the old albums. It slipped out, accidentally. My dad must have known, but he never let on, never acted like I wasn't his daughter."

"So when she lost her ring—" Peri said.

"She was heartsick that she had lost the only link to my father I had."

"Didn't you notice it was gone when she passed?"

Jeanine nodded. "It got a little nasty with Ms. Castillo at that point. I accused the staff of stealing the ring. Ms. Castillo wouldn't even question them. She claimed the ring must have been missing when Mum *wandered away*, as she put it."

"Did you try filing a report with the police?"

"No, the ring wasn't worth anything, it was just sentimental, although I do wish I could get it back." She looked down at the photos. "It meant so much to Mum."

"The Conway family is having an auction to sell the rest of their heirlooms," Peri told her. "Have you heard about it?"

"No, I don't pay much attention to them."

"The auction will include the Forever Roses ring. Wish you could have some of the proceeds?"

"No." Jeanine shook her head. "Don't get me wrong, a little extra money is always good to have, but I've got everything I need. My husband was very generous in the divorce, so my house is paid for, and I don't have any big expenses."

"No children?" Peri asked.

Jeanine nodded toward the photos on the mantle. "Only stepchildren. We wanted our own, but I just couldn't carry one to term. It definitely put a strain on us."

Peri set her iced tea on a coaster. "Jeanine, do you still have the clothes your mom was wearing when they found her? And something with her DNA, like a comb or toothbrush?"

"Yes. Why?"

"I have a hunch about who took her coat, but an analysis of her things might confirm it."

Jeanine went back down the hallway and returned with a small bundle. She studied them, smoothing the wrinkles. "So light, they wouldn't have protected her in the night air."

Taking the clothes from her, Peri said, "Jeanine, I think this is the place where I tell you the Placentia Police Department has a ring that looks like your mom's."

"Really? If I can identify it, can I get it back?"

"Not right away. There are a couple of problems. One is that it was discovered on the finger of a dead girl, who, I believe, was wearing your mom's coat."

"Oh, no," Jeanine said. "What's the other problem?"

"Do you remember the first time you saw the ring?"

"God, I can't say," she said. "She just always had it."

"Do you know if she ever received any visits from Conway?"

"Oh, no, I don't think so. At least, I don't remember."

"Here's the thing," Peri said. "The ring we found on the dead girl is *the* Forever Roses ring. The Conway family has the replica."

Much like the ring, the look on Jeanine Ressler's face was priceless.

CHAPTER 17

Peri stopped at a Rite-Aid pharmacy on her way out of town. She grabbed a pregnancy test, paid and left in as little time as possible. Sticking the package in her tote, she headed back to Orange County.

Her cell phone rang as she passed the Cabazon shopping outlet.

"We're bringing Waters in for some more questioning," Skip said. "I thought you might want to sit in."

Peri glanced at the time. Three o'clock. "Is he there now? When are you starting?"

"They just put him in Interrogation. I thought I'd let him stew a bit first."

"Geez, Skip, I want to be there, but I'm just coming back from Palm Springs," she said. "I don't suppose you can let him stew for another hour."

"No, I've got too much to do," Skip told her. "Why were you in Palm Springs?"

"Interviewing Sylvia Banks' daughter, Jeanine."

She could feel his annoyance burning through the phone. "Peri, what did I tell you about letting me know where you are when you're investigating this case?"

"Sorry, Skip, but I didn't think a Palm Springs matron posed much of a risk. Besides, I got a lot of information. I think I'm on to the link between Sylvia Banks and Marnie Russell. And I've got some possible evidence to test."

"You promised to be careful."

"And I will," Peri said. "I'm going to spend a nice, quiet evening at home."

Her interview with Jeanine still occupied her thoughts as she pushed her cart through Ralph's, picking up groceries for the week. It took forever to meander through the aisles, making decisions about whether to buy canned vegetables and eat them from the tin, or get fresh produce and watch it rot in her fridge. By the time she left the store, the sun had become a sinking ball, casting long shadows across the parking lot.

Peri stopped at the office before she went home, to pick up a manual. Her new client, Mrs. Cheavers, had rescheduled for tomorrow, so she straightened her desk and wiped the dust away. As she locked her office door, she thought about the test kit in her tote, and wondered how Sylvia Banks felt when she found herself pregnant and alone.

"Hey, bitch," someone said and spun her around by the shoulder.

She got a brief glimpse of David Waters, his arm cocked back. Then she felt pain in her head, and the wall against her back. His face drew close to hers, the smell of beer and bad sinuses engulfing her as he said, "Hit me with that bag again and I'll kill you."

Her legs buckled and she slid to the floor. She looked up to see him standing over her, swinging his leg back. Waiting for the top of the kick, she managed to turn away and get half of the blow.

It still hurt like hell, she thought, as the world went dark.

CHAPTER 18

Peri heard footsteps.

She felt hands on her arms, and painful jostling, but couldn't open her eyes to see what was going on.

"Ma'am?"

Forcing her eyes open, she saw a young man's face. The ground lurched and rolled under her. She reached up and grabbed at the oxygen mask over her mouth. Ripping it off, she rolled to her side and threw up on his blue uniform.

"Sorry."

"No problem, ma'am. We're taking you to the hospital. You probably have a concussion, and some cracked ribs."

"David Waters," she said.

The EMT gave her a quizzical look. "Is that your name?"

"No, you bonehead, David Waters attacked me." She rolled back onto the cot, wincing. "Sorry, getting beat up makes me cranky."

"That's okay, ma'am," he said, replacing her mask. "I've been called worse."

"My name," she told him, her voice muffled, "Peri Minneopa. I'm a P.I. Call Skip Carlton, Placentia PD." She began to feel drowsy.

"He'll want to…to…to do something."

She awoke again on a cold table, a light in her eyes and a new face peering into hers.

"How do you feel?" the doctor asked her.

"My head hurts."

"You are hit very hard," he said. She couldn't place the accent, but his eyes were kind. "You have a concussion and two bruised ribs, not broken. It's not too bad, but we will keep you here tonight, for observation."

His words were precise and left no room for argument.

"Could I have my own PJs?"

He smiled. "Certainly. We will call your husband?"

"No, call Blanche Debussy at the Coroner's."

She wished she could bottle the look of horror on his face, just to sell for Halloween. "Blanche is my friend," she told him.

Peri was holding an ice pack against her face, drifting in and out of sleep, when Blanche rushed into the room. She placed one hand on Peri's forehead, and gripped her wrist with the other, taking her pulse.

"Peri, sweetie, thank God you're okay," she said.

"You know, we've got nurses to do that," Peri told her.

"I know, but I can't help it." She gently hugged her friend. "What happened?"

"Give me some decent clothes and I'll tell you."

Peri slipped out of the shapeless, backless, hospital gown and into her purple nightshirt while she told Blanche about the attack.

"God, Peri, it's bad, but he could have done so much worse. You could have been raped, or killed."

"I know," she said. "I think he must have heard someone coming, otherwise, he'd have probably kept kicking. It doesn't seem like I laid there very long."

"Have they arrested the creep? Where's Skip? Are you pregnant?"

"Not yet, I don't know, and I don't know."

"Peri—"

"Have a heart, Beebs. My brain aches, my side hurts, and either the pain killers they're giving me are wimpy or they haven't kicked in yet. I'm not even sure if I still know the stuff I used to know."

Blanche took Peri's hand. "I'm sorry, sweetie. I just thought, if the doctor examined you, he might have noticed if you were expecting."

Peri raised her eyebrows. "That's not the end I got hit at. Oh, wait, should I have pain killers if I'm pregnant? What the hell, it can't be good for the baby if Mommy's hurting."

"I think maybe they're starting to work," Blanche told her. "Did you at least get a test kit?"

"Yes, I bought one in Palm Springs." Peri looked around. "Hey, where's my bag?"

"It's over here," Blanche said, and handed the tote to her.

Peri dug through the vastness. "Dammit, he took my wallet," she said. "And I can't find that kit."

"What kit?" Skip asked as he walked in.

Peri and Blanche looked at him, mouths agape.

"My sewing kit," Peri said. "It must have fallen out of my bag."

Skip gave Peri a delicate kiss. "Heard you didn't quite go the fifteen rounds."

"He caught me by surprise. It was David Waters, you need to arrest him."

"Already done. And thanks to you, we can keep him in a cell while we toss his apartment."

"Glad to be of service." Peri adjusted her position in bed. "By the way, Jeanine Ressler will probably be calling you about the ring."

"Not another one."

"Oh, yeah, only this one's interesting. According to her, Melvin Conway gave Sylvia Banks a replica of the Forever Roses ring."

"So Sylvia didn't know she had the real thing?"

"Nope, and she had something else of Conway's. His child. Jeanine is Melvin Conway's daughter."

"You're kidding," Skip said. "Did you tell her our ring was real?"

"Of course."

Skip shook his head. "This is definitely going to throw a monkey wrench in Kevin Conway's plans."

"A monkey wrench?" Blanche said. "That's an understatement. It'll be in the courts for years."

CHAPTER 19

Peri rolled over gingerly and rubbed her eyes, then stopped. Her left temple still felt sore. Someone stood in the doorway, holding a tray.

"Breakfast, Miss Peri," the nurse's aide told her.

"Thanks," she said.

She staggered to the bathroom and looked at her face, expecting the worst. A large bruise of variegated colors ran up her temple and down her cheek. Not too bad, she thought as she lifted her nightshirt and checked out her left side. It, too, showed signs of Waters' rage, in a boot-shaped purple mark across her ribs.

Peri returned from the bathroom and turned on the TV. A morning news show prattled on about the perfect barbeque for the Fourth of July. The segment ended and a new one began, a report about Christie's upcoming auction. Peri turned the volume up.

"This fall, you'll have a chance to own a piece of history," the smiling host told the camera, as he explained that the Conway estate would be auctioned off, including the Forever Roses ring.

The camera showed a close-up of the magnificent, if fake, jewels. Peri waited to hear something about the controversy, that the ring was part of a murder investigation, but the man didn't mention it.

She grabbed her clothes, swallowing down mouthfuls of Cheerios in between dressing. The nurse came in and stopped in the doorway.

"Peri, the doctor hasn't released you yet," she said.

"I know, but I'm fine and I need to get to work."

"Let's at least have the doctor look at your pupils and sign the form," the nurse told her.

"Is he on his way?"

"Well, I don't know, but he'll be in sometime today."

Peri picked her tote up and dug out her phone. "Okay, I don't have time for *sometime today*. If he's interested, tell him to stop by my office and he can take my temperature."

She dialed Skip's number as she left the building. "Skipper, can you take me to my car? Have you seen the news this morning? Kevin Conway is proceeding with the auction. He's advertising the fake ring as if it's real. You guys didn't release the ring to him, did you?"

"Whoa, Nelly," Skip told her. "Let's have one question at a time. Yes, I can take you to your car. No, we didn't release the ring. No, wait, what was your other question?"

"Did you know about the auction?"

"Oh. No. I'll come right over and get you."

Fifteen minutes later, Peri and Skip were headed south on Rose Drive, toward Alta Vista Street.

"I'm a little surprised the doctor released you so early," Skip said.

Peri shrugged. "They needed the bed."

"Well, just for your info, we found a hacksaw with blood on it in Waters' apartment. It's at the lab right now. We also found your wallet when we picked him up."

"Any cash in it? When can I get it back?"

"No, took the money, but left the cards," he told her. "You can probably get it all back by tomorrow. In the meantime, here's your license and ATM card, at least."

"Thanks. Has trace come back on Marnie's clothes?"

"Yeah, the report's in my office. Hairs on the coat, some from the same donor as the hair on the ring, plus a third party hair and rust stains on the sleeve."

"I've got more in my car for trace," she told him as they stopped at her office. She handed him the bag of clothes. "Sylvia Banks' clothes that she was wearing when she wandered off, plus a hairbrush for identifying her DNA."

"Why do we need these?"

"Because I'm thinking the hair in the ring and on Marnie's coat are Sylvia's, and Marnie Russell's hair or DNA is on Sylvia's jacket. I think she met up with Sylvia somewhere and exchanged coats with her. Mrs. Lopez told us the ring was too big for Miss Banks' finger and kept falling into the pocket. It's possible Marnie saw Sylvia, wanted a warmer coat, and ended up with more than she bargained for."

"Yeah," Skip said. "Death."

"So, what are we going to do about Kevin Conway?"

Skip looked at her. "What needs to be done?"

"He can't sell that ring as real. It's a fake."

"Peri, this may come as a surprise to you, but you can't control what everyone does. The auction may or may not proceed. At some point down the road, the ring will be discovered. It's not our problem."

"But it's fraud," she said. "And you know it."

"It's fraud if it happens." He drew her in close to him and kissed her. "I'm glad you're okay. Go home and rest."

CHAPTER 20

Peri sat in her office, waiting for Mrs. Cheavers. She hoped Skip wouldn't stop by her house to see if she needed chicken soup. He had made her promise to rest today, but she'd already scheduled the appointment with her client and she needed the money.

At precisely ten o'clock, the door opened and a woman walked in. Her golden, form-fitting dress accentuated both her glowing tan and her curves. Peri guessed her to be older than she looked and either cosmetically enhanced or wearing a gravity-defying foundation garment. Long, auburn curls cascaded around her flawless face. She attempted a smile as she entered, although Peri thought the Botox must have made it difficult.

"Mrs. Cheavers? Call me Peri."

The woman stared at Peri, aghast.

"Oh, this," Peri pointed to her face. "You should see the other guy."

"I'm so sorry," Mrs. Cheavers said. "Does it hurt? Shouldn't you be resting?"

"Oh, no, I'm okay. Now, let's talk about your husband."

They sat and chatted for an hour, most of their conversation revolving around what a rat Mr. Cheavers could be, and that he might be hiding his wealth with one hand while he cuddled younger women with the other. Peri took notes about his known habits, got out a contract for Mrs. Cheavers to sign, and collected her much-needed fee.

After Mrs. Cheavers left, Peri scheduled the rest of her week to coincide with Mr. Cheavers' workday, then called her doctor. The hospital painkillers had begun to wear off, and she had checked herself out before the hospital doctor could give her a prescription. Unfortunately, neither Dr. Ngo nor any of her staff would write Peri a prescription sight unseen. She'd have to come into the office.

Peri had just enough time to go home and shower, before heading down Yorba Linda Boulevard toward Dr. Ngo's office on Prospect Avenue. A grouping of single-story buildings, the medical offices sat on the edge of Placentia and Yorba Linda, with tract homes to the north and horse properties to the south.

"Oh dear, Peri, what happened?" the doctor asked, as she read her chart.

"Sometimes my job has side effects. The ER doctor said it was just a mild concussion and two bruised ribs."

"Yes, I see that. I also see you checked yourself out, AMA." The petite woman looked over her half-glasses at Peri. "Why would we do that?"

"I had an appointment this morning."

"That couldn't be rescheduled?"

Peri shrugged. "Yes, but I didn't want to. Oddly, if I want to pay my hospital bill, I need to work."

Dr. Ngo scribbled on a pad, and then handed Peri the results. "Here's a script for a mild painkiller. Be careful, dear, and if you have any problems breathing, or blurred vision with a headache, call me right away." She looked back at the chart. "And you might want to watch your diet. It says here you've gained a little weight. It's common at your age, but I know you like to stay in shape."

"Okay, Dr. Ngo."

Why didn't I ask her for a pregnancy test? Peri got into her car and headed for the pharmacy. It would have been easy. *I could have known for certain. Gawd, why am I putting this off?*

She considered her reluctance to find out, while she waited for her prescription to be filled, then as she drove back to her house.

The answer occurred to her as she pulled into her driveway. If she was pregnant, there would be expectations from the world. Everyone would hold their collective breath waiting to hear if she was going to continue the pregnancy. If she didn't, there would be judgments from people, telling her she'd regret her decision. If she did, there would be demands from people, telling her what she could and couldn't do. Skip would be the worst. Whether he was happy about the child or not, he'd expect her to drop the Russell case. He'd use her run-in with David Waters as the perfect example of why it was too dangerous.

"I'll find out later," she decided as she walked to her front door.

A small, white paper bag awaited her on the porch. Blanche's handwriting said, "You so owe me," on the outside. Peri opened the bag and looked at the contents. It was a pregnancy test.

She carried the bag inside and set it on the counter while she got a glass out of the cupboard and filled it with cold water. The phone rang as she swallowed down her pain medication.

"You resting?" Blanche asked.

"Sure," Peri told her, loading dishes into her dishwasher. "Relaxing on the sofa, watching TV."

"Liar. You weren't home when I dropped my present off. Did you get it?"

"Yes, and you're right. I owe you, big time."

"Make sure you read the directions," Blanche said. "I think you have to pee on it first thing in the morning."

"Yes, Mom."

"And be careful, Peri. Honestly, I wouldn't have recommended the change of careers if I thought you'd be in danger."

"Oh, Beebs," Peri said. "Surveillance is safe. The only reason I got on this case is because Benny talked me into cleaning his freezer."

Peri walked into her living room and collapsed onto her couch. She flipped through the TV channels, but nothing captured her attention, so she got out her notes and reviewed them again, trying to determine the connection between Sylvia Banks and Marnie Russell. Did they actually meet, or did Sylvia leave her coat where Marnie could have found it? HIS House and Bradford Square were only a block apart. Could they have met in the middle?

The codeine in her medication closed her eyes. She dreamed of a refrigerator with hands reaching out to clutch her, pulling her into the coldness. The phone interrupted her fantasy.

"Hey, Doll," Skip said. "Feel like coming down to give your statement?"

"Hmm," she replied. "As soon as I wake up."

"We're holding Waters right now. I was hoping you'd press charges before we have to let him go."

Peri's eyes opened. "Give me twenty minutes."

She walked into the bathroom and stared into the mirror. Her bruise looked worse than it had this morning. As a matter of fact, she looked worse than she did this morning.

"Fifty year olds should avoid fistfights," she said, looking at the discolorations, the puffiness, and the wrinkles. A layer of make-up did nothing for the bruise, but made her look like she wasn't trying to frighten anyone.

David Waters emerged from the interrogation room as Peri entered the station. He glared at her, but said nothing, so she returned the favor and went to Skip's office. Skip looked up from his paperwork and regarded her colorful face.

"You look," he paused as he searched for a word. "Nice."

Peri laughed. "I look like crap, Skipper. Let's get this statement written so I can go home and take more drugs."

She filled out the report while Skip told her about Waters' interview.

"He still insists the last time he saw Marnie was Sunday night. His hacksaw had blood on it, but turns out it's his. According to him, he got a little drunk and couldn't figure out how to open a box of pizza, so he tried to use the hacksaw on it."

"Sounds like him. How about Marnie's baby? Any ideas on the dad?"

"No, but we've ruled out David Waters. Wrong blood type."

"Really?" Peri autographed her work, then stood up. "Skip, we need to go back to HIS House. Somebody must know who else Marnie was seeing."

Clutching her side, she added, "Let me just take another pill, first."

CHAPTER 21

Karen Anderson greeted Skip and Peri at the front door to HIS House. She looked as high-strung and impatient as the first time.

"Mrs. Anderson, we need some more information about Marnie's friends," Skip said. "Could you tell us who was close to her?"

"I don't know that Marnie had a lot of close friends here," she said. "Most of our residents are families. Not a lot of single girls, or guys."

As they moved into the kitchen, Peri took off her sunglasses.

"Oh my goodness," Karen said. "Your face looks awful. What happened?"

Peri put her hand up to her cheekbone, feeling embarrassed. "I'm fine. Just part of the job."

"Is there anyone around here we can talk to who knew Marnie?" Skip said.

Karen introduced them to Denise. Short, with spiky blonde hair, she pulled her t-shirt down over her bare midriff, trying to make it meet her cutoff jeans.

"I heard about poor Marnie," Denise said. "She played with my girls sometimes. She was real nice."

"Did she have any boyfriends?" Peri asked.

"Yeah, she was seeing someone."

"We mean, before David Waters," Skip told her.

"David who?" Denise said. "I only know about Carlos."

"Carlos?" Peri asked. "Do you know anything more about him? His last name, or where he works?"

"No, we wasn't that close. Marnie just mentioned him from time to time. She'd tell Clarissel and Maribella, those is my babies, she'd tell them that she couldn't play no more 'cause she had to meet Carlos.'"

"Did you ever see him pick her up?" Skip said.

"No, sir. She walked to meet him, I don't know where."

A little dark haired girl in bright yellow shorts and a striped shirt ran in to the living room and threw herself into Denise's lap. "This is Clarissel, my oldest," Denise told them.

"Clarissel, what a pretty name," Peri said. "How old are you?"

"Seven," the young girl replied.

"Did you like playing games with Marnie?"

Clarissel looked to her mom, who told her, "Miss Russell, sweetie."

The little girl nodded.

"Did she ever talk about her friend Carlos?"

Clarissel frowned and shook her head. "No, just when she went outside. She'd look at the clock and say, 'it's time to meet Carlos'. Then she'd go out the door and walk to the church."

"Did she stop at the church?" Skip asked.

The little girl looked at the detective, then hid her face in her mother's shirt.

"I'm sorry, Officer," Denise said. "She's a little shy around men."

Skip sat back, and looked at Peri.

"Clarissel, sweetie," she said. "Did you see Miss Russell go past the church?"

Clarissel nodded.

"Well, thank you, Clarissel, for helping us." Looking up at Denise, Peri said, "Mrs. Anderson told me she had to break up a fight between Marnie and David Waters. Did you ever see anything like that?"

Denise seemed puzzled. "I don't know who that is, but I never saw Marnie argue with anyone." Lowering her voice, she added, "Except Mrs. Anderson."

"Mrs. Anderson?" Skip said. "What did she fight with her about?"

"Mrs. Anderson don't like Marnie living here, 'cause she was a single gal. She only wants families around. So she was always on her case about something."

Skip and Peri exchanged looks.

"Thank you, Denise," Skip told her. "You've been very helpful."

"Some guy named Carlos," Peri said as Skip drove her back to the station. "He shouldn't be too hard to find in Orange County."

"Maybe Waters knows him."

"Maybe. And what was that about Mrs. Anderson fighting with Marnie? Sounds like she didn't quite tell us the truth." She paused. "I'm beginning to think maybe Waters could have killed Marnie, although I'm still not convinced he cut off her hands."

"No, I think you're right," Skip said. "If he'd wanted that ring, he could've gotten it some other way. But I could see him killing her, especially if he knew she was carrying someone else's baby."

Peri looked out the window of the SUV, thinking about Marnie's baby, and the possibility of her own.

"Hey, how are you feeling?" Skip asked her suddenly. "Are you going to be okay by yourself tonight?"

"What did you have in mind?"

He smiled. "Well, if you were a little apprehensive about being alone, I could spend the night."

"Wow, the sacrifices you'd make for me, Skipper."

"I'll even let you be on top," he said, winking.

"Whoa, there, Stud. I'm a little too broken for any action yet."

"Even with the drugs?"

Peri laughed. "If you don't mind, I'd rather be conscious during our playtime."

"I was just joking. But if you'd feel safer with me asleep on the couch, I'm there."

"I'm okay," Peri told him. "Waters is locked up, so I'm not in any danger. Besides, I plan on taking one of those lovely little pills tonight and sleeping as soundly as I can, without rolling on my ribs."

At five o'clock in the morning, Peri had to pee. Standing by the toilet, barely conscious, she tried to open the test kit. Her fingernails dug into the cellophane, but she couldn't get more than a few strips off at a time. She finally got the end open and pulled on the box. It held firm, so she ran her thumbnail under the tab, slicing her flesh in the process.

"Ouch—" She put her thumb in her mouth.

Persevering, Peri yanked on the cardboard until it finally gave way. She pulled out the narrow plastic envelope and a set of instructions, which immediately fell into the toilet. Fishing the paper out, she spread it on the counter to dry.

At last, basic instinct overcame scientific experimentation.

"Screw it," she said and sat down. "I'll take the test when the directions dry out."

She returned to bed and slept until ten, after which she moved into the living room and tried to do some work. The pain pills made it hard for her to focus. Every report she attempted to write quickly disintegrated into nonsense as she dozed off, her fingers resting on the keyboard.

At two in the afternoon, a knock at the door woke her. She stretched carefully, unfolding her legs from their cramped position on the couch. A key turned in the lock and she heard Skip's voice.

"Peri? You awake in there?"

"Kinda." Peri immediately smelled the pungent odor of hot and sour soup.

"I brought you some lunch." Skip reached down and kissed her. "Can't stay, I gotta be in court at three. You still having dinner at Blanche's tonight?"

She sat up and leaned over the container, inhaling the delicious aroma while her stomach growled impatiently.

"Well, I was invited. I'd rather not miss the opportunity to meet the Goth saxophonist, especially when Dani's been hiding him for months." Peri took a mouthful of soup and sighed. "Mmm, thanks, Skipper, this is great."

"You're welcome, Doll. Listen, be careful. Don't go driving around if you can't stay awake."

Peri smiled. "You know me, Skip. I'm always careful."

CHAPTER 22

After the day of rest, Peri decided to join the Debussy family for dinner. In an attempt to heed Skip's advice, she only took half a pain pill, so she wouldn't fall asleep at the wheel. She had mixed emotions about her decision as she drove to Blanche's. Although she was wide awake, her side reminded her of her injury with every bump in the road. At last, she pulled into the driveway and inched her body out of her car.

As usual, she rang the bell then opened the door.

"Come on in, Peri," Blanche called from the kitchen.

Peri walked around the corner to witness the chaotic normalcy of a Debussy family meal. Two teenagers propped up the kitchen counter while their mother ran back and forth, shoving plates in their hands and giving them precise orders.

"Your lasagna's starting to burn," Peri said.

"Thank you," Blanche replied. "And it's cannelloni."

She looked around for the oven mitts, but Peri grabbed them first and opened the oven door.

"Here, let me help," she told her, and lifted the pan to safety. "Dani, could you be a dear and put the salad together for me? Everything's in that bag I brought."

Nick elbowed Danielle, who peeled her body away from the counter as though attached by Velcro. She opened the grocery bag and took out the contents, slowly, as if hoping an adult would tell her to hurry up, and then take the task away from her. It worked.

"Dani, we'll never eat if you move like a slug," her mother told her. "Give me that and go put water glasses on the table instead."

The doorbell rang.

"That's him," Dani said and ran toward the door. "Nick, put the glasses on the table."

"Hey, Mom told you to do it," he yelled. Blanche thrust a pair of tall glasses at him, and pointed him toward the dining room.

Alone in the kitchen with Peri, Blanche asked, "So? What did the test say?"

Peri took the salad bag from her. "Nothing yet."

"What?"

"Don't snap at me. Do you know how hard it is to open cellophane at five in the morning?"

"Peri, you've got to stop procrastinating. If you think you might be at all—"

"Are you expecting something?" Dani asked as she walked around the corner.

Surprised, Peri pulled the salad bag with such force it exploded, sending lettuce skyward.

Dani held up a package. "This came for you, Mom. Did you send for something?"

Peri broke out into nervous laughter. "Guess I don't have to toss the salad," she said, picking greens off the counter.

"Just put it on the hall table, dear," Blanche said.

"Okay, Mom. I'm gonna go wait for Chad." With a flip of her ponytail, the girl left the room.

"Chad?" Peri asked. "A Goth saxophonist named Chad? Isn't that just so, so Yorba Linda?"

"That's what I thought," Paul said as he walked in. He gave Peri a kiss on the cheek, then turned to his wife. "What can I do to help?"

Dark eyed, with wavy auburn hair, Paul Debussy was a perfectly handsome counterpart to his pretty wife. He had worked his way up the company ladder at one of the many aerospace companies in southern California, survived the mergers, and now sat at the top of middle management. His employees respected the fact that he had started as an engineer. It meant he knew what they did for a living.

"So, Peri, I heard about your fight," he said. "How—"

"Shh," Blanche told him. "I think Chad's here."

Silence overwhelmed the kitchen as everyone strained to listen to the conversation at the front door. Two muted voices could be heard, one a mewling entreaty and the other a begrudging rumble. Finally, footsteps sounded and four pairs of eyes turned toward the entrance, waiting for Chad.

Dani entered first, her expression a mix of nonchalance and dread. Behind her walked a surprise.

Peri's contact with Goths had been limited to the clumps of kids in black at the mall, in trench coats, combat boots, and kohl-darkened eyes. They stood around like feral cats, their sinuous backbones turned to the world, as if they dared anyone to care about them.

The young man extending his hand to her looked like the Rolls Royce of Goth. Tall and muscled, his black wool slacks and Burberry trench coat fit him well. Inky curls framed his face, touching his shoulders. Peri noted a touch of black eyeliner, subtle and elegant.

"Chad Geary," he said, shaking everyone's hand.

Looking over at Dani's parents, Peri saw a look of relief on Blanche's face and worry on Paul's. She immediately decided this would be an interesting evening.

Everyone took his or her place around the table. Chad still had his coat on as he pulled Dani's chair out for her.

"Think the roof's going to leak, Chad?" Peri asked.

"Um, no," he said, bewildered.

"Then take off the raincoat. We're not dining al fresco."

Dani rolled her eyes, but Chad removed his coat, revealing a black silk tee shirt that hugged his chiseled biceps. Blanche stifled a gasp, but her eyes popped, briefly, from their sockets. Dani watched her mother and smiled a little.

"Dani, one, Beebs, zero," Peri whispered to her friend.

Blanche pinched her arm in retaliation.

"Wine, Peri?" Paul asked.

"Not this evening, thanks." She put her hand over her glass. "I'm still on medication for my injuries. Alcohol doesn't mix well with codeine."

"I heard about the fight, Aunt Peri," said Nick. "That guy's an asshole."

"Nick," Paul said. "Language."

"Sorry."

"How are you healing?" Paul asked.

"Fine, thanks. So far, the worst part is trying to cover the bruise up with enough make-up to keep small children from screaming."

They all dished their food quietly, and began eating in the awkward silence.

"So, Chad, Danielle says you're a saxophonist," Paul said. "Where does your band play?"

"We haven't been together that long," he replied. "But we have played Steamers in Fullerton, and the street fair in Brea. We're also scheduled for one of those park concerts at Tri-City in August."

"Wow, that's pretty good for not being together long," Peri told him. "What kind of music do you play?"

"It's a kind of fusion, jazz, and punk," Chad said.

"It's really good," Dani added.

"So, bebop with dark undertones, or what?" Peri asked.

Chad looked at her. "What's bebop?"

"A style of jazz," Paul said. "What kind of jazz did you fuse with the punk?"

"Huh?"

"I mean, Latin, swing, smooth?"

"What kind of musical training have you actually had, Chad?" Blanche asked.

Peri thought she could hear wheels squeaking underneath the young man's curls. She suddenly felt sorry for him, a lovely young man being devoured by parental wolves.

"Beebs," she said. "Did you ever get anything back on that trace we got from Benny's house?"

Blanche looked at her. "What trace?"

141

"The blood from the freezer."

Peri saw Chad's eyes widen. "Oh, it's okay, dear," she told him. "Dani's mom works in the Coroner's Office."

Chad turned to Dani. "I thought you said your mom filed reports for the county."

"Oh, Danielle, you're too modest," Peri said. "Chad, Dani's mom is an Assistant Coroner, so she gets first look at most of the Orange County corpses. I'll bet a Goth like you would have a million questions for someone like her."

"Aunt Peri—" Dani looked at Peri, eyes pleading.

"What?" Peri asked. "Chad, are you a Goth or not?"

"Yes ma'am."

"So, death and the macabre interest you, don't they?"

Chad stared at Peri, his eyes as dark as a limo's tinted windows. "Actually, they do. I'm personally not rushing to the grave, but I am fascinated by where the spirit goes when the body stops ticking."

"Ever see a dead body?"

Dani groaned at Peri's question and looked to her mom, her eyes begging her to change the subject. Blanche stared back at her daughter with a little shrug, as if to ask her what she expected.

Peri smiled, knowing Paul wouldn't help his daughter, either. He never interfered with his wife's antics. At the first mention of evidence and the coroner, he began a quiet conversation with Nick about his recent track meet.

"I've never seen one, ma'am," Chad told Peri. "Except for my grandma at the funeral, but she looked kind of fake, you know? All made up."

"I know what you mean," Peri said. "I saw my first dead body, in the raw, so to speak, the other day. They look a lot different without the embalming fluid and make-up."

"I'll bet. I'd love to see one, just to look into their eyes."

"Ever read *Firestarter*?" Peri smiled. "Stephen King?"

Chad smiled back. "Yeah, his villain—what was his name? He liked to look into people's eyes when he killed them, to see their soul leave, or something."

"John Rainbird." Peri sat back and took a sip of her iced tea. She stared into Chad's eyes, her eyebrow cocked. "I hope you don't plan on watching people's souls leave, Chad."

The room took on a silence, as if all sound had been sucked out. Everyone turned to Chad for his answer.

"Oh, no, no," he said. "I'm not that kind of guy."

"See that you're not, young man," Peri told him. "I'd hate for you to end up in jail. Or on Mrs. Debussy's slab."

Peri looked over at Blanche, and then burst into loud, throaty laughter. The rest of the table stared, until Blanche started laughing, too.

"So, getting back to the trace, Beebs," Peri said. "Was it blood?"

"Yes, it was, a little diluted, but blood. Skip should have the report by now."

"Wow," Chad said. "It must be fascinating to work with a laboratory and try to figure things out. Like how someone was killed, and who did it." He looked at Dani. "Why didn't you tell me your mom did this for a living?"

Dani focused on her plate, nibbling at the pasta. "I didn't think it was important."

"It's not important, it's just cool."

"I suppose," Dani told him, shooting a glare at Peri.

After dinner, Paul and Nick cleared the table while Blanche put the leftovers away and Peri loaded the dishwasher. They heard the front door slam and Dani's angry footsteps marching upstairs.

"I think that's my fault," Peri said, and went to the teenager's door.

"Dani?" she called, knocking softly.

The muffled response told her to come in. The tears around it told her to tread lightly. Dani sat in her overstuffed chair, legs curled up underneath her, clutching a stuffed dog, floppy from years of affection. Peri took a seat on the ottoman in front of her, noting the smell of lavender and vanilla from the lit candles in the room.

"Hon, I'm sorry if I was too forward, too—" Peri searched for a word. "Too me, at dinner."

The young girl sniffled. "It's okay, Aunt Peri. It's not like I told you not to talk about your work, or Mom's."

"I don't understand. Are you ashamed of what your mom does?"

Dani brushed at her watery eyes. "No, that's not it. When I met Chad, he's just so cute, but he's a Goth, right? I wanted him to like me for me, not because I might have access to dead bodies."

"Well, he seems to like you for you."

"I thought he did, but all he could talk about when we said goodnight was what a cool job Mom has and how I must be able to hear and see a lot of interesting things, pictures, and stuff." She let out an enormous, trembling sigh. "He's already forgotten me. Now it's all about whether I've got an *in* with the dead."

"Maybe not," Peri told her. "Tonight, he may just be excited about the newness of it all, finding out about your mom. Before, he thought you were a hot chick. Now, you're a hot chick who has something in common with his passion."

"But it's not my passion, Auntie." She pulled at the ear of her doggie. "He's so cute, but we don't have anything in common."

"Then explore your differences," Peri said, then realized the double meaning of her advice. "I mean your different interests. Not your different, you know, physical, um, your likes and dislikes, not your body parts, um. Oh, hell, I'm talking about talking, not about sex. Just say no, and all that."

Dani laughed through her tears. "Oh, Auntie, don't worry about that. I'm a—what do you call it? A smart cookie." She gave her a hug. "It's a good thing you don't have kids. You'd tell them to have a good time, then spend an hour explaining what you meant by that."

"Yeah, lucky for them," Peri said, thinking about the test kit at home.

CHAPTER 23

The battering and resulting medications caught up with Peri on Sunday. She woke at eleven, then at two, then at five. A quick read of the Sunday paper and a peanut butter sandwich later, she gave up and went back to bed.

By seven o'clock the next morning, Peri had forgotten to take her test. Instead, she overslept, causing her to throw on a t-shirt and shorts, and run out the door to catch up with Mr. Cheavers, who left for work promptly at eight. After watching him drive away from his house, she followed him to his office and parked her car in the lot across from the Century Bank Plaza in Irvine.

Camera in her lap, she sat low in her car, a ball cap over her blonde hair, watching. Mr. Cheavers rewarded her by crossing Main Street and strolling toward his workplace, while Peri took pictures. Fortunately, the morning was warm, so she could roll down her window without being noticed. She spoke softly into a digital voice recorder, giving a monologue describing the scene.

He didn't leave his office until Peri had drunk three cups of coffee, ate a bag of chocolate covered pretzels, and had to pee. She followed him to a fitness club, where she snapped a few frames of his entrance into the tinted glass doors, a gym bag across his shoulder. Fortunately, she could see his car in the lot from her vantage point, across the street in front of the Seven-Eleven. Peri scampered into the store to use the restroom and buy more junk food.

Her phone played a merry tune as she returned to her car. Throwing the bag of salt and vinegar chips aside, she dug it out of her tote and answered.

"Miss Minneopa, we need to talk."

"Hello, Kevin," she said. "How can I help you?"

"I must have that ring back." His voice sounded depressed, haggard.

"Kevin, I can't help you. The ring will stay in custody until either a trial is held or, if the case goes unsolved, you have to petition the court for its release."

"Can't you convince the police to release it now? Surely you have enough pictures and evidence from it."

"Christie's appraiser on your tail? You know, you really should hold up the auction until ownership can be established."

"Miss Minneopa, I shall be blunt. The market has not been kind to me. I lost a lot of money on my investments, and I need this auction to pay off my creditors."

Peri whistled. "You must be drowning in debt, to need the money from that ring."

"I'm afraid it's a rather sticky situation," he said. "With the ring, the collection will fetch about three times what it would get without it."

"But what's the collection actually worth?"

"No one knows. What's a script worth? It's just words on paper, even if it is signed by the great Melvin Conway. The interest generated by the ring rubs off on everything around it. Even Christie's is treating the auction specially, because of the ring."

"It's truly sad, Kevin, but I'm not going to help you."

"You have got to. The people I owe—"

She cut him off. "Okay, that's it. I've got to go."

"Not until you agree to help me."

"You're not my client, and it's not my problem. Goodbye, Kevin."

His voice took a hard edge. "I'm not finished with you. Not nearly."

"Yeah, take a number, pal," she said as she closed the phone.

Her cell phone rang again, immediately. She snapped it open.

"Leave me the hell alone."

"What the hell's your problem?" Skip asked.

"Oh, hey, Skip, sorry. I just got off the phone with Kevin Conway. He was trying to strong-arm me, if you can imagine."

"Are you okay? What did he want?"

"Of course I'm okay. Even on my worst day, I'm bigger and meaner than he is. He wants his ring back. I don't know how he thinks I'm going to help him."

Skip sighed. "Peri, I wish you'd leave this case alone. I'm getting worried about you."

"Skipper, you're so sweet. I'll be fine. David Waters is in jail and Kevin Conway's too pretty to fight with me."

"Yes, but Conway's rich enough to hire someone to do his fighting for him."

"He's not that rich. He just told me he's got a lot of creditors, of the bad variety. Maybe you should pull his financials. He's banking on the sale of that ring to get him out of debt."

Peri turned to see Mr. Cheavers leave the building. "Gotta go, Skip. I'll talk to you later."

The rest of her day was spent chasing her client's husband between the office and various errands, all benign. He finally turned into the family estate at nine o'clock, and Peri drove home, beating herself up all the way. I must live in a perfect world, where no one cheats their insurance company and husbands are all faithful. Either that, or I'm really bad at this.

Too tired to call Skip, she collapsed on her sofa and turned on the TV. Her favorite movie, *The Big Sleep*, was playing on the classics channel, so she microwaved a bag of popcorn and sat back down to enjoy Bogart and Bacall. The phone rang to interrupt her.

"Hey, Doll, just checking in." Skip would have made a perfect Marlowe.

"I got home about ten minutes ago," she told him. "Safe and sound, no loss of limbs. Hey, by the way, Beebs said she gave you the report on the blood Jason found in the freezer. Was it Benny's?"

"No. It has thirteen alleles in common with Benny, though, so I figure it's his mom's."

"How about evidence from Sylvia Banks?"

"The hair in the ring and on Marnie's coat are definitely Sylvia's. And you were right about the jacket, they found Marnie's hair on the collar."

Peri looked up to see Philip Marlowe pull his ear lobe and speculate about a clue. Her hand reached up and rubbed her own ear. "So, Marnie and Sylvia met and exchanged coats. Skip, did you talk to anyone at McDonald's? Maybe that's where we'll find this Carlos."

"No, I haven't yet. Wanna meet me there tomorrow morning, say, seven?"

"Um, can it be earlier? I'm on a surveillance case."

"I can do the interview," Skip offered. "I'll just let you read my notes afterward."

Peri laughed. "You know I can't read your chicken scratches. I'll be there at 6:30. If you're not there, you can read my notes."

After hanging up from Skip, Peri downloaded her pictures from the day onto her laptop. She flipped through each one, looking at Mr. Cheavers, his wardrobe, his body language, searching for infidelity clues.

Nothing caught her eye. An older man, he didn't strike Peri as particularly handsome or homely, just a normal Joe. He walked with his body upright, his shoulders back, confident. His gray hair was slightly longer than Skip's, full and wavy on the top.

His hair. Peri looked at the pictures of him going into the gym, then coming out. His hair looked the same, entering and exiting.

"Shouldn't your hair be wet from the shower, Larry?" she said to the computer screen. "Or are you hygienically challenged?"

Her plans made for the next day, Peri read the pregnancy test directions. It seemed simple enough. Open the package, remove the plastic guard, and anoint the stick. She placed the package on her bathroom counter, then went to bed, prepared to discover the truth in the morning.

At five o'clock, Peri rose and went into the bathroom. She opened the package, removed the guard and sat down to answer the question: was she pregnant? As she lowered the stick, the phone rang, startling her in the morning darkness. She felt the cold water splash up as the test hit the bowl.

"Goddammit," she exhaled, and looked down. The test stick floated around the surface, thoroughly wet and completely ruined.

"Blanche is going to kill me," she said aloud as she listened to the answering machine. No one ever delivered good news at five o'clock in the morning.

"Beep. Beep. Beep." Someone's fax machine tried to send her voicemail a document.

"Goddammit," she repeated.

CHAPTER 24

"What can I get for you this morning?" June, a smiling, gray-haired woman greeted Peri at the counter of McDonald's.

"I'll take a Sausage McMuffin, no egg, and orange juice," Peri told her, inhaling the scent of salt and grease. "And, could I speak to the manager?"

Rita Mills, the day manager, came out from behind the grill. She looked a little younger than June, but not as young as some of the fast food managers Peri had encountered. A soccer mom, no doubt, who was trying to earn a little spare change.

"How may I help you?"

Peri introduced herself, then took a picture out of her tote. "I'm investigating the death of Marnie Russell, and I was told she worked here for awhile. I don't know which shift she worked."

"Yes, Marnie," Rita replied. "I saw the article in the paper. How awful. She worked the day shift. I was her supervisor."

"Can you tell me anything about her friends? Specifically, her male friends?"

"Our schedule is usually too busy for a lot of chit chat, so I didn't get to know her very well." Rita paused. "She worked here for about five or six months. At first, there was a young Hispanic man who would show up as she got off work. He was very nice, polite, clean cut."

"Do you remember his name?" Peri asked.

"Carlos. I don't know the last name."

"You said, 'at first.' When did Carlos stop coming around?"

"Oh, I don't know," Rita replied.

"It was about a month ago," June said. "I remember, because she came to work crying, on Mother's Day. I asked if she was sad about her mother, her being an orphan and all. She said, no, she broke up with Carlos."

Rita nodded. "That sounds right. Shortly after that, David showed up."

"David Waters?"

"I never got his last name." June frowned. "Scraggly, sneaky, horrible man."

"How did they act together, like boyfriend and girlfriend?"

Rita and June looked at each other. "No," Rita said. "I wouldn't say she looked at him like that."

"Not like she looked at Carlos," June added.

"Could you describe Carlos?" Peri asked. "Or do you know anything else about him, where he worked or anything?"

"Slender, but broad shouldered, like he worked out," Rita said. "Very handsome, dark hair and eyes."

"He works at Ralph's," June told her. "Sometimes, he wore one of their shirts."

Peri jotted down the information. "Thank you, both, very much."

She grabbed her breakfast and left for the gym.

Arriving at the fitness club forty-five minutes before Mr. Cheavers was scheduled to arrive, Peri parked in a different lot, and waited. He walked in right on time.

She gave him ten minutes, then entered the club. A tall, athletic girl leaned over the counter, chatting with one of the male members. Peri strode to the desk and stood, staring at the employee. She waited for their flirtation to either run out, or the date to be set. Finally, she walked forward and stretched her arms across the counter, her shoulder brushing the young man.

"Excuse me, but are you accepting new members?" she asked.

The girl looked at her, smiling but perplexed. "Why, of course."

"Oh, good. I thought perhaps you were full and didn't need any more money."

A tall man, lean and muscled, in the company uniform, walked over. "May I help you?"

"Yes," Peri replied. "My husband and I are interested in joining your club. I thought this young woman could give me a tour as soon as she was available."

The manager glared at his employee, then extended his hand. "My name is Bob Haynes. Let me show you our facilities."

They walked through the club, Peri feigning interest while Bob pointed out the latest equipment for reducing her body fat and increasing her muscle mass. Peri held her cell phone up here and there, taking pictures.

"My husband will want to see this," she said.

Around a corner, standing by the pool, were two bodies in swimsuits. Larry Cheavers stood tall, allowing a young blonde to lean into him softly. His head bowed toward hers, whispering something in her ear. They looked very cozy.

"Wow, look at this pool," Peri told the manager, holding up her camera. "Ted will love it."

She spent the next fifteen minutes in the office, getting the manager's spiel about the discounts he could give her if she signed the contract today. After fending him off while still appearing interested, she took an armload of brochures and left, feeling quite proud of her skills.

Once out of the building, Peri lingered by the planters to the side, scratching at her hair through her plain, brown baseball cap, her blue eyes covered by sunglasses. She took a water bottle out of her tote and wiped it down as she waited. Soon, she saw Cheavers' young blonde leaving the club, her long, tanned legs at a brisk walk.

Peri suddenly moved toward her, water bottle in hand, searching through her tote for something. She planned her path carefully, appearing distracted, until she bumped into the blonde. Gasping in surprise, she dropped her water bottle and her tote.

"Oh, I'm so sorry," she said as she reached for her bag. "I wasn't watching where I was going."

"It's okay," the woman replied in a high, breathy voice. She picked Peri's bottle up and handed it to her. "I get distracted all the time."

"Thanks. Again, I'm so sorry."

At least she's polite, Peri thought as she watched the young woman walk away, then reached deep in her tote and pulled out a plastic bag. Carefully placing the bottle inside, she went back to her car and watched for the blonde to leave the lot. As the deep red Beemer convertible pulled out, Peri jotted down the license plate number.

Remaining a few cars behind, Peri followed the little red sports car to South Coast Plaza. The blonde parked in the employees' lot and walked into Nordstrom's.

Looking at the time, Peri took off her baseball cap and jacket, fluffed her long blonde hair, and put on a pair of tortoiseshell glasses with clear lenses. Once her appearance had been altered, she entered the store. Nordstrom's exemplified the high-end look. The aisles were wide, leading to elegant displays and neatly arranged racks of clothing.

She wandered around, stopping to touch a blouse here, hold up a skirt there, like any window shopper. From behind a rack of fancy workout gear, she saw a glimpse of blonde hair coming out of the changing room in Petites. Cheavers' girlfriend carried a dark suit on a hanger. Peri watched her ring up the sale for the customer, a beautiful Asian girl with blue-black hair.

Nice store, Peri thought, *but how do you afford a Beemer on a sales girl's salary?*

She returned to her car and drove back to Placentia. Skip called as she exited the freeway onto Tustin Avenue.

"I missed you this morning," he told her.

"I missed you, too, Skipper. Could you help me run a license number? Also, I have fingerprints."

"You just use me, don't you?"

"It's true, you're only good for sex and information."

Skip chuckled. "Feel like using me tonight, or are you still too sore?"

"I don't think my rib cage can take it. Did you talk to the McDonald's ladies?"

They compared notes, finding that the women gave each of them the same information.

"I went past Ralph's after I left them," Skip told her. "Got a list of everyone named Carlos who worked there in the last six months."

"Is it under a hundred names?"

"Surprisingly, there are only sixteen. I thought you might want to help me narrow it down."

"Sure," Peri said. "If you'll help me out with my surveillance case."

"And if I don't?"

"I could hack into the system, Skipper, but I hate to make you sad."

"Come on over to the station. We'll work together."

Peri ambled into Skip's office and took her notes out of her tote bag. Skip got up and closed the door. She looked up at him, her eyebrows knitted in a frown.

"What's up?" she asked.

"I don't want you to worry, Doll," Skip said. "But when I got back to the station today, I found out Waters has been released."

"Released? Who the hell would release a guy who assaulted someone?"

"The lawyer who posted his bail."

"Well, what idiot would take his case?"

Skip shook his head. "Everybody deserves a good defense."

"What's defensible about what he did?"

"Peri, not to stand up for him, but you did hit him in the head with a tote bag."

"And didn't even leave a mark. He hit me in the head and the ribs," she told him. "So not fair."

"Maybe not, but he's out on bail, and I'll be spending more time keeping you safe." Skip handed her a sheet of paper. "Here's a list of guys named Carlos and their addresses. I've already narrowed them down by the appropriate age. See if anyone jumps out at you."

"And here's the license number," Peri said.

Peri read the list, checking the addresses against the map of north Orange County.

"It looks like there are three that live in the area," she said. "Ramirez, Barragan, and Lopez. We should start with them."

"Sounds good to me." Skip picked up a paper from the printer. "Here's the ID on that car, owned by Heidi Watson, in Costa Mesa. I'll have the prints run later, if you need them."

He leaned over the desk. "Now then, I think we should go get some dinner and get you home. I'll just need to stop and pick up a few things."

"My own personal bodyguard?"

Skip smiled. "Placentia's best, at your service."

"All right, I'll pick up some Chinese, and meet you at my place."

Peri got two three-item plates at the Flaming Wok. She liked this place because she could get ten pounds of food for five dollars. As she pulled into the drive, her phone rang.

"Okay, tell me you've taken the test now," Blanche said.

"No, and I don't know when I'm going to, Beebs."

"Peri, Goddammit, pee on the stick."

"Wow, someone's testy, aren't they?"

"Let's just say, I don't have to worry about being pregnant this month," Blanche replied. "What about you?"

"Okay, I was all set to take the test this morning, and I dropped the damn stick in the toilet."

Blanche laughed. "Only you. So go get a new one."

"Here's the thing, Beebs. David Waters made bail today, which means Skip is worried about me, which means he's going to be spending a few nights at my place."

"For how long?"

Peri sighed. "I don't know. But I can't take the test with him around."

"You could certainly get pregnant with him around."

"Good God, Beebs, go eat some chocolate or something. I'm not ready to share this with him."

She shut off the engine and opened the car door. *I'm not even ready to share this with myself.*

CHAPTER 25

Peri shuffled through the living room at six A.M., on her way to make coffee. She held her side in an attempt to support her ribs. Skip sat at the kitchen table, reading the paper.

"I guess I should have asked where the coffee was last night," he said.

She opened the freezer and reached into the back, wincing slightly. Skip dropped the paper and went to her side.

"Here, let me do that," he said. "Still hurting?"

"Mostly when I get up in the morning. I think it's from the change of positions."

Peri let him make the coffee, instructing him on the number of scoops, amount of water, and everything else he touched.

"I've made coffee before, you know," he told her.

"I know. I've tasted it."

By the time they were ready to visit Ralph's grocery store, Peri's movements came easier, due in part to the pain relievers she had swallowed down with her java.

The Ralph's grocery chain could be seen everywhere in southern California. The store on Yorba Linda Boulevard had competed with Alpha Beta, Lucky's, and Albertson's before finally triumphing.

Merging, all the merging, Peri thought as she eased her way out of the car and made her way into the store with Skip. Nothing stays the same.

She and Skip introduced themselves to the manager, who told them two of the men named Carlos were currently at work. The third Carlos worked nights. The manager called the two employees to the front. Peri watched them approach. They were about the same height, and same build. One had a darker complexion, although they were both very neat and clean-cut.

"Carlos Lopez, and Carlos Ramirez," the manager said. He then turned and told the men, in Spanish, that Peri and Skip needed to speak with them.

Peri stepped forward. "My name is Peri Minneopa. I apologize for taking you away from your jobs, but Detective Carlton and I need to ask you some questions."

The Carlos on the right smiled at Peri blankly, while the Carlos to the left told her, "Thank you, it's okay."

"Did you know Marnie Russell, Mr. Lopez?" she asked him, noting his red eyes.

He lowered his head. "Yes."

Skip nodded to the manager, who dismissed the other Carlos.

"Mr. Lopez, how well did you know Marnie?" Skip asked.

"She and I were together." His accent made the words sound lyrical, and his sadness made them heartbreaking.

"When did you see her last?"

"Two weeks ago," he replied with certainty. "It was a Monday."

"Can you tell us what you talked about?" Peri asked.

He looked at Peri, his black eyes searching hers. "It's my fault she's dead," he said, covering his face with his hands.

Skip put his hand on Carlos' shoulder and directed him outside to sit on a bench. Peri followed and sat down next to him.

"Why is it your fault, Carlos?" she asked.

"We fought." He stared at the ground. "A few weeks ago, we fought, and we broke up. It was my fault, for being stupid."

"Was it about the baby?"

He nodded. "Si. Yes. I was a fool. She told me she is going to have a baby, and instead of being happy, I am afraid. I tell her we cannot be a family, because she is white and my parents will not accept her."

"She must have been very upset."

He put his head in his hands again. "She cried, so much."

"So, you didn't see her for awhile after that," Skip said.

"No, I go to work and I try to forget. But I love her, so I decide it's okay, let's marry. I go to McDonald's on Monday to ask her to take me back." He frowned. "She said no."

"Did that make you mad?" Skip asked.

"No, I'm not mad at her. She feels frightened and alone, and it is my fault. I am only mad at myself for being weak, and at David for taking advantage."

Peri looked up from her notes. "So you knew that she was seeing David?"

"Si. But she doesn't love him. He is just something to grab because she is drowning."

"Did anyone see you talking to her that Monday?" Skip asked.

"I guess. We were in the parking lot after work. People are walking by."

"Carlos, how did you know David?" Peri said.

"He worked here, at Ralph's, for a little while. They fired him for sleeping on the job." He shook his head. "He's not a good man. He's not good for her."

"I have one more request," Skip told him. "We'd like to verify that Marnie's child was yours, so, could I get a swab of your cheek to compare the DNA?"

"Yes, of course."

Skip collected the evidence, then shook Carlos' hand. "Thank you, Carlos. Here's my card. If you think of anything, please call."

"Please find who did this to her," Carlos said. "And my baby."

Peri returned with Skip to his car. As she adjusted her seatbelt, she felt the familiar stomach churning, flash fire that continued to plague her. She opened her window and lay her head on the frame, hoping the cool air would make her feel better.

"Are you okay?" Skip asked.

"Sure," she told him. "I just feel bad for Carlos. He seems so heartbroken." Peri started to say more, but her lip quivered and tears filled her eyes.

"Dammit. What the hell am I crying for?"

"I've never seen you like this," Skip said. "He really got to you."

"No, I'm just, I don't know," She wiped moisture from her temples as she stared at the road. "It's probably a side effect of my—"

She couldn't find a word for *injuries* that didn't make her want to weep. "Sorry. My ribs hurt, my head is aching, but if I take the pain pills too often, I get groggy." In an attempt to block thoughts of pregnancy from her mind, she began to ramble. "And I did get…jumped. I mean, I'm a tough cookie and I can take a few knocks here and there, but having a big lug punch me is a little disconcerting. Plus, the kick didn't help. You know, most normal women would have a meltdown after the punch, let alone the kick. I think I'm doing pretty well, considering. I should be allowed to have one minor breakdown."

"You need some rest," Skip told her.

"No, no, I've got work to do. It's just a momentary glitch, like a case of hiccups." Or it may be hormonal, and not in a good way.

"By the way, how did you zero in on Lopez?"

"Because he spoke English. We never had any hint that Marnie spoke Spanish, so I assumed they'd need a common language." Her sweat and depression subsided. "Plus, he looked so sad, his eyes all red and everything."

As they left Ralph's, Skip turned right on Yorba Linda Boulevard.

"Where are you going?" Peri asked. "I need to go home."

"I think it'd be better if you came to the station with me."

"But I've got work to do today."

"So do it in my office," he told her. "Where you're nice and safe."

Peri frowned. "I can't tail Heidi from your office. If I don't complete this case, I don't get paid. If I don't get paid, I can't pay the doctor bills, and they repossess my ribs."

"Wandering around in your car is a great way for Waters to get you alone. I don't want his behavior to escalate. He's just the kind of guy to take a chance on killing you to get rid of a witness. Especially since this assault charge is his third strike."

"Skipper, I'll be careful. I can't suspend my life because David Waters is running loose."

Skip said nothing, but continued to drive toward the police station.

"Either take me home now, Skip," Peri told him. "Or I'll just walk to my house."

"You are the most stubborn woman," he said.

"I'm not stubborn. I just want what I want. Now, take me home."

"Fine." Skip turned down Madison Avenue, to Peri's house.

They didn't speak again until he pulled into the driveway.

"Could you at least call me to check in? Frequently?"

She leaned over, wincing, and kissed him. "If I haven't called by four, send the Cavalry." She got out of the car. "And that dog with the keg around his neck."

CHAPTER 26

Peri parked her car across from Heidi Watson's town home and waited, a cooler of Diet Coke by her side. She had not seen Heidi with her client's husband anywhere outside the gym, but they must be meeting somewhere. After finding out the woman lived alone in a rather expensive condo, Peri took a chance. Maybe that was their love nest.

While she sat, she sifted through her notes on Benny's case, still looking for the link between Marnie and Sylvia. A thought occurred to her, so she called Skip.

"Skipper, this is a long shot, but Carlos has the same last name as the woman who took care of Sylvia Banks at Bradford Square. Is it possible they're related?"

"I don't know, Peri, Lopez is a pretty common name."

"Yeah, but there's got to be some way that Marnie met Sylvia. If Carlos had access to Bradford Square and Marnie was with Carlos…you see how they could meet?"

"Sounds reasonable, if the connection is there," Skip said. "I'll check it out while you're at your 'other' job. How's that going, by the way."

"Boringly, thank you. I'd like to have another Diet Coke to keep me awake, but I'll have to find a bathroom if I do."

Skip laughed. "Welcome to surveillance. Maybe you should invest in some Depends."

"I think not. What time should I expect you tonight? What are you bringing for dinner?"

"Will pizza at eight do the trick?"

"Perfect," Peri said. She went back to her work, sitting in her car with her camera ready.

At six thirty, Heidi's Beemer pulled into the development and into her garage. A few minutes later, Peri heard another engine and tires rolling against the pavement. She sunk down into her seat and glanced at the rear view mirror. Larry Cheavers parked his car, then walked to Heidi's front door. As soon as the door opened, Peri snapped away, taking as many pictures as possible of the couple embracing and kissing. She felt especially proud of her last shot, a close-up of Heidi's hand on Larry's butt, her fingers pressing firmly into his dark wool slacks.

On her way home, Peri thought about Sylvia Banks' night of wandering. They found her behind Ralph's, Mrs. Lopez said. Peri doubted anyone had treated it like a crime scene. An elderly woman meandered two blocks, crossed the street, and collapsed, and it happened weeks ago, so any evidence at the scene had to have disappeared.

Still, Peri decided to stop at the local fire station to chat with the paramedics. The station on Bradford seemed like the most likely candidate to answer a call at Ralph's, so she pulled into their lot and walked into the office.

A man looked up from his computer. "I'm Chief Danes. May I help you?"

Peri introduced herself. "I'm looking for information about an incident that happened about three weeks ago. An elderly lady was found behind Ralph's. I think she was suffering from exposure."

"I remember that. Tom's the one who went out on the call. Let me introduce you to him."

Peri followed him down a corridor and through a large, gray door. She could smell a mixture of chicken, chili powder, and corn tortillas, no doubt their supper. Six men sat around a table, eating. The chief called Tom Flores over to meet Peri.

"Please don't interrupt your dinner," she told him, sitting down at the table. "We can talk while you eat."

Tom, a broad man with the complexion of cinnamon, smiled. "What can I do for you?"

"Chief Danes tells me you helped an elderly lady about three weeks ago, the woman found behind Ralph's."

"Oh, yes," he replied. "Poor thing, she had been in the night air too long. She was borderline hypothermia, and kept drifting in and out of consciousness."

"Did you assume she was homeless?"

"No, homeless people are more equipped for temperature changes. They generally have too many clothes on. This lady only wore a nightgown and a cotton jacket. I suspected she came from either Bradford Square or a private residence."

"Where exactly did you find her?"

"Over here behind this Ralph's." He gestured to the north. "She was lying in between two dumpsters."

"Who told you she was there?"

"Hmm, I think it was an anonymous phone call, but you'd have to check with dispatch for that."

"So, they logged the time and number, right?"

"Yes, they actually record the call, although I'm not sure how long the calls are stored." Tom took a bite of casserole. "I can try to get the information for you. Why are you investigating this?"

"It's kind of connected to the murder of that girl in the park," Peri told him. "Thanks for all your help."

Peri glanced at her watch. Seven-thirty. She knew she should head for home, but she couldn't wait to look at the scene. Driving past her street, she turned in at the Crossroads Shopping Center and wound her car around to the back of the stores. From the front, the Center had been updated to feature stone architecture and golden tones. The back, however, still maintained the white, blockish look of a warehouse.

Like a Hollywood set, faking everyone out.

She got out of her car, and put her cell phone in her pocket. The dumpsters had been filled and emptied a number of times in three weeks, so she didn't think she'd find any evidence in them. However, she hoped there might still be a shred of Sylvia's visit somewhere.

The sun still gave light, but the shadows were lengthening, so Peri got her flashlight out to help. She walked around the dumpsters, shining the beam on pieces of paper and cloth, anything that might be important. As she moved around to the opposite side of the furthest dumpster, she noted a shopping cart, bent and rusted, resting against the block wall in the back.

Sylvia was so frail, she thought, how would she have gotten here? No one found a wheelchair at the scene, and Bradford Square didn't report one missing. Is it possible that someone put her in a shopping cart?

Using her flashlight, Peri examined the cart. On the handle, stuck in the corners, she saw hairs. She went back to her car to get her camera, and called Skip.

"It's eight o'clock, where the hell are you?" His voice mixed anger and fear.

"Sorry, Skip, but I'm behind Ralph's, where Sylvia was found. There's a shopping cart here with hairs stuck in it. I'm wondering if it was used to cart Sylvia to the dumpsters."

"You don't listen to me at all, do you? Lock yourself in your car and I'll be right there."

"Skipper, stop freaking out."

"Promise me," he said.

"Yes, sir."

Peri opened her car door to get in as Skip requested, then decided to take pictures instead. She focused and clicked, taking close-ups and far shots of the green dumpsters and shopping cart against the gray block wall.

"Starting a new career?" A raspy voice said behind her.

Peri wheeled and saw David Waters, leaning against her car, smiling.

"Returning to the scene of the crime?" she asked.

"Crime?" He spat. "What crime?"

"Your crime, of dragging Sylvia Banks down here against her will to rob her."

"Why would I need to drag her down here?" he asked. "I coulda robbed her at the old folks' home."

Peri smiled. "And how did you know who she was or where she lived, David?"

"None of your business, Bitch."

He pushed himself off her car and strode toward her. She moved away from him, put the camera down and gripped her flashlight. David ran forward and reached for her arms, trying to push her. She swung the flashlight at him, connecting with his chin.

He stepped back, shaking his head, and she followed him, swinging the light as if she were warming up in the batter's box. Each swing caused him to duck or bend or otherwise contort his body to stay out of the way, until at last he couldn't stand and fell backward, his head making a thwacking noise on the pavement.

"Not as easy to smack me around the second time, is it?" Peri asked, her breath raw and gasping.

David rolled to his hands and knees, slowly, groaning. Headlights caught him on the rise, like a coyote in traffic. Skip jumped out of his car and ran over to Peri.

"Are you all right? What happened?"

Peri leaned into Skip, holding her sore ribs. "We were just having a conversation. Mr. Waters knew Sylvia. He even knew where she lived."

"Really?" Skip asked. "What else do you know, Waters?"

The scraggly young man stood and glared at them. "Nothing," he said, then turned and ran.

Peri started to chase him, but Skip held her back. He punched a number in his phone and spoke. "Tony? It's Skip. Listen, put out a BOLO on David Waters. Last seen behind Ralph's on Yorba Linda, he's wanted for questioning in Sylvia Banks' abduction."

Turning to Peri, he put his arm around her. "Let someone else chase him. Our pizza's getting cold."

"First, process this cart," she said. "Look at the hairs. And there are probably prints."

Skip laughed and kissed her head. "Okay, Bulldog, let me call Jason."

After Officer Bonham arrived to collect the evidence, they returned to Peri's house for the evening.

"I have to say," Peri told Skip in between bites of pizza. "Waters has a point—why take Sylvia so far away to rob her? He could have broken into her room some night and done it."

"Maybe he had another reason, like, kidnapping."

"Or maybe she caught him in the act and started making a lot of noise, so he had to go to Plan B," Peri said. "Take her out and dump her. He doesn't need to actually kill her, but if she dies, oh well."

Skip nodded. "Maybe."

"We need to get those hairs and prints analyzed." She reached across Skip for the TV remote, to watch the news. As she did, he nuzzled her neck, running his hand down her back. She sighed contentedly and turned to kiss him.

"Hold me for awhile, Skipper," she said. "I'm so tired."

CHAPTER 27

"Subject was observed paying close attention to blonde woman at LA Fitness," Peri typed on her laptop. Looking at the photo, she needed to describe it factually without being offensive. She stopped and stared out of her office window, observing the flowers in bloom. Ornamental bamboo stretched over the coleus and ferns, while the deep primary colors of the bird-of-paradise flowers soaked up the sun. Light dappled through the atrium, filtering through the morning mist.

She could have written the report at home, but she felt the need to be in a structured surrounding. Moreover, she wanted to get her three hundred dollars' worth out of the space. After a few minutes of reverie, she went back to her writing.

The printer had just completed its job when the door opened and a tall, muscular man entered. His suit looked expensive, but he did not. Acne scars defined his shiny face, his small dark eyes were shadowed by thick, tangled brows. If baboons wore Armani, this is what they'd look like.

"You the private dick?"

"Private investigator," she told him. "How may I help you?"

He stood close to her desk, leaning slightly forward, his feet apart, and hands clasped together in front. "I represent a client who is interested in the Forever Roses ring. My client would like to be sure the ring goes to the rightful owner."

"Tell Kevin Conway I still can't help him," Peri said. "It's in police custody."

Baboon Face's eyebrows lifted, slightly. "Although I'm not at liberty to discuss my client's identity, I can assure you it is not a member of the Conway clan."

"Well, pal, I don't care if you're an agent of the Queen. I can't help you."

"We know Kevin Conway isn't the only person who believes they have a stake in the ring. And we know your relationship with Detective Carlton gives you certain privileges and access to police information. I am prepared to offer you fifty-thousand dollars to ensure that the ring's final resting place is in our hands."

Peri picked up her phone. "And I'm prepared to call Detective Carlton and ask him to arrest your ass if you don't get out of my office." As she said this, she put the phone to her ear.

"Very well, Miss Minneopa. We were prepared to reward you for your efforts, but we will now proceed without your help." He turned and left, slamming the door.

"Did I just wander into a Jimmy Cagney movie?" she asked herself. Looking at her phone, Peri pressed the button to save the picture she'd taken. Then she called Skip.

"I'm sending you a picture," she told him, before explaining about her visitor. "Sounds like we need to dig a little deeper into this ring."

"Don't suppose you got any prints?"

"Sure. Come on over and dust my doorknob."

"You bet," he said. "What's on your schedule today?"

Peri leaned back in her chair. "I'm having lunch with Blanche, then dropping off Mrs. Cheavers' report. Then, I was thinking about re-visiting the park where we found Marnie, just to look around."

"Think you'll find what the police overlooked?"

"No, Skip, it's not like that. I just want to think about the case, see if I can come up with any ideas about why she was in the park."

"Doll, why don't you let me come to the park with you? I'll bring home cheesecake."

"From the Cheesecake Factory?"

"Is there any other kind?"

"Okay, Skipper, you win. See you at home."

Peri waited at an outdoor table of Zov's Bakery for Blanche, watching the lunchtime crowd rush in and out. The temperature had inched toward eighty degrees. By three it would have crossed that threshold and more. People in suits came into the restaurant, beads of perspiration on their foreheads. Peri felt a little underdressed in her cotton skirt and spaghetti-strapped top, however, at least she wasn't sweating.

She relaxed, and tore off small pieces of warm pita bread, dipping it in baba ghanoush. Finally, a petite brunette in a navy suit scurried down the sidewalk and sat down at her table.

"Sorry, sorry, always running," Blanche said.

"Sit, breathe in and out, repeat if necessary," Peri told her. "I already ordered an iced tea and the aram for you."

As Blanche took off her jacket, her cell phone began playing a happy tune. She dug her phone out of her purse.

"Crap," she said, looking at the number before answering it.

The waitress arrived and served their plates: beautiful pinwheels of roast beef and dill in cracker bread. The young woman opened her mouth to ask if there would be anything else, when Blanche yelled into the phone, "John, just cut the fingers off and plump them in fabric softener. You'll be able to get prints that way."

Peri looked up at the waitress, who seemed a little pale. She smiled and shrugged, knowing it was better left unexplained.

Blanche hung up and turned to Peri. "I suppose I shouldn't bother asking you if you've taken your test yet."

"I suppose not," Peri replied. "Here's what I figure— I'm not officially late until a month has gone by." She took a bite of her sandwich. "Besides, it's not going to change anything if I know now or a week from now."

"Are you saying you'd have this baby?"

Peri shrugged. "I guess so. I don't have much of a choice."

"Yes, you do."

"Yeah, I know, women's rights, I could have an abortion, yadda yadda. In theory, it sounds like a perfect solution. In practice, it comes with a huge, social price tag."

"I've never known you to be pressured by what other people think."

"It's not a matter of caring what people think, it's a matter of losing clients because they suddenly abhor you for one single action." She took a long drink of her tea. "If you keep it a secret, it lays in your brain like a big lump of coal, not to mention leaving you open to blackmail if anyone finds out. That's a career killer in my line of work."

"And if you don't keep it a secret?"

"Then all of your job skills mean nothing, because you elected to terminate a pregnancy. I suppose I could try to get employment at an agency, where they can't discriminate against me, but I could kiss my days as a self-employed P.I. goodbye."

"So you'd raise the baby?"

Peri shook her head. "I said I'd have the baby. I didn't say I'd keep the baby."

"Oh, Peri, why not? You get along great with kids."

"Yes I do. I love playing with them. Then I love handing them back to their parents and going home to my orderly house and my orderly life. A gal's got to know her limitations. So the only down side to not knowing," she added, "is that I feel like I should be taking better care of myself until I know for sure."

Blanche smiled. "Okay, I'm closing the subject until you bring it up again."

"Ha ha, as if," Peri said. "I'll bet you ask me tomorrow."

"You're on. So, what else is new?"

Peri brought her friend up to speed on her latest escapades. "By the way, did you ever get a mold of Marnie's head injury?"

"Yes, didn't Skip show you? There was an odd depression on her front left temple, rectangular with deep ridges on the top and bottom. But the one that killed her was an almost puncture-like dent in the back. There were also white paint flecks in the wound that I sent to trace. I gave the report to Skip."

"Darn that Skip. If I don't ask for it, he doesn't volunteer."

"Men," Blanche said. "Can't live with 'em—"

"Can't cut their fingers off and plump them in fabric softener," Peri finished.

"Speak for yourself, girlfriend."

"By the way, how are the teenaged lovebirds?"

"Oddly, now that we've gotten to know and like Chad, Dani's bored with him." Blanche sipped her drink. "I don't think they're going to last the summer."

"You starting a pool? Put me down for August first, eight o'clock."

They finished their lunch talking about the upcoming Fourth of July celebration and what to do for Paul's birthday. At last, Blanche had to run back to the lab and Peri had to turn in her report on the wandering Mr. Cheavers.

As she drove back from the Cheavers home, Peri decided that delivering bad news to a client sucked. She did not feel like she had performed a good job. Instead, she felt like a rat. Mrs. Cheavers took the news fairly well. There were no tears or angry words from her. Peri got the impression the woman had been preparing for the worst all along. She acted relieved to know the truth.

Maybe Mr. Cheavers would be relieved when he got home, too. Relieved of his home, half his income, and possibly his gonads.

Peri had turned right onto Yorba Linda Boulevard and was headed west toward her house, when her cell phone rang. A panicked Benny yelped unintelligibly.

"MissPeriyougottahelpme."

"Benny, slow down. I don't understand you. Did the police come back?"

"No, Miss Peri, you gotta help me," he said, his voice high and nervous. "Someone's sneaking around in my yard."

"Benny, hang up and call 9-1-1," she told him. "I'm on my way."

"I don't want the police here."

"Oh, dear God, Benny, stop acting like a loony tune and call the freakin' cops. I'll call Skip. I'm coming from Yorba Linda, but I'll be there as soon as I can."

She rushed to Benny's house, calling Skip as she drove. When she arrived fifteen minutes later, two squad cars had beaten her to the site, and Benny stood outside, leaning against one of the cars with his hands behind his back, body stiff with apoplexy. Peri parked and ran over to him.

"Benny, what happened?" she asked.

"Miss Peri," he said. "They think I killed him."

"Killed who?" Peri looked past Benny to his yard. A body lay crumpled, in the overgrown grass.

"I don't know," he replied. "The guy who was sneaking."

Peri walked around to the fence, and ran into Officer Monroe.

"Who was it?"

"ID says David Waters," he told her. "Stabbed with a bread knife."

"And what makes you think Benny did it?"

Officer Monroe shrugged. "It was his knife."

Skip drove up and got out of his car. Peri walked over to him.

"You can cancel that BOLO on David Waters," she said.

They went to view the body. Waters sprawled on his back, staring upward, the hilt of Benny's bread knife at right angles to his chest. Blood had saturated his tee-shirt, pooling to his left and adding a coppery odor to the overall scene. He smelled worse than Marnie, somehow. Peri thought it had to do with the freshness of all the bodily fluids he had expelled.

"You check the body," Peri said. "I'm going to talk to Benny."

Skip stared at her. "When did the tail start wagging the dog?"

"Sorry, Skip. I mean, well, whatever you do right now, I'm going to talk to Benny." She walked to the officer and asked to speak to her client. The officer released Benny from his stance against the car and moved away.

"Benny, can you tell me what happened?"

His face shone with perspiration as he turned to her, his eyes swollen and red. "Miss Peri, I didn't kill him."

"Of course you didn't," she said. "Start from the top."

"I went to the store and got some spaghetti sauce. Ralph's had a sale, with coupons, two jars for two dollars. Mom used to make a great sauce, but I—"

"That's nice, Ben, but let's move along."

He frowned. "Anyway, I came home and my stuff was rearranged, like it is sometimes, so I thought Dino was looking for something again. Then I heard someone on my front porch. Dino never comes through the front door, so I knew it wasn't him. I could hear someone rustling around in the bushes. That's when I called you."

"That was around eight o'clock," Peri said.

"I guess. I heard a sound, like someone grunting, so I went outside. I saw the body. I screamed." He shrugged. "Next thing I know, there's a police officer standing over me, slapping my face."

"It's true ma'am." Officer Monroe had walked over to them. "He was passed out when I found him."

Skip joined them. "Benny, is that the knife we returned to you?"

Benny glanced in the direction of the body. "I don't know. Maybe. The handle looks the same."

"Where was it?"

"I was busy when the officer brought my knives back, so I told him to leave them on the porch." Benny pointed toward a small table by the front door. Peri could still see the box that held the carving knife. "I forgot to bring them in and put them away."

"So anybody could have picked it up," Peri said.

"Sure," Benny replied. "Anybody."

"Well, Benny," Skip told him. "Your front yard is going to be a crime scene for awhile."

"And if someone was in your house," Peri said. "I'd suggest some fingerprinting."

Benny's eyes widened. "No. Not in my house."

"Not your stuff, Ben," Peri said. "Although, it would help you find out if someone's been moving your things. I was thinking about your doors, especially the front door."

This calmed Benny down a little.

"Anyway, the police will have to process the scene," Skip said. "I'm not going to arrest you now, but you should stay in town. We think you should check into a hotel, or stay with someone, until we've finished the investigation."

"Leave my memories?" Benny sounded distressed.

Peri put her hand on his shoulder. "Benny, no one will touch your stuff. Detective Carlton won't let them."

"I guess I could stay with Aunt Esmy, although her house kind of creeps me out."

"Why?" Peri asked.

"It's so crowded in there," he replied. "She collects the weirdest stuff."

CHAPTER 28

The cool morning air made Peri slip on her sweatshirt after she stepped out of her car. She looked around the park, and noted the trampled grass where the crowds had gathered a few days ago, hoping to get a glimpse of a corpse, just to turn away from it in horror. The yellow tape had been torn down. She walked up to the shrubbery where the body had been found.

The oleander bushes still lay flattened away from the building, branches snapped and leaves torn. Peri took out her camera and snapped several close-ups of the ground and the flora. Standing where the body had been, she looked around the park grounds. The gentle roll of green grass, interrupted by trees and picnic tables, made it a popular place for families on the weekend, and young lovers all the time.

Peri imagined the killer, hitting Marnie in the head with something hard. She'd seen the pictures and the molds of the impressions. They had hit her hard on the forehead, then harder in the back of the skull. The forehead dent looked rectangular, although the longer sides curved inward, and the shorter sides were deeper. The wound in the back of the head was deep but rounded, almost like a small shovel, or a tough spatula.

Head trauma didn't usually result in instant death, so it was possible this wasn't the crime scene. Maybe Marnie got hit somewhere else and wandered here, collapsing in the bushes.

But why against the building? Peri called Blanche.

"Hey, Beebs, what was the lividity like on Marnie?"

"There were two pooling sites, on her left hip and her back," Blanche replied. "There was very little blood at the scene, so we assumed the body was moved, probably by whoever cut her hands off. It was all in the report."

"I know, but those things are harder to read than I thought they'd be. Thanks, Beebs."

Peri went back to her car, pausing to throw her empty coffee cup in the trash. The park trash cans were not emptied as often as they should be, so she had to push a layer aside to fit her cup in. Below a Taco Bell sack, a piece of dark green plastic caught her attention. She saw golden fibers on the folds, the same color as Marnie's wool coat.

After taking pictures of the plastic in the trash, Peri slipped on a pair of disposable gloves and picked it out. It was a lawn and leaf bag, torn at the seams to elongate it. To transport a body, she thought. She stuck the plastic in a paper bag and headed to the police station.

"Skip," she said, rushing into his office. "I think I found something."

She held up the plastic bag.

Skip looked up from his report. "What's it supposed to be?"

Peri explained her theory while he watched her. "I found it in the park trash. I think it may have been used to move Marnie's body from the original crime scene."

"I thought you were going to wait for me to go to the park with you," he said.

"That's when Waters was alive," she told him.

"So, I guess you don't need a bodyguard service anymore, with Waters dead."

"What? No, I don't. Were you even listening to my idea?"

"Sure, the body was moved, we'll find coat fibers and maybe more on the plastic." He sat back in his chair. "We got the prints back on the knife that killed Waters. They weren't Benny's."

"Great, that gets him off the hook. Whose were they?"

"There were three sets. Waters', Officer Chou's," Skip stared at her. "And yours."

Peri's smile froze, then melted away. "Ah, Skip, that's insane. I can't be the killer."

"I know that," he told her. "But we have to convince the D.A. When would your prints have gotten on the knife?"

"Geepers," Peri said. "I washed that knife for Mrs. Needles all the time, and put it back in the drawer. Although, when I showed it to Officer Chou, I know I didn't touch it."

She gasped. "Wait. I know when I touched it last. I was looking for something to help me scrape the ice off when I was cleaning the freezer."

Peri watched Skip write in his notebook while she talked.

"I can't believe you're writing me up about this," she said. "I have an alibi, for God's sake. I was at Mrs. Cheavers' house."

"Peri, I still gotta write it all down and present it to the D.A. so they don't stick your pretty tush behind bars."

"That's just stupid. It could have been Officer Chou."

"Except that Officer Chou has no motive."

"And I do?"

"There's a rumor that Waters was going to file a complaint about you hitting him with your bag."

"When were you going to tell me this?"

Skip shrugged. "I was waiting for that nanosecond between rumor and fact."

"Nice. Did you process Benny's house?"

"Waters may have been on the porch, but he didn't enter. We found Benny's and a print that matched the one on his freezer, and the partials on the bag. It's frustrating that we can't get a match in the system on that one."

"What could Waters have wanted at Benny's?"

Skip shook his head. "I don't know, but I was going to go back to his apartment to see if there were any clues."

"Can I come?"

"No, I don't think that's a good idea, Peri."

"Skip, I didn't murder David Waters. I want to find out who killed him."

He looked at her, frowning. "Are you being paid by anyone to find out who killed Waters?"

"No, but—"

"Then you have no business working this case," he told her, rising from his chair and grabbing his keys.

Peri threw the bag of evidence against his chest. "Here, take this to trace on your way."

"I know you're mad, Doll, but I'd be tainting my case if you came along."

"I know you're right." Her words were conciliatory, but her tone was not. "But I'm still just going to be mad for awhile."

CHAPTER 29

Skip let himself into David Waters' apartment. The last time Skip saw the one-bedroom unit, it had looked like a typical bachelor sty. Nothing had changed. Empty pizza boxes and beer cans were stacked on the kitchen counter. The living room furniture consisted of a beanbag chair, and an old portable TV, perched on the college student's bookcase of cinderblocks and boards. If the police had tossed the place, he couldn't tell.

Previously, Skip had been hunting for a weapon that could have cut off Marnie Russell's hands. This trip would be more of a paper search, rummaging around for names, receipts, anything that would tell him who Waters knew and why.

He turned toward the kitchen and began to work. The drawers were mostly empty. Some contained cheap Bic pens and the free notepads distributed by realtors, their names across the top, to encourage people to call them and buy a house.

In a bottom cabinet, a lone quart-sized pot sat on the shelf. Skip pulled it out and took off the lid.

Jackpot.

Inside were racing slips, dozens of them. They all indicated bets of between twenty and two hundred dollars apiece. Skip counted up the amounts. It seemed Mr. Waters could not pick a winner, at least not consistently. He had lost ten thousand.

I hope you won that much back, buddy, Skip thought, placing the bets into an evidence bag.

Underneath the slips he saw a business card. It surprised him to see that it was for the Bradford Square facility, with Maria Castillo's number. He added this to the bag and continued to search.

At last satisfied he'd looked under every piece of furniture and in every cabinet, Skip locked up Waters' apartment and left.

He drove back to the police station, taking stock of what he did and didn't know. There were fewer items on the 'didn't know' list, but the remaining ones, who killed Marnie Russell and David Waters, and who cut off Marnie's hands, loomed the largest. He still felt that Waters was involved in Marnie's death, but proving it would be harder now.

The only good part about Waters' death was that Skip could relax about Peri's safety. He hadn't been thrilled when she opened her investigation business, even though she insisted she would only be taking low-risk assignments. Any investigation could turn ugly, if the people under the microscope didn't want to be scrutinized.

Now if he could just figure out how to make Peri marry him. He knew she loved him, they had a great relationship, but he couldn't get her to commit. Maybe she had a point. They hadn't been successful in their previous relationships, so perhaps their commitment to separate lives and a mutual affection worked the best.

Back at the office, he sat down at his desk and dialed her number. He could at least tell her about Waters' gambling.

"Playing the ponies," Peri said. "I wonder if it has anything to do with that goon who visited me."

"Maybe. By the way, that guy's prints came back this morning. Name's Ken Meade. Been arrested for assault, mostly."

"Any idea who he works for?"

"No one in particular. He's a contractor," Skip said. "He used to work for Johnny Sox until Johnny got put away for tax evasion."

"So now you think he's working for Conway's creditors?" Peri asked.

"I'm still working on that, but you stay away from him. If he comes to your office again, call me right away."

"Oh, good God, Skip, since when are you my dad? Let's change the subject before I get mad again. What else did you find?"

"A business card for Maria Castillo at Bradford Square."

"Wow, how coincidental is that? Are you going to go talk to her?"

"Actually, I had a better idea. I thought I'd pull her financials and phone records first. I figure, if she's got anything to hide, I'll be ahead of her."

"Ooh, Skipper, that's brilliant," Peri said. "I'd love to be there to hear you confront her with the evidence."

He was silent for a moment, afraid of starting a fight. "I know you would, Doll, but you can't."

"Am I at least cleared yet?"

"I wouldn't say you've been cleared. The only time you're cleared with the D.A. is when we find the killer. So far, no one's looked twice at you, and the chief hasn't called me off the case. And the lab found a hair on Waters' shirt that doesn't match his or yours. No hits in CODIS, but I'm hoping it's our killer's."

Peri sighed. "All the more reason for me to want to find out who did it."

"Peri—"

"But I'll let you do it. By the way, did you find out about Carlos? Is he Claudia Lopez's son?"

"No, I haven't had time," Skip said. "Maybe you could run that down for me?"

"And what are you going to do for me?" Peri teased.

"Come over tonight and I'll show you."

He hoped she could hear his smile through the phone.

"Skipper," Peri said as she walked in his back door. "I brought the ribs."

He walked around the corner, wearing sweatpants and drying his hair with a towel. "Want a beer?" he asked, opening the refrigerator.

"No, I'm laying off the alcohol for awhile," she told him. "It doesn't mix with the pain pills."

They sat in front of the TV, watching the news and eating Brian's barbeque.

"How are the ribs?" Skip asked.

"They're good," Peri said, licking sauce off her fingers. "Brian's makes the best babybacks."

"Not those ribs, your ribs, you goof."

Peri laughed. "Ow, they're still a little sore. But my face is looking better, isn't it?"

Skip held her chin and tilted her head to the light. "Not too bad. It's taking on a greenish yellow glow." He leaned forward and licked the sauce from her chin.

They kissed, and laughed, and kissed again, tasting the spicy barbeque on their lips. The meal pushed aside, the two made careful but delicious love on the couch, Skip watching for any signs that Peri might be in pain.

"You okay?" he whispered as she arched her body into his, wincing a little. "Am I hurting you?"

"Only in the best way," she told him, and kissed his neck.

Afterward, they relaxed on the couch, Skip picking at the leftover meal while Peri's head rested in his lap.

"You staying tonight?"

Peri stretched her legs out. "No, my files are at home. I want to go over my notes."

"Don't you ever take a day off?"

"I'm building a business, Skipper. I've got to get my name out there, especially with insurance companies and wealthy women suspicious about their husbands."

She sat up and kissed him. "Someday, when you retire from the force and come to work with me, you'll thank me."

Skip laughed. "Oh, no. When I retire, I'm headed straight to the golf course."

CHAPTER 30

Early the following morning, Peri sat in her office, looking at Marnie Russell's forensic report, when the phone rang.

"Miss Minneopa, what have you done?" Kevin's voice sounded one note below frantic.

"I don't know, Kevin, what do you think I've done?"

"Christie's got an anonymous phone call, alerting them to the *unusual* nature of my Forever Roses ring."

"You mean, that it's fake."

"Do you know what this is doing to my credit? Do you know what my creditors are doing right now? They're trying to seize the entire collection, plus my home."

"I am sorry, Kevin, but I didn't leak that information to Christie's. Your fraudulent activities aren't my problem."

"Then who did? That police officer who blew me off?"

"No, I can't imagine Detective Carlton calling them. He doesn't consider it within his jurisdiction."

"Then who else knew?" Kevin asked.

"I don't know, Kevin." Peri thought about it. "It's not exactly a secret that the police have an expensive ring in evidence, but I don't remember telling anyone yours is a replica."

"Then how did they know?"

"Who are *they*? Does one of them look like a goon? No neck, pock-faced?"

She heard him gasp. "You've seen him?"

"He came to my office to make his own deal," she said. "I know his name's Ken Meade, but who does he work for?"

"I can't tell you his name, but I owe him a lot of money. You can see why I need that ring, or I, at least, need to know that I can have it by the September auction."

His voice sounded weak, trembling. "You don't know these people. They want their money. They want it now."

"Well, I wouldn't count on getting that ring, Sport. The police and the court probably won't be finished with it by September."

"Can't I file a claim for it?"

"You can. Of course, you should know there's another party filing a claim."

Kevin's voice sucked in a stammering, "What?"

"It seems you're not quite the end of the Conway line, after all."

Her office door opened, so Peri ended her conversation with Conway and stood to greet her new client. She couldn't mask a look of surprise when Mr. Cheavers walked into the room.

"Are you the bitch who ratted me out?"

"No," she said. "I'm the private investigator who was paid to rat you out."

"You bitches are all alike. Do you know what you've done? You've cost me everything."

"Are you saying that the photos I took of you and Heidi were misconstrued somehow? That her hand squeezing your ass isn't what it looks like?"

"I'm saying it's none of your business." His face glowed crimson with anger. "It's between me and my wife."

"And your girlfriend. And now, your divorce lawyer."

"Stupid bitch—" He lunged toward her.

Larry Cheavers may have been a regular at the gym, but he had no practice fighting. Peri stepped into him, hard, pushing him backward. He stumbled and fell against the door.

"You're an idiot," Peri said, disgusted. "Get out of my office."

He unhooked his rib cage from the doorknob and backed into the hall.

"I'm not done with you," he told her.

"Get in line, buddy."

A tall woman stood at the door, waiting for Cheavers to exit before she entered. Her head slowly moved up and down as she looked him over, one eyebrow arched, her mouth firmly set. She reminded Peri of an egret, sharp angles dressed in white, a hint of knobby knees below the skirt.

"Miss Minneopa? I'm Kathryn Riley Waters."

Peri held out a chair for her, then took her seat behind the desk. She watched the older woman set a pale leather clutch on the desk, open it and remove a compact. The woman scrutinized her makeup, touched a shiny spot here and there with powder, and traced her red lipstick with her red nails. With one more glance at her wavy silver hair, she closed the compact and turned her attention to Peri.

"Did you know that Minneopa is a Dakota word?" Mrs. Waters asked, smoothing her skirt. "Is your family Native American?"

Peri laughed and held up her freckled arm. "My dad's from Minnesota, Mrs. Waters, very blond and Viking. I don't know how we got an Indian name, but I'm guessing my Viking forebears plundered it." She picked up her pad and a pen. "How may I help you?"

"I want you to find out who murdered my son. His name was David Waters."

Well, today's just one surprise after another, Peri thought.

"Mrs. Waters, I'm afraid I can't take this case. Your son and I had an antagonistic relationship."

"I'm well aware you had accused him of battery."

Peri didn't like the way she made it sound, like her pain killers were for her 'alleged' bruises. "I'd like to find out who killed him, too," she said. "But I'm too personally involved in the current investigation."

Mrs. Waters pulled twenty one-hundred dollar bills from her purse. "Well, now you can find out and get paid for it." She held the money out to Peri. "It's the best of both worlds."

Much as she hated doing it, Peri pushed her palms outward. "Mrs. Waters, I can't take the case, but perhaps I could help. Could we talk about David for a few minutes?"

The older woman bowed her head, pressing the bridge of her nose to stop any tears. "I realize David did not lead an exemplary life. He was an only child and I indulged his every whim. It has become painfully clear to me that I did not equip him to be a responsible citizen." She took a deep breath. "Now it's too late."

"Do you know if David had any enemies?" Peri asked. Or any friends?

"I assume so. He was constantly in debt to people, bad people. The first few times, I gave him the money to bail him out. But I found that, instead of paying what he owed, he used the money to bet more."

Peri jotted down notes. "So he was addicted to gambling."

Mrs. Waters chuckled. "David was addicted to everything, dear."

"I don't suppose you know the name of any of these people he owed money to."

"There was a bookie named Rodney or Ronnie or Rory," she replied. "He was always in debt to that man."

"Could it have been Rory Green?"

Mrs. Waters drummed her manicured nails on the desk. "Rory Green…that might have been the name. Rory Green. Yes, I think it might have been."

"Thank you, Mrs. Waters," Peri said. "That information is very helpful. As I've said, I can't take the case, but I can pass this information on to the Placentia Police Department. I know they're actively trying to find your son's killer."

"You mean that detective, Charleston or Carlston?"

"Skip Carlton?"

"I don't care for him. Very brusque. An unpleasant man. Acted as though David was a common grifter."

"Mrs. Waters, I think you may have gotten the wrong impression of the detective. He's very interested in solving your son's murder." Peri stood up and held out her hand. "If you can give him one more chance, I think you and he can become allies."

Mrs. Waters smiled a little and nodded, before standing and offering Peri a lifeless handshake. She turned and walked toward the door.

"All right, Miss Minneopa," she said. "Just one more."

Peri stuffed her notes into her bag and drove to the police station. Skip's office was empty, so she sat down behind his desk and started reading through the case file on Marnie, comparing it to her notes. She had been studying them for an hour when she heard a knock on the doorjamb.

"Excuse me, I'm looking for Detective Carlton."

She looked up and smiled. "Hey, Skip. I was just reviewing the case."

"And, coincidentally, I was just telling the Chief that you weren't helping on the Waters case."

"No, not Waters, I was looking at Marnie's file." She batted her eyes at him. "Honest, Skip, I was being good. Hey, guess who stopped by to see me? Waters' mom."

"You're kidding. She wouldn't talk to me when I went to her home."

"Ooh, where does she live? She came into the office so hoity-toity. Mrs. Kathryn Riley Waters. Is she in one of those big old houses in Fullerton?"

Skip laughed. "Hardly. She lives in the Amberwood Apartments in Brea."

"No joke? She acted like the lady of the manor." Peri filled him in on her conversation with Mrs. Waters. "She said she thought Rory Green, the guy who got fired from Bradford Square, was his bookie."

"Maybe." He held up a folder. "I've got the reports on Maria Castillo here. I was just going to read them."

"Great," Peri said, her feet still propped on his desk.

"Alone."

She rose and walked toward the door. "Fine. I'm going to go talk to Mrs. Lopez, see if there's any connection to Carlos."

"See you later, Doll."

Since Peri had to drive by Bradford Square on her way home, she decided to stop there and see if Mrs. Lopez was on duty. The nurse had just completed her shift and met her in the lobby.

"Mrs. Lopez, do you have a son who works at Ralph's?"

"Yes, my son, Carlos, has worked for them since high school. He is paying for his classes at Fullerton College."

"Did you know Marnie Russell?"

The small Hispanic woman lowered her head. "Yes, I know her. Carlos date her for awhile." She crossed herself. "I am so sorry to hear."

"Did you disapprove of their dating?"

"No," Mrs. Lopez said. "She is a lovely girl, and she make Carlos so happy."

"Mrs. Lopez, we spoke with Carlos. He indicated that his family would not have liked it if he had married Marnie."

"It is a little true. I would not care, but my husband still has his heart in the old country. He would not have accepted it, at least not at first." She clasped her hands, kneading her fingers. "Roberto can be stubborn. He might take a long time to accept a gringa into our family."

Peri wondered if she should tell Mrs. Lopez about the baby. She decided against it. It would be Carlos' burden to share, if he chose.

On a hunch, Peri asked, "Mrs. Lopez, does Carlos come here to visit you? Did he ever bring Marnie?"

"Si, yes."

"When they visited, were you taking care of Miss Banks?"

"Maybe." She paused. "Yes, I remember, they come in one day when I am taking Miss Banks to her room."

"So, they would have seen her pretty ring?"

Mrs. Lopez laughed. "Yes, but they know it is not valuable At least, Carlos knows."

Yes, Peri thought, Carlos knows a lot of things. "Mrs. Lopez, do you know where Rory went after he was fired?"

"Si, I hear Ms. Castillo on the phone one day. She say Rory is cleaning tables at Mikey's for his cousin."

"Thank you so much for all of your help," Peri told her.

Halfway back to her house, Peri thought about getting a new test kit. She felt increasingly cantankerous about taking the test. As a child, school testing had always made her peevish. She usually aced them, but not without adding a cynical flavor to her written answers. She even managed to make her multiple choice tests seem suspiciously sarcastic.

Her report cards usually said something like, "Periwinkle is a bright girl, but she doesn't seem to take her studies seriously."

She thought she took her studies very seriously, just not her teachers.

I probably deserve to have a daughter like me. She remembered her late mother, telling her, "Someday your chickens will come home to roost," and could swear she heard the heavens laughing.

Driving past her house, Peri headed south on Kraemer Boulevard toward the city of Orange. She found a drugstore on the corner of Katella and ran in to purchase a pregnancy test. In addition to a kit, she also picked up shampoo, chocolate covered pretzels and a Diet Coke, hoping somehow to keep the salesgirl from focusing on the package that screamed, "I MAY BE PREGNANT."

The clerk, a young, raven-haired girl with five hoops in each ear and a silver ball below her lip, behaved as if she didn't care if Peri bought a vat of butter and a copy of Buff Dudes magazine.

Her purchases complete, Peri got back in her car and drove north to Mikey's.

Mikey's Sports Bar sat in the corner of a strip mall, bordered on one side by a sushi restaurant and on the other by a dentist's office, a fact that always made Peri laugh, picturing the dentist waiting by the door while the drunks fell and knocked their teeth out. A ramp wound its way up to a mini-patio holding a few small iron tables and chairs. The glass doors and windows were tinted, with drink and food specials painted in large, colorful letters.

Peri entered the bar and stood for a moment, letting her eyes become accustomed to the dark. Several long, high tables sat perpendicular to the wall, with bar stools tucked underneath. On her way to the bar, she saw a couple of pool tables in the back corner.

A few people sat around the tables, having pizza and beer while they watched the Angels game on ESPN. Peri didn't recognize any of them, but she did know the guy leaning over the bar.

Skip had his badge out, talking to the bartender.

Peri slid in to the seat next to him. "Hey, Copper, how's business?"

"What are you doing here?"

The bartender looked at her. "Diet Coke," she said before turning back to Skip. "Thought I'd see if Rory was working today."

"First of all, for the millionth time, you're not working the Waters case. Second of all, he's not here today." Skip winked at her.

She took a drink of soda and smiled at him. "I'm not working the Waters case. I want to talk to Rory about the night Sylvia Banks went for her little adventure."

Swiveling around on the bar stool, she said, "It's a pity Rory's not working today."

She noticed a young, pasty-faced man with a black *Mikey's Pizza* polo shirt at one of the tables. He flinched at the mention of his name, and kept his eyes on the pizza he was serving as his body turned toward the sound of their voices.

They watched the server walk around the corner, toward the kitchen, so Skip followed. Peri hung back. The young man set his tray atop the stack, and then turned to go back to the tables, nearly running into her.

"Whoa, there, Rory," she said, smiling.

Rory backed up, his eyes wide, as Skip stepped around to block his movement. After introducing themselves, the detective placed his large hand on Rory's neck.

"Why don't you have a seat, Mr. Green." Skip pressed down on his shoulder. Rory resisted for a split second, then sank into a chair, flanked by Peri and Skip. He crossed his arms, defensive and defiant.

"I'm interviewing people who know David Waters," Skip said.

"So who said I know him?" Rory replied.

"David's mom," he told him. "So you might as well talk to us."

"Okay, so I know Waters, so what?"

"Where did you know him from?"

Rory shrugged. "He comes in here to watch a game, have a beer, that's all."

"Sure you didn't know him from Bradford Square?" Peri asked.

"What? No, I, no."

"Really, Sport?" She smiled. "Because I heard he's been placing his bets with you since last February, and you've only worked here for a month."

"Hold it, I ain't no bookie. Dave's my friend, okay? So, he likes to play the ponies, and I know a guy, that's all." Rory turned away from her. "I just hooked him up."

"When did you see him last?" Skip wrote in his notebook as he spoke.

"Don't remember. Maybe last week, Tuesday."

Skip looked at Rory. "How much did he owe you?"

He leaned back against the table behind him, his pale eyes darting from Skip to Peri to the floor. "I said I wasn't no bookie."

"Don't act stupid, Rory," Skip said. "We know he was in hock to you."

"He ain't in hock to me, I tell ya. But, I heard he owes somebody at least five grand."

Peri could feel her stomach wobbling and organs heating again. She didn't want to be here while she felt like this. Pulling information out of this man seemed like picking cat hair off velvet.

"Oh, for Pete's sake," she said, fanning herself with one of the menus. "We haven't got time to dance around. We just want to know who might have wanted Waters dead."

"Dead?" Rory's eyes went wide.

"Didn't you know, Sport?" Peri said. "Dave's dead."

He ran his hands through his hair, squeezing his scalp. "Oh, man, oh man."

"So, who was the guy?" Skip asked. "We need to know who you hooked him up with."

"If I tell you, I'm screwed."

"If you don't, you're going into the station," Skip told him. "So we can find a suitable jail cell for you, for withholding evidence."

Rory groaned and huffed and panted for a few more minutes before finally surrendering. "Ken Meade. He wouldn't want Dave dead, would he? Not if Dave owed him money, right?"

Peri and Skip glanced at each other.

"That's for the police to figure out, Sherlock," Peri said. "Had Dave mentioned how he was going to pay Meade off?"

The young man slumped back down in his chair, his eyes shifting toward the floor. "He did mention a possible job. Sounded like a lot of money for a little bit of work."

"Too good to be true?" Peri asked.

Rory looked up, his eyes meeting hers and holding, before darting away. He nodded.

"Thanks for your cooperation," Skip told him.

"We need to talk about something else, Rory," Peri said. "Suppose you tell me what happened the night Sylvia Banks wandered away from Bradford Square."

"That was not my fault." He pounded his fist on the table. "I told them not to put me on nights, I can't stay awake."

"So you fell asleep on your watch?"

He nodded. "I drank a bunch of coffee, too, which I hate, but I wanted to stay awake. I was sitting at my station, pouring cup after cup of that crap out of a thermos, and I still couldn't keep my eyes open."

"A thermos?" Peri asked. "Don't they have a coffee pot at the facility?"

"Sure, but Ms. Castillo came by with a thermos. She knows I don't stay awake so good, so she made me a special brew, to help me."

"Too bad you don't still have it," Skip remarked.

"The thermos? I still got it, in the back of my truck. I tossed it back there when they fired my ass the next morning."

"Have you cleaned it?" Peri asked.

"Nah, I forgot about it, so it's still rattling around in my truck bed. I should throw it away. It's probably too moldy to use now."

"Rory, could we have the thermos?" Peri glanced at Skip. "Detective Carlton would like to see what kind of magic formula Ms. Castillo brewed for you."

"Sure."

He walked outside with them, over to a faded Toyota truck parked in the corner space. Skip took the black, insulated bottle from him.

"Hope you don't have any vacation plans in the next few weeks," Skip said.

"With what money?" Roy shrugged, then returned to the bar.

Skip walked Peri to her car. "I was going to stop by Bradford Square to ask Ms. Castillo why she called Waters several times a day for weeks, and if it had anything to do with the fact that she recently dug herself out of a lot of debt. Two months behind in her house payment, six months in her credit cards, collection agencies chasing her all over town. Suddenly, last month, she's caught up."

"Maybe you should wait until you get that analyzed," Peri said, pointing to the thermos Rory had given him.

Skip nodded. "I figured Waters had to be doing some kind of job for her. If she drugged Rory on the job, it might explain what she was having Waters do."

"Stealing from the residents?"

"Probably gave Waters a portion of the take," Skip said.

"Has anyone there been reporting any thefts?"

"I don't know," he said. "Jim Stanton works robbery detail, I'll have to read the logs. I would imagine things disappear from a residence like that all the time. Even without the Alzheimer's patients, let's face it, old people lose stuff."

"You'd think the families would kick up a fuss."

"Maybe, but if they didn't take it to us, we'll never know. I'll bet the home doesn't keep those records. Of course, we still don't know why Waters took Sylvia Banks from the home."

Peri frowned, shaking her head. "Unless she screamed so much that he took her outside so she wouldn't wake up the other residents. But why all the way to Ralph's? Did you get the results from the shopping cart?"

"Yeah, it was Miss Banks' hair in the cart, and Waters' fingerprints on the handle. So we know he took her."

"Maybe Ms. Castillo can tell us why." Peri leaned in close to him. "Can I be there when you interview her? For Marnie?"

"I don't know, Doll, I'll have to pass it by the chief. It'll probably be a couple of days to get the results of the thermos back." He glanced at his watch. "I should get over to the college. My class starts in half an hour."

He smiled. "You in the mood for company later?"

"I'll leave the light on for you."

CHAPTER 31

Feeling restless at six A.M., Peri got up and slipped on her running shorts. Three miles later, she felt relaxed, and looked forward to a cup of coffee and the newspaper. She opened her back door and found Skip at the kitchen table, reading the sports section.

"Hey, you're up," she said. "My legs were twitchy, so I went for a run."

She poured herself a cup of coffee and turned to join him at the table. That's when she saw the box. Skip folded the paper and looked at it, then her.

"I was only looking for more toilet paper," he said. "Do you always keep a spare pregnancy test in the cabinet?"

Peri felt distinctly like wildlife in the middle of a busy road. "Maybe."

"Talk to me, Doll."

She sat down at the table, collapsing her shoulders with a sigh. "I know we're careful, but I am a little late. I didn't want to tell you until—unless I was certain."

"So I'm guessing you don't know yet."

"No, I can't seem to get the test taken." She laughed. "You don't know how hard it is to pee on a stick."

"What do you plan to do if you are?"

"First, I was going to tell you. After that, I wasn't sure." She rubbed the back of her neck. "I'm still not."

"You know, that offer of marriage is still good."

Peri smiled. "Skip, I love you fiercely, don't ever doubt that. I'm also fifty years old, and realistic about what I can and can't do. When did we try living together, what's it been, five years ago? We thought we were both so compatible, it had to work, but it didn't. I was always pissy at not having enough alone time. You constantly worried about keeping our finances separate and what that meant. In the end, I was just thrilled we were able to split up without splitting up. Marriage and a baby would force us to pool our resources. How would you feel about that? And I'd have a lot less alone time, which I'd hate."

She shrugged. "I'm not saying I've decided what to do, I'm just telling you what I'm thinking about."

Skip reached across the table and placed his hand on hers. "All excellent points, Peri. And I'm not saying I think marriage would solve everything. Hell, I'm fifty, too. It's no time to be starting a family. But I love you. You're the first woman who doesn't need me to hang constantly by her side. I like your independence, and the freedom we can give each other without feeling jealous. I just want you know that whatever you decide to do, I'll support you."

"Thanks, Skipper." She picked up the test kit. "And when I finally get this test taken, you'll be the first to know."

Peri got up and kissed his forehead. "Now then, how about some breakfast?"

She opened the refrigerator and fished out eggs, onions, cheese, and last night's steak. Skip chopped ingredients while she heated the pan. Ten minutes later, they sat down to eat their leftover scramble and read the paper. Peri stretched her legs out under the table, her feet across Skip's thighs.

I wonder if there's something wrong with me, that I can't seem to play house with this lovely man.

On her way to the office, Peri stopped by the police station to see if any more reports had come in. Skip wasn't at his desk, so she walked around to sit in his chair, then reconsidered and took the visitor's seat instead. She glanced around at the folders on his desk, looking for any new reports.

"Hey, Doll." Skip walked in with an envelope. He threw it on his desk and sat down across from her. "Here's the latest. It's the analysis of the trash bag you found."

Peri grabbed up the report and read. "Hair and epithelium from Marnie, wow, so this is what she was wrapped up in. Wool fibers, consistent with her coat, no prints, red nylon fibers."

"Yeah," Skip said. "I'd trade the fibers for prints any day."

"The nylon is different." She paused. "Maybe fabric from a car trunk?"

"Maybe, but whose car upholstery is red?"

"I know someone." Peri frowned. "Does a black 1960 Cadillac Coupe de Ville sound familiar?"

"Benny. I have to admit, he's growing on me, but I don't like the way we keep ending up back at his house."

"Well, at least this time we won't be at his house," she told him. "He's still staying with Aunt Esmy."

Skip and Peri drove into Fullerton for the warrant, and then headed for the southeast end of Placentia. On the way, Peri listened as Skip called Jason Bonham to meet them, for trace processing.

Aunt Esmy's house stood in the middle of a middle class neighborhood, indistinguishable from the other three-bedroom, two bath models in the tract. Benny's Caddy sat in the driveway.

"Why, Peri, what a pleasant surprise," Aunt Esmy said as she opened the door. "And Detective, how nice to see you again. You haven't come to arrest Benny, have you?"

"No, Esmy," Skip replied. "But we do need to talk to him."

"He's in the kitchen. Come on in." The small, plump woman pointed toward the back of the house.

Peri and Skip walked through the open floor plan, looking around at the décor. Mounted animals hovered, hanging on every wall, and perched on every shelf. An owl, in mid-flight, hung over the doorway, wings spread and talons extended. Glassy-eyed deer watched over the dining room table, raccoons clung to banisters, and an assortment of squirrels and small birds graced the top of practically every piece of furniture in every room.

"Your house is certainly…unusual," Peri told Esmy, wondering how many other normal-looking tract homes were decorated in early American road kill.

"Do you like them? Taxidermy is my hobby." The older woman stroked a small dog, curled in eternal repose. "After I retired, I needed something to do with my time."

"You've clearly been busy."

"Yes, well, I began with Mr. Whiskers, there on the piano," she said, pointing to a cat staring blankly into space. "And I liked it so much, I mounted all of my pets when they passed away, then started collecting dead things around town."

The thought of this round, over-coifed woman walking around collecting animal corpses made Peri stifle a laugh. "Why, Esmy, I thought volunteering at the church and the homeless shelter would take up all of your energy."

"Oh, goodness, no, dear." Benny's aunt began to take cans out of a bag on the counter.

"Miss Peri," Benny said, sitting at the kitchen table with a glass of iced tea. "What are you doing here? And Detective?"

"We've come about your car, Benny," Skip told him. "I have another warrant here to look in your trunk."

Benny's eyes widened. "Why would you want to look in there?"

"Officer Bonham wants to see if you had a plastic bag in your trunk."

"Oh," he said with a nervous giggle. "Well, sure, of course I've had plastic bags in there. I always keep plastic bags in there. I don't want to mess up the carpet."

Jason arrived at the door, so Skip went outside with Benny's car keys while Peri stayed inside with Esmy and her nephew. As Benny stood by the window and watched what they were doing to his car, Peri looked around the kitchen. A pale, plastic mold of a familiar shape stood on a craft table, surrounded by knives, glue and other tools.

"Wow, a coyote," Peri said.

"Oh, yes, that was a great find," Esmy replied. "He was on Carbon Canyon Road, all four paws in the air. Usually, there's a lot of road rash, but his skin was in great shape."

"You have a real passion for your hobby, don't you?"

"I think everyone needs to have something they love to do." Esmy looked at her nephew. "Or collect. Benny, dear, why don't you come and help me put these cans on the top shelf."

After about fifteen minutes, Skip returned to the kitchen. "Thanks for your cooperation, Benny. You ready, Peri?"

On the way back, they discussed Benny's car.

"Jason didn't find any trace at all," Skip told her. "That car is so clean it looks brand new."

"Even with Luminol?"

"Nope, no blood found. Jason took some fibers to compare, but all we can really tell is whether the carpet's comparable or not. Carpet fibers aren't unique."

Peri sighed. "Well, it was worth a shot. It might at least prove the body wasn't in Benny's car."

They were silent for a moment.

"So, what did you think of Esmy's house?" Peri asked.

Skip laughed. "Benny's into Dino and Esmy's into Fido. What a family."

"I agree with Esmy that everyone's got to have a passion," Peri said. "But that family's genes have passion overload."

Peri watched the daylilies and oleander bushes whip by as they drove down Chapman Avenue.

"Passion," she said, and then paused. "Skip, Benny's all about Dean Martin, right? Remember the first time you went to his house? He asked you if he could have the ring, if no one claimed it."

"So?"

"So why would he want something that's not related to Dino?"

"Simple. Because it's worth a fortune."

"We didn't know that at the time, though." She grabbed his arm. "Seriously, I thought his eyes were going to leap out and hug that ring when I unwrapped it. Why would he care about it?"

Skip thought about it. "Good question. We may need to ask him."

"I think I'd like to research a connection first. If he wants that ring because it has some link to Dean Martin, he's been very quiet about it so far."

He shook his head. "Damn Benny. I hate that we keep coming back to him, without finding any evidence."

"I think everybody knows more than they're telling," Peri said.

"Welcome to my world."

CHAPTER 32

Peri sat on her patio, enjoying the afternoon sun while she worked on her laptop. Once in awhile, she looked around at her yard, wishing she had enough money to pay for proper landscaping. She thought about Kevin Conway's house, so beautifully lush. Her small space, bordered by walls of cinderblock, contained uneven patches of grass, surrounded by yellow-leafed rose bushes. In the far corner, a bougainvillea hung halfway over the yard, dripping hot pink flowers.

It's better this way, she thought. *If I had it professionally landscaped, I'd have to hire a live-in gardener to keep things from dying. I don't have the extra room for that, much less the cash.*

Turning back to her work, she searched through websites in an attempt to find six degrees of Dean Martin. The only reason Benny would want that ring is if it had some connection to his hero. A Google of Marnie Russell revealed nothing, as she expected. Thinking that Benny saw the ring on Sylvia's hand, she looked for a correlation between Dino and Sylvia Banks.

"Nothing," she said aloud. "Damn."

Peri got up and went into her kitchen. She grabbed a pint of mocha toffee ice cream from the freezer and a spoon from the drawer, then went back outside.

"Not Sylvia," she said, suddenly. "Elizabeth."

Benny may not have known about Sylvia, but he'd definitely know the ring as belonging to Elizabeth Marquette. She searched the Internet for a Dean Martin link to Marquette, or Melvin Conway. It took her three pages and six websites to find it. In his early career, Martin had a walk-on in one of the many high-society melodramas starring the famous couple. Peri dug deeper into the trivia and discovered Melvin had given his wife the Forever Roses ring during the filming of that movie.

"Score," she said. She scraped another spoonful of ice cream from the carton, turning the bowl upside down in her mouth, allowing the rich flavor to fill her senses.

After a few more bites, Peri returned the ice cream to the freezer, threw her laptop in the car and headed out on her rounds. Her first stop was the fire station. She wanted more information about the night they found Sylvia. Tom Flores waited for her in the lounge. She had called ahead to see if he would be on duty.

"Thanks for meeting me again, Tom," Peri told him. "I was wondering if you had a chance to check the phone records for the night you found Sylvia Banks."

"Yes," he replied, handing her a printout. "We only got one call that night. Here's a printout of the message, along with the number."

"That's great. When you arrived, was Miss Banks lying on the ground?"

"Actually, no, she was propped up against one of dumpsters." He looked at the ground. "She was shivering and whimpering like a little child. I see a lot of people in trouble, but little old ladies in distress really get to me."

"I'm sure she was happy to see you, Tom. You saved her life." She looked at the printout and nodded. "I won't take up any more of your time. Thanks. You've helped me a lot."

She left and drove to the police station, armed with the phone records. Skip was in his office, standing at his whiteboard and writing clues, drawing lines from one point to the next. She watched over his shoulder while he scribbled something on the board.

"Bibs cat chickens out?" Peri read.

"It says, 'Benny's car checks out'," Skip told her. "It's perfectly legible."

"Yeah, right. Hey, I've got a list of things I need from you."

"Like what?"

Peri dug her notepad out of her tote. "Number one, have you found out who Ken Meade is working for? Two, what did forensics say about the thermos? Three—"

A young woman in uniform burst into the office, her tanned face pale. "Detective? We have a problem."

"What's wrong, Ella?" Skip asked.

Ella Mason, the officer in charge of the property and evidence room, opened her mouth to speak, her eyes wide, as if afraid of what she had to say.

"There's been a break-in, sir. The evidence lock-up has been robbed."

"What did they take?"

"The ring, sir."

They rushed down the hall to the Dutch door that allowed access to all of the evidence collected in the small city's crimes. The door stood ajar, although the locks had no marks on them.

"I took an early lunch, but I'm certain that I locked up," Ella said. "When I came back, it was standing open. I asked around to see who had opened the locker, but Steve and Tony were the only ones here and they said they didn't. Nothing looked out of place, so I checked the guns first. They were all still here. That's when I thought about the ring." She pointed to a standard, cardboard box, a red and white label on the corner with a case number and date written in black marker.

Skip put on gloves, then set the box on a table in the middle of the room and emptied the contents. He picked up every bag, looking it over, then placing it in the box. No ring could be found.

"I don't suppose they'd be stupid enough to leave fingerprints?" Peri said.

"I'll have Jason dust it, but I'm not hopeful."

"This makes no sense. Who would know which box to look in?"

"They're in our database. If someone hacked in, they could find out easily."

"Even more stupid," Peri said. "Why would anyone steal it? It's so famous, you couldn't sell it whole. And if you dismantled it and sold the stones individually, they wouldn't be worth as much as the entire ring."

"Well, first on my list would be Kevin Conway," Skip replied. "He's desperate to get out of debt."

"Running a close second might be Ken Meade."

Skip stepped out into the hall. "Jason," he called. "You around?"

While Jason collected traces of anyone who might have touched the doors and boxes, Skip and Peri jumped into the SUV and headed toward the Hollywood Hills.

Skip fumed as he drove. "Dammit, I didn't need this."

"I still don't get it," Peri said. "Why steal something you can't sell?"

"Well, if Meade took it, he'd have two reasons. He might want to collect what Waters owes him. Or, if he's working for his boss on Conway, they might be willing to take less for the stones in order to collect what Conway owes them. If someone else took it, who knows? They might even be a collector, in which case they just want to own it, even if no one else knows they have it."

"That sounds like Benny, but I can't imagine him walking into the police station on his own, much less breaking into the locker."

Skip laughed. "Yeah, I'm thinking Meade is a better bet. We've got to convince Conway to tell us who Meade is working for, before we drag him in for questioning."

"Am I supposed to be the good cop or the bad cop?" Peri asked.

"First of all, you're not a cop. Second, I've seen you in action—you seem to cover both of those extremes within one interview."

She shrugged. "I may have been a little hormonal lately."

"About that," Skip said. "No pressure or anything, but have you found out whether, you know…"

"Not yet. I have to take the test first thing in the morning." She watched out the window. "I plan to do it tomorrow."

CHAPTER 33

Peri thought navigating the roads to Conway's house was difficult in her Honda, but in Skip's Chevy Trailblazer, she could only hold her breath and be glad he drove. He picked his way cautiously through the maze of parked cars that left one lane available for driving. At last, they arrived at Kevin's driveway. Peri said a little prayer of thanks as they teetered to a stop, the front bumper kissing the garage door and rear bumper hanging out into the street.

Kevin opened the door to his house, his eyes registering surprise at seeing them.

"Mr. Conway, we're here to discuss your ring," Skip said.

He smiled and led them to the living room. "When do I get it back?"

"Well, that depends," Skip replied. "Where were you this morning? Say, about eleven thirty?"

"Rick and I were at the lawyer's office until almost eleven." Kevin sank into the couch, a lean, sand-colored cat winding itself around his shoulder. "Then he dropped me off at home and went to his office, while I fixed myself some lunch."

He picked up a tumbler of what appeared to be a Bloody Mary. "May I fix you one?"

"No thanks," Peri said.

"Is your ring still in your vault?" Skip asked.

"Why, no, I have it in my safe now."

"May we see it?"

Kevin disappeared down the hall. A few minutes later, they heard the soft footsteps of his return. He held a box out to Skip, then resumed his position on the sofa.

Skip turned the ring over and looked at the inside, then the outside, while Peri looked over his shoulder. He looked at Peri and shook his head. It was beautiful, but not as beautiful as the real ring, and it was missing the unique mark given to it when it was checked into evidence.

"How are your financial woes, Kevin?" she asked.

He frowned. "Not good, Miss Minneopa. Christie's is pressuring me to call off the auction, saying that without the ring, I may not make enough to cover their costs. I've had to change my phone number twice in a month to avoid my creditors." He took a long drink and closed his eyes, tears clinging to his lashes. "I need that ring back. Rick is getting very tired of the drama."

"So are we, Kevin," Peri said.

He looked at her, puzzled.

"Someone stole the ring from the police station," Skip told him.

Kevin gasped. "What? No."

"Mr. Conway," Skip said. "We think maybe Ken Meade stole it. He implied he might try it. We think he'd try to sell the individual stones to get some of the money back that you owe his employer."

This didn't appear to make Kevin feel better. "But, he can't get the full value of the ring for just the stones. If I'm lucky, it would pay only half of what I owe."

"That's why we need to find out who Mr. Meade works for, Kevin," Peri told him.

"And if I help you, what do I get in return?"

"The undying thanks of a grateful nation," Peri replied.

"Not nearly enough," Kevin said. "If I help you, I expect you to help me get my ring back. It's my ring, *my* ring, do you understand?"

Skip stood up and walked over to him, leaning his tall frame over the couch. "And I expect you to tell us who Meade works for, or I'm going to take you into custody for interfering with a police investigation."

Kevin scowled. "But you don't know for certain if Meade stole it."

"I can still lock you up for twenty-four hours while I establish whether he did or didn't. And right now, it's him and you on my short list of suspects."

"Me? Why would I steal it?"

"Duh, because you think it's yours and you want it back," Peri told him.

"Okay, okay," he said. "His name is Leigh. Alexander Leigh."

"Thank you, Mr. Conway." Skip handed him his card. "If you are contacted by either Meade or Leigh about the ring, please call me. I'd hate to arrest you for receiving stolen goods. That's a felony."

Peri looked up at the house as they drove away. Kevin stood at the entrance, the cat in his arms.

"I'm so hating the possibility that he'll end up with the ring," she said. "He's obviously a spoiled brat who never learned how to manage money."

"True. I don't understand people who keep spending until it's gone, then look around perplexed, like someone dug up their money tree."

"Did Jeanine Ressler contact you?"

Skip nodded. "A couple of days ago. I told her how to file a claim for the ring. I think she's got a good case for it."

"Of course, we have to find the ring before anyone claims it," Peri said.

"We discovered the theft quickly, so maybe, we'll get lucky."

Peri watched Skip command his SUV out of the hills and onto the freeway. "I'm impressed, Skipper," she said. "The way you drive these narrow streets with such confidence."

He smiled. "Well, I am the captain of my ship."

"But are you the master of your domain?"

"When I have to be." He laughed.

Peri reached over and stroked his neck. "You don't have to be tonight."

"Do you think that's a good idea?" Skip asked. "I mean, if you're going to take the test tomorrow and all?"

"It's not like I have to study for it."

"I just mean, I don't want to hurt you. Or anything."

"Good God, Skip, how many pregnancies have you gone through? Two?" Peri smiled. "You're acting like some kind of weird, '50s husband."

"Be nice, Doll. I'm trying to be sensitive and supportive."

"And I appreciate it, Skipper, I do." She leaned over and kissed his cheek. "Okay, we'll find out for certain tomorrow and go from there."

An hour later, they had returned to the police station. Peri drove home and indulged in her two favorite things: sweats and a pint of ice cream. Turning on the TV, she spread her notes over the floor while Jessica Fletcher looked for clues on *Murder, She Wrote*.

"Screw it, I can't figure this out," she said after studying her scraps of information for half an hour. She gazed at the TV screen. "Jessica, what am I missing?"

Before going to bed, she opened the pregnancy test kit and made certain everything was ready to go for the morning. Reviewing the instructions once more, she went to bed, confident she would know soon whether her life was about to change. It took her awhile to go to sleep, as she realized the thought of finding out excited her.

The sun had barely crawled over the horizon when Peri awoke. She went into the bathroom and picked up the package. Carefully tearing the plastic at the notch, she removed the test stick, and then took the clear plastic guard off. As she did so, the absorbent fiber came off of the stick and lodged in the guard.

Peri dug the fiber out and tried to re-attach it, but had no luck. She sat down, flabbergasted, and threw the defective test across the bathroom. It hit the tile above the tub and clattered downward, settling at last on top of the drain.

"What the hell do I have to do to pee on a stick around here?" she said to the morning light.

Unable to get back to sleep, she made a cup of coffee and did a little more research before making out her list of things to do for the day. She showered and dressed, in a beige skirt and navy blue V-neck shirt. Before stepping out for her first errand, she called Dr. Ngo's office and made an appointment. Happily, the doctor had an opening that afternoon.

Screw this at-home testing, Dr. Ngo will be able to tell me if I'm pregnant.

Peri drove to Ralph's and entered, looking for Carlos Lopez. She found him in the back, wheeling out a large cart with cereal on the racks.

"Good morning, Carlos," she said. "I'd like to talk to you a little more about Marnie. When is your break?"

He looked at his watch. "Not for half an hour."

Peri walked down to the Starbuck's on the corner, for a cup of coffee. The rich smell of coffee, the deep colors of the shelves and walls displaying products, accompanied by the smooth singing of James Taylor, almost overwhelmed her finely tuned senses. She stood in line behind three other customers, all women in heels, tapping them impatiently.

The display case held a range of pastries. Peri's skirt tugged at her hips, reminding her she should order a simple cup of dark roast. As if that's possible at Starbuck's, she thought. She should have a regular coffee, black, but she wanted a latté, a vanilla latté, and more. That crumbly coffee cake looked good, or maybe a lemon bar.

"What can I get for you today?" the young man at the counter asked.

"A tall, Sumatra blend," Peri said, while her head screamed, *latté, Latté, LATTÉ, you bad witch.*

She picked up her cup and went outside to sit at one of the tables. This Starbuck's didn't actually have an official patio. Small tables and chairs littered the sidewalk in front of the store, pretending to be a veranda while cars whipped by, belching their exhaust at the customers. Peri watched the cars drive in and out of the shopping center, perhaps five feet from where she sat. The drivers were an interesting mix of harried women in minivans, construction workers in trucks, and men in suits and Beemers.

"I hear you've been looking for me."

Peri looked up to see Ken Meade towering over her.

"Yes, Mr. Meade, Detective Carlton is very interested in talking to you." Smiling, she pointed to the chair across from her. "Or you could talk to me."

The large man stared at her for a moment. Her invitation had been a very faint attempt to use her femininity, trying to entice him to talk to a pretty woman instead of a dour police officer. From his blank expression, she thought it had gone over like a lead balloon. After a few awkward seconds, he lowered himself into the chair.

"Might as well talk to the private dick."

"You are a very coincidental man," Peri said. "We know David Waters owed money to you. We also know you work for someone to whom Kevin Conway owes money."

He shrugged and said nothing.

"Look, Mr. Meade, the Placentia Police Department doesn't care who owes you what, as long as you're not assaulting anyone to collect your money."

"I didn't kill Waters."

Peri shook her head. "No, it doesn't seem logical that you would kill the man who owed you, how much?"

"Five grand."

"But you might see an opportunity to get some of the money back by selling off a piece of police evidence."

At last, an expression crossed his face, one of surprise and confusion.

"Something disappeared yesterday," Peri told him. "Something valuable, especially to Kevin Conway. And Alexander Leigh."

"The ring?" His mouth hung open.

Now it was Peri's turn to stare at Meade.

"Oh, no," he said. "Don't be pinning this on me. How would I even break into the police station?"

She had to agree. Even the blindest receptionist would have seen a man the size of the Titanic sailing by the front desk.

"You could have paid someone to do it. Just be aware, Mr. Meade, the PPD has called the media and alerted all buyers to be looking for that ring, or the stones from it. If you stole it, you can't sell it."

He stood up. "Miss, I did not steal that ring." His anger gave an eerie undertone to his voice. "Even the loose stones would be impossible to sell. They are large enough and unique enough to be recognizable to any jeweler. David Waters aside, my employer needs Kevin Conway to have that ring if he wants to get his money back."

"One more thing," Peri said. "David Waters had indicated he was going to be able to pay you back soon. Do you have any idea how he was going to do that?"

"He had already begun to pay me back. His original debt was ten thousand. I don't know how he was earning the money, but he paid his debt down by half just within the last month."

"When's the last time you spoke with him?"

"Last Monday, when I called him. He told me he'd have the rest of the money by the end of the week."

Peri spied Carlos coming out of Ralph's, so she stood. "Thank you for your candor, Mr. Meade. I highly recommend you give Detective Carlton a call and explain this to him. I can relay the information, but it will look better for you if you volunteer it."

The big man nodded, then turned and walked to his car. Peri walked toward Ralph's, keeping track of Meade's movements. He drove by her in a cream Buick. She memorized his license plate and wrote it down as soon as he had disappeared around the corner. Motioning to a bench outside the grocery store, she and Carlos sat down.

"Carlos, you strike me as a very nice young man," Peri said. "I think you like to help people, just like your mother."

He smiled and shrugged, modest.

"How often do you visit her at Bradford Square?"

"Many times," he replied. "Sometimes I drive her to work."

"And you've gotten to know some of the residents, yes?"

"Yes. Some are very friendly."

Peri took a folder from her bag and pulled out a picture. "Did you know Sylvia Banks?"

His smile faded to a look of worry. "A little."

"Carlos, I need you to know that I've already spoken to your mom about you. She said you knew about Sylvia's ring."

He paled. "Miss Peri, I know that the ring is not valuable. I told them it is not valuable." Running his hands through his hair, he added, "It is my fault, it is all my fault."

"Let me guess." She put her hand on his forearm to quiet him. "Marnie felt alone, frightened because she's pregnant. She decided she needs money for an abortion."

Carlos looked at her, glaring. "No," he said, then softened. "I know she wants money. I don't want to believe it's for an abortion, but I don't know why else she would need it."

"David Waters also needs money. Somehow, they get together and decide on a plan, to rob Sylvia Banks."

"I told her that the ring is not real, it is not valuable. But when we visit my mother and she sees the lady's hand with the pretty jewels, I don't know…" His voice trailed off. "Marnie's eyes get so bright, so shiny when she looks at it."

"Carlos, I suspect David was stealing from the other residents. The police are investigating."

The young man nodded, beginning to understand. "Marnie thinks it is real, so she tells David. They decide to steal it and split the money."

"The only thing I can't figure out is why they brought Miss Banks here."

"I don't know." Carlos stared at the ground.

Peri held up the report from the fire station dispatcher. "This is the report from the dispatcher that night, Carlos. It says that an anonymous caller told them about Sylvia Banks." She paused. "The call came from your phone."

"I don't want to get involved. I'm afraid I will be in trouble, or my mother, because we introduce Marnie to Miss Banks."

"Please don't blame yourself, Carlos, no one thinks it's your fault. Tell me what happened."

"The manager asks me to empty the trash that night. I walk outside and see David and Marnie, leaning over a shopping cart. Then I hear a little voice, pleading with them to let her go, telling them that she does not have it. David lifts something out of the cart—I see that it is Miss Banks. She is so small, so helpless. Marnie is running her hands up and down the lady's clothes. I yell, 'what are you doing?' and they turn to look at me."

Carlos shook his head. "They are not afraid. Marnie says, 'she won't give us the ring' and I tell her it's only a fake, leave her alone. 'That's what you think,' David says. I decide to call 9-1-1, but I cannot tell them that Marnie is doing this. So I tell them there is an old lady behind Ralph's and that she is hurt. I go back outside to make certain they haven't hurt her. They hear the sirens and David runs. Marnie says, 'at least I should have something for my trouble.' She takes her jacket off, then takes Miss Banks' coat and runs away. I sat Miss Banks down and wrap Marnie's coat around her, to make her comfortable. Then I went back inside."

"So that's how Marnie got the ring," Peri said. "Either she didn't feel it buried in the coat pocket, or she did and was scamming Waters."

He nodded again. "I found out later that she had Miss Banks' ring. I tried to talk to her again, to make her give back the coat, the ring, to be a good girl and marry me." Carlos looked up at Peri. "If I had not been such a fool, she would not have done this thing."

"Don't blame yourself, Carlos. You gave her the opportunity to set things right and she didn't. That's not your fault."

She stood up. "You'd probably better get back to work. Thank you so much for talking to me. You've helped me understand a lot."

CHAPTER 34

"How are you healing?" Dr. Ngo asked Peri, tilting her chin up and examining her fading bruises.

"The ribs are still a little sensitive, but I'm feeling much better."

The doctor wrote in her chart. "Is that all you needed to talk about today?"

"Not really." Peri paused and took a deep breath. "I need to know if I'm pregnant."

Dr. Ngo smiled. "My dear, you could buy a test from the store for that."

"Apparently, I can't." Dr. Ngo looked bewildered, so Peri said, "It would just be easier if you did it."

"Well, why don't you tell me about your symptoms."

Peri described it all, from her disrupted monthly cycle, to her heart-pounding, hot-blooded nausea. Dr. Ngo listened, nodding, smiling a little.

"We'll test you for pregnancy, but I'd also like to do some blood work," she told her. "Do you know when your mother began menopause?"

"No, she had a hysterectomy in her thirties."

"Pity, usually, a woman's cycle tends to follow her mother's. But your hormone levels will tell us plenty."

Gayle Carline

"Menopause?"

"You are fifty," the doctor said. "It wouldn't be a surprise. Let me get the nurse and we'll do some testing."

The nurse escorted Peri to the restroom for a sample to test, then directed her to a small room in the back to draw her blood. The chair reminded Peri of one of those classroom chair-desk combinations, except that the desk portion had padding. Jackie, the phlebotomist, had just positioned the needle securely in Peri's vein when Dr. Ngo walked in.

"So, how's the rabbit, Doc?" Peri asked.

Dr. Ngo looked puzzled. "What?"

"Sorry, just making a joke," she said. "In the old days, they used to say 'the rabbit died' when a pregnancy test was positive."

"Ah, yes, because they used to use rabbits." Dr. Ngo laughed. "That's good, I'll have to remember it."

She looked at the chart. "In your case, the rabbit is very healthy. You aren't pregnant."

Peri's heart began to race as her internal core heated. "Good," she said, touching the back of her hand to her moist temple.

"But that hot flash you're having tells me you are probably at least peri-menopausal," Dr. Ngo told her.

"Hot flash?" Peri asked. "Shit—sorry—darn."

Jackie burst out laughing. "That's okay, sister, we've all been there and done that."

"But what about my nausea?"

Dr. Ngo smiled. "For some women, the sudden increase in temperature makes them sick to their stomach, especially if the hot flashes are intense."

"So I'm just lucky."

"Make an appointment for next week sometime," Dr. Ngo said. "I'll have the results back from the lab and we'll talk about what to do to control the symptoms. In the meantime, I recommend the herbal remedies. Black cohosh, oil of evening primrose, especially a combination of herbs, Vitamin E, may reduce your flare-ups. Here's a brochure with a list."

Peri stopped at Trader Joe's on her way to the police station and bought a little bit of every herb on Dr. Ngo's list. She figured one of them would do the trick. Then she drove to the station, wondering why she felt so blue. She didn't want a child, so the news should have made her want to dance in the street. Instead, she wanted to cry.

She walked into Skip's office and sat down. Skip worked at his computer, focused on entering information from a report. Peri knew he tended to be single-minded about completing a task, and he often didn't acknowledge her until he had entered the last letter or checked the last box. Still, today, the longer he ignored her, the more alone and hurt she felt, and the less she understood herself. By the time he looked up, her eyes shone with tears.

"Hey, Doll, what's up," he said, his voice upbeat, until he saw her face. "What's wrong?"

He got up and shut his office door. "Peri, are you pregnant?"

She smiled and shook her head. "You can break out the Grey Goose again." Her voice trembled. "There's no baby."

The tears spilled down her face, which glowed scarlet with embarrassment.

"Doll, I thought you'd be happy."

Peri wiped her face. "I am, I don't know what's the matter with me. I didn't want a baby, you didn't want one. I ended up going to see the doctor and she took some blood. She thinks I'm starting menopause."

Skip handed her a tissue, while she sat back and took some deep breaths. "I guess, if I wasn't pregnant, I just didn't want to be old."

"Oh, Peri, you're not old," he said. "You're a perfect age."

He kissed the top of her head. "Now then, would you like the latest reports on Marnie's case?"

She nodded, sniffles subsiding. "And afterward, maybe an evening at Brian's?"

"You bet." He smiled. "The good news is that the thermos Ms. Castillo so graciously provided to Rory contained just enough pentobarbital to keep an adult male dozing for about four hours. Her fingerprints on the thermos put one more nail in the coffin."

"Great," Peri told him, wiping at her smudged mascara. "Any word on Benny's carpet?"

Skip shook his head. "That's the bad news. The carpet fibers didn't match the dye or the consistency of the ones on the plastic bag. So Benny's car didn't transport Marnie to the park."

"I'm going to go talk to him about the ring, anyway. I know he's hiding something. Say, did Ken Meade get in touch with you yet?"

"Actually, yeah, I got a phone call from him. He's coming in for questioning in about an hour."

"He doesn't have a lot of information, but Carlos told me quite the story about the night Sylvia Banks had her little adventure." Peri told Skip what Carlos had said. "We may never know why Waters took Sylvia all the way to Ralph's. But we know he did it, and we know he was looking for the ring."

"Okay, Doll," Skip said, rubbing her shoulders. "You've answered the question of how Marnie got Sylvia's ring. We need to find out where it is now."

"Did Jason find any prints?"

Skip shook his head. "Just police staff."

Laying the report on the desk, Peri stood up and straightened her skirt. "I'm off to talk to Benny. Give me a call and we'll meet up for drinks at Brian's. I think I deserve it."

The afternoon sun beamed at an awkward angle, making Peri cautious as she turned her car west out of the parking lot. She arrived at Benny's a few moments later and pulled up at the curb. As she shut off the engine, she saw Benny's door open and a large shadow step out to the porch.

Even after he moved into the sunlight, it took her a moment to recognize him. Officer Tony Monroe looked different in civilian clothes. A bright Hawaiian shirt sailed over his enormous frame, and baggy gray shorts sat low on his girth, pockets sinking where there should have been an ass.

Benny appeared at the door, smiling. They shook hands, both looking happy, before Tony turned and walked toward the street. Peri slunk down in her seat, raised her camera to window level and pressed the button multiple times. She lowered the camera and waited to hear a car start.

Instead, she heard footsteps coming closer. Hiding her five foot, nine inch frame in a Honda Accord was next to impossible, but she pushed herself as far down to the floor as she could, and hoped for the best. The footsteps were coming slower now. Standard operating procedure, she thought, to approach with caution. They stopped and Peri held her breath.

Suddenly her heart began to race, and her temperature shot skyward. This is not a good time for a dress rehearsal for Hell, she told herself, but there was no stopping the hot flash. Curled sideways close to the floor, her nausea felt close to producing results this time. Throwing up would be neither pleasant nor easy to clean. She waited for the sound of someone at her door. What she heard was a car door slamming, and then an engine starting. Peeking up over the dashboard, she saw Tony Monroe had gotten into the truck parked in front of hers and was driving away.

Peri returned to her seat and leaned it back. She turned her car on and cranked the air conditioning to Mach I. After a few seconds, she felt better.

"At least with a pregnancy, it'd be over in nine months. Does this ever stop?"

She turned the car off, and began to get out, then decided not to question Benny. Instead, she waited. And waited.

When Skip called her at six thirty, she still sat outside Benny's house.

"You ready to go for that martini?" he asked.

"I guess. I've been waiting for Benny to leave so I could snoop around his house, but he's still home."

"Peri, you cannot break into his home. That's definitely against the law."

"I know, but I want to get in there without Benny's hovering. Guess who was leaving his house as I drove up?"

Skip sounded surprised. "Monroe? What was he doing in there?"

"I don't know, but wouldn't it be great to get into Benny's place when he's not there?" Peri asked. "I bet he's got a ton of Dino's old clothes. You'd look great in them."

She heard him laugh. "I'm not ending my career by breaking into a house and trying on clothes."

"Fine, Spoil-Sport, I'll meet you at Brian's in ten."

In addition to serving the best barbeque in town, Brian's Beer and Billiards had a long-standing reputation as a neighborhood favorite. University students met there on Wednesday nights for cheap beer, and engineers stopped by after work to watch an inning on one of the large TVs before heading home. A small patio in front for the smokers led into a long, dark room with two pool tables and a dart board to the right, and a bar and dining tables to the left.

Peri walked past the smokers watching ESPN and took a seat at the bar. Skip hadn't arrived yet, so she scrounged enough money for a light beer and waited. She sipped her drink and relaxed, checking out the crowd.

There were at least twenty people, some watching an Angels game, some playing pool, and all of them young. Peri looked at the pool players, two men and two women. Boys and girls described them better, teasing each other, flirting with every gesture.

Fanning herself with a bar menu, Peri wondered why she still felt like one of the youngsters in her soul, when her body obviously disagreed. Maybe that's why the doctor's diagnosis bothered her. Even though she had never thought about having children, she still considered herself to be young and fertile enough to have one.

Before Peri could become too maudlin about her advancing twilight, she saw Karen Anderson enter the bar. Peri detected the slightest frown on Karen's face as she recognized the P.I., a wisp of dislike, before she smiled and greeted her.

"How nice to see you," Karen said.

"Girls' night out?"

"No, my husband and I are meeting another couple here for drinks before we go to dinner."

"So the shelter gives you some time off."

"Oh, yes, I only work there five days a week. Then we have a night manager, and a lady who comes in on weekends."

"That's nice. Usually, nonprofit organizations wring every minute they can out of their employees."

Karen smiled, that soulless cold-eyed grin Peri had seen before. "The church has been very generous, very understanding that we have families to raise."

Both women turned toward the door, hoping one of their men would walk through to save them from this conversation.

"Have you found out who killed Marnie yet?"

"We're working on a few leads."

"That poor girl," Karen said, shaking her head. "She was so bright, so sweet."

Peri remembered her discussion with Denise. "Do you get a lot of single people staying at HIS House?"

"Not a lot, but it's a nice balance when they come. Families can be so busy. A single person often brings a sense of quiet and calm."

Relief came finally, as Skip walked in the door, followed by a couple whom Karen recognized. Grateful for the escape, Peri and Karen smiled and parted, each to be in company they preferred more.

"Feeling better?" Skip asked.

Peri shrugged. "I'll be perfect once you buy me that dirty martini."

"Why didn't you order one?"

"You know me, Skip. I never have enough money for Grey Goose."

He sat down at the bar and gave the order to the bartender, the martini for Peri and a Bass Ale for himself. "I don't know why you think a civil servant can afford the expensive vodka."

Peri smiled. "I figure, don't ask, don't tell."

"So, what did you and Mrs. Anderson have to discuss?"

She told him about the conversation. "Karen's attitude doesn't jive with what Denise told us, but I figured she'd stonewall if I pressed her further. I think I'll go visit HIS House on Karen's day off and see what the other residents have to say."

"Good idea. Sorry I was late, but after I talked to you, I decided to look at the evidence Jason collected from our little burglary." He leaned into Peri, lowering his voice. "Tony Monroe's prints were on the box and some of the bags. Why was he digging through that evidence?"

He sat back up and took a drink of his beer. "He probably thought that, even if we dusted for prints, an officer's wouldn't be suspicious."

"But are his prints, and his visit to Benny enough for a search warrant?"

"No. We've got to get more, somehow. And I'm stumped as to what else we can find."

Peri played with the skewer of giant olives in her glass. "If Benny paid him for procuring it, think Tony would put the money in the bank immediately?"

Skip shook his head. "I can check it, but he might try to hide it from the wife. The way he tells it around the squad room, she holds the purse strings, and they're tied pretty tight."

"Well, I've got an idea for squeezing some info out of Benny," Peri told him, eating the last olive. "Why don't we head back to my place? I've got some chicken and potato salad in the fridge."

She leaned into him, putting her lips to his ear. "And I'm feeling much better."

CHAPTER 35

"You can relax, Beebs," Peri told her friend over the phone. "The stork won't be visiting my house."

"Thank God," Blanche said. "I mean, if that's what you want."

"What do you think?" Peri groped for words. "Actually, I feel happy, but not. I can't explain it, Beebs, but I'll want to talk about it when I get it figured out."

After she got dressed for the day, Peri headed back to HIS House for another round of digging for truth. Today, she saw three children playing in the yard. A large brunette woman, possibly in her twenties, sat at the patio table and smoked, watching the trio chase each other in and out of the lawn furniture.

"Good morning," Peri said, and introduced herself. "Did you know Marnie Russell?"

The young woman nodded. "She was quiet, liked to play with the kids."

"How would you describe her relationship with Mrs. Anderson?"

"Not good. Mrs. Anderson don't like her, you can tell."

"How?"

She took another drag on her cigarette. "Just the way Marnie always had to take out the trash, and Marnie always got yelled at if the TV was too loud or a dish was broken. Didn't matter whether she done it or not, Mrs. Anderson made it her fault, somehow."

Peri smiled. "And, could I ask how you and Mrs. Anderson get along?"

"Oh, she treats me fine, I got no problem with her." She looked past Peri to the children. "Ronnie, you let go of Summer's hair," she yelled. "Don't make me come over there."

Thanking the woman for her help, Peri went into the house. One family sat around the kitchen table, while another woman washed dishes. A group of adults and children sat in the living room, watching a movie.

Peri interviewed them all and got the same story: Mrs. Anderson treated Marnie Russell as though she hated her. She made certain she got names and exact quotes in her notebook before leaving.

Maybe Karen just didn't want to speak ill of the dead, maybe she felt some remorse about the way she treated Marnie. Or maybe she's just lying to me.

Skip wasn't in his office when she arrived at the station. She stood in his doorway, trying to decide whether to wait for him or leave him a note. Jason Bonham loped toward her, an envelope in his hand.

"Hey, Jason, do you know where Skip is?"

"Sure, he's in Interrogation, with some lady."

'Some lady' could only be Ms. Castillo. Peri knew she shouldn't listen in. She knew she'd be yelled at, but she couldn't help it. Quietly opening the door to the viewing room, she peeked inside. No one watched Skip interviewing Ms. Castillo, so she slipped in, leaving the light off to avoid attracting attention.

Skip sat with his back to the two-way window. Maria Castillo sat in front of him. Papers were spread on the table between them. Peri recognized them as phone and bank records. Ms. Castillo appeared tense, as wide-eyed as any frightened rabbit. Peri had read that rabbits could actually be frightened to death. Ms. Castillo looked like she could be close to that now.

"You see how it looks, Maria," Skip said. "We know you were calling David Waters on a regular basis, and we know you were paying off bills with money we can't account for in your normal paychecks."

He pulled out another report as she sat, silent. "I've been doing a little investigating. Many of your residents are very forgetful, and seem to lose their valuables. Too many, compared to other facilities."

Skip's voice softened. Peri smiled as she watched him work his magic.

"I have to ask myself, Maria, if I were desperate for money, what would I do? If I hired someone to help me steal, I might feel badly and want to stop. But what if they didn't want to stop? What would I do to make them stop?"

Ms. Castillo looked up at Skip as though she might physically explode from her restrained emotions. She sat, staring at him for a few seconds before clamping her hand over her mouth. A gasp escaped, followed by ragged, weeping breaths.

"I couldn't help it, I couldn't help it," she told him in between sobs. "I swear to God I did not kill him."

She buried her head in her arms, sobbing uncontrollably, and begging for mercy.

"I'd like to believe you, Maria, but do you have an alibi? Can you tell me where you were last Thursday around eight?"

Ms. Castillo managed to stop crying long enough to tell him. "I was in Temecula, at Pechanga. I was gambling." She hung her head. "I was gambling."

Peri watched Skip lean back in his chair. She knew his expression would be one of disapproval. "Trying to win enough to cover your debts?"

The woman began crying again.

"We'll check out your alibi, but it sounds like you're off the hook for Waters' murder."

Peri knew she'd get into trouble, but she couldn't help herself. She picked up the phone and called him. "Skip, ask her if she knows of any of his other gambling and thieving friends who would've had the opportunity to kill him."

He turned and looked at the mirror, a scowl on his face. "What are you doing?"

"Never mind, just ask her about any common associates." She knew he couldn't see her, but she smiled anyway.

"Fine." He turned his back, slamming the phone down.

Ms. Castillo shrugged when she heard the question. "There was someone else. I know it was a woman, but I never knew her name."

"Not Marnie Russell?"

"No, definitely not her. This was a married woman. David always made the big show of protecting her reputation, like he was some kind of gentleman."

Although the interview had been taped on the room's video camera, Skip wrote in his notebook, and then handed her the phone. "I know you didn't want a lawyer before, but I think you should call one now."

Seeing him get up from the table, Peri hustled out of the room. She went back to his office and waited for him.

Skip walked in and threw his notebook on the desk. He did not look happy.

"Goddammit, Peri, do you know what kind of trouble you can get me into?"

"I know, Skip, I'm sorry, but I just had to hear what Maria had to say about Waters. I keep thinking there's got to be a connection to Marnie's death."

Skip's voice grew louder. "Even if you have no evidence, no proof of any kind? Your little question-and-answer sessions with these people are only enough to imply things, not enough to prove anything."

Peri's voice rose to match his. "Yes, even though I'm just a private dick, and a newbie at that. Waters and Marnie planned to steal Sylvia Banks' ring, according to Carlos. Marnie told Waters she didn't have it, even though she did. Then she died. Then Waters died. What kind of map do you need to show you they were on the same road?"

"Most of what you just told me is strictly from Carlos. What makes you think he's telling the truth? Where's your corroboration?"

"What would make him lie?"

Skip rolled his eyes. "Oh, I don't know, maybe because he killed them both in a jealous rage. Ever think of that?"

Peri rose and walked to the door, furious and sweating. "Fine."

"Where are you going?"

"To get Carlos' alibi," she said, slamming the door behind her.

CHAPTER 36

When Peri arrived at Bradford Square, the facility hummed with chaos. As she walked to the office, she could see someone standing in the middle of boxes and papers, all strewn over the floor. This had to be the night manager, Lawrence Dreyfus, a small, balding man who shuffled through the mess as the phone rang incessantly.

The scene fed Peri's anger at Skip, and anger with herself for feeling inadequate. She should have checked on Carlos. It was a stupid, naïve mistake to believe what people told her. The Ralph's manager said Carlos wouldn't be in until Friday. She couldn't wait that long to cover her bases.

Sticking her head in the office door, Peri asked, "Excuse me, but is Claudia Lopez on duty today?"

Mr. Dreyfus looked at her as though he didn't understand the version of English being spoken to him. "I'm sorry? Lopez? Yes, let me page her."

Mrs. Lopez joined Peri in the lobby, her eyes wide with the gossip that wanted to leap from her throat.

"Did you hear about Ms. Castillo? Dios mio, we did not think such a thing, even though we see the man around, Waters is his name? We think he is some kind of delivery man. He only ever speak to Ms. Castillo."

Peri finally had to interrupt her. "Mrs. Lopez, Carlos doesn't work today and I need to get in touch with him. His phone number is back at my office, so I thought I'd stop by and see if you could give it to me."

"Si, yes," she replied. "I hope he's not in trouble."

"No, he's actually been very helpful. I just need to confirm a couple of things with him."

He answered after two rings. Peri identified herself and asked if he had time to meet her today.

"I need a little more information," she said. "I'd be happy to buy you lunch somewhere."

An hour later, she and Carlos sat in the local Quizno's, having warm sandwiches and cold drinks.

"I'm sorry to have to ask you this, Carlos," Peri said. "But for the police, I need to know where you were when Marnie and David were murdered. I can tell you are a good man, but the police don't know you. They want proof."

Carlos looked down. "I remember when I hear about Marnie. The paper said late Saturday night or early Sunday morning. I remember thinking that I had been working the night shift at the store. We restock everything after Memorial Day."

He glanced up at Peri. "I felt bad that I was not there to stop it."

"Well, that's a good alibi. The manager can verify it. How about last Thursday, around eight?"

"Last Thursday was my brother's birthday. We are all at my mother's house, having a little party."

Peri frowned. "Usually, it's better to have witnesses who aren't family members. Of course, if you have a large family and they're all telling the same story, time-wise, it will be okay."

She rose from the chair. "Thank you, Carlos. I knew you were telling me the truth."

So there, Skip Carlton, she thought as she returned to her office.

Sitting at her desk, Peri typed up her notes. She owed Benny a report on her progress. He had been calling her every day, wondering about the case. The same questions every day: did she know who killed Marnie, were the police coming back to his house, could he have the ring if no one claimed it?

She noted that yesterday his voice had cooled when he asked about the ring. As if he suddenly didn't need to ask anymore.

CHAPTER 37

Peri settled into the corner booth of Capone's and checked her watch. If she played the evening correctly, she might solve a crime. The waitress brought a glass of merlot and a plate of their delicious garlic-cheese bread. Peri nibbled at a piece of bread and sipped her wine.

Benny appeared in the doorway, hands in his pockets, cigarette behind his ear. When he saw Peri, his shoulders caved a little and his hands came out to wring themselves. Peri smiled and beckoned him over.

"Benny, it's so nice to see you again," she said. "Please sit. Would you like a glass of wine?"

"No, water is fine." He picked up the menu. "I don't know why I bother reading this thing, I know it by heart."

The waitress passed by their table. "Are you ready to order?"

Benny nodded, but Peri said, "Not yet, thanks. We have one more person joining us."

"The detective?" Benny looked stricken.

"No," Peri told him. "A surprise."

She looked up and saw a willowy brunette. Making eye contact with Peri, the woman walked over to the booth.

"I'm so glad you could make it, Jeanine," Peri told her, and then turned to Benny. "Jeanine, this is Benny Needles. Benny, this is Jeanine Ressler."

Jeanine took off her jacket and sat down in the booth, next to Peri.

"Benny," Peri said. "Jeanine's mom and dad were in the movies. Her mom's name was Sylvia Banks. Her dad was Melvin Conway."

His eyes went wide. "You're Melvin Conway's daughter?"

"Yes," Jeanine replied. "He and my mother met on the set of *A Woman Knows*."

Benny leaned forward. "True? That's the movie right after the one Melvin Conway made with Dean Martin."

"Peri thought you might like to hear about Melvin Conway," Jeanine said. "And Elizabeth Marquette."

They placed their order, and then continued to talk.

"Mom said Melvin Conway was very dashing, a real charmer. She thought, perhaps, Dean Martin took some tips from his acting style."

"Did your mom ever meet Dean Martin?"

"No, but she met Frank Sinatra once," Jeanine told him. "She said he was very nice."

The waitress brought bowls of spicy, warm minestrone.

"This reminds me of Mum," Jeanine said. "She cooked great Italian food, had a wonderful recipe for minestrone."

"My mom was a good cook, too," Benny said. "Not Italian, though. She made fried chicken, apple pie, meatloaf—what a meatloaf. I miss her cooking."

"How long has she been gone?"

"A year. How about yours?"

"Just a month."

Peri sat back and watched the two of them get to know each other.

"Hey, Peri, what about your mom?" Benny asked.

"My mom's been dead for seven years," she replied. "And no, she couldn't cook. I used to think 'peel cover back and heat for three minutes' was an old family recipe."

"That's too bad," Jeanine said. "So, did you ever learn?"

"Not really." Peri took a sip of her wine. "Practically everything I try turns out looking like scrambled eggs."

Soon, the meals arrived. Benny dove into his lasagna while the women nibbled more gracefully on their pasta dishes. In between bites, Jeanine retold the stories she had heard as a child, about the pranks Errol Flynn played on the set, and the time Melvin Conway nearly killed himself taking a fall from a horse. Benny leaned forward, as if he savored every word. Once their appetites had been satisfied and the coffee had been served, Peri asked Jeanine to get out her photos.

"Jeanine's got some great old pictures of her mom and the stars," she told Benny.

Benny smiled.

"Oh, look, there's Tyrone Power with your mom."

"Yes, Mum was one of the young maidens in one of those pirate movies, I forget which one. She said he was sweet, but kind of a wolf."

"Weren't they all?" Peri smiled.

Benny and Jeanine flipped through the book, talking about each star and what they were like.

"Your mom was real pretty," Benny said. "Too bad she was never in a movie with Dino."

"I know," Jeanine replied, turning the page. "Ah, here's my favorite picture." She pointed to the photo she had shown Peri originally. Sylvia stood, timeless, laughing at the camera outside Grauman's. Benny saw the ring on her finger immediately, just as Peri thought he would.

"The Forever Roses ring," he said. "What's it doing on your mom's finger?"

"That's not the real ring," Jeanine told him. "It's a replica. Melvin Conway had it made for my mum. Elizabeth Marquette had the real one."

She smoothed the page down, letting her hand pause at the photo of Conway with Sylvia. "He had it made for my mum because of me. Because he felt badly that he couldn't marry her and give me his name."

Jeanine sighed. "And now it's gone. My only link to my father, gone." She pressed the back of a finger to the corner of her eye, to stop a tear in its tracks.

"Oh, well," she said, picking up her coffee cup. "I guess I'll have to settle for my pictures. It's better than having no memories at all."

Peri had watched Benny's face while Jeanine spoke. He turned pink, then red, then crimson. His eyes became glassy with tears. At last, he exploded like a pressure cooker.

"I did it. I'm sorry, I took the ring."

"Oh, Benny," Peri said. "You're so sweet to feel bad, but there's no way the police would have let you back in the evidence locker."

"No, I didn't take it myself. I paid Officer Monroe to take it for me." He wiped his eyes. "You wouldn't believe how pitiful his salary is. I don't know how people live on so little."

He turned to Jeanine. "I'm so sorry, but you gotta understand. When I was little, my mom loved Dean Martin. She used to watch his movies, listen to his records. Every Thursday night, we'd sit and watch his TV show together. My hair used to be curly and black. She'd run her fingers through my hair and tell me, 'Benny, darling, he's so dreamy.' So I watched him, and listened to his records, and then started dressing like him. Mom liked it. When Mom died, I bought an autographed picture of Dino. I thought it would've made her happy. Then I bought another to make her happy, then another. Now I keep thinking the next thing I get will make Mom happy enough, so I can stop."

He hung his head. "You see why I needed that ring. But it's not Elizabeth Marquette's, it's Sylvia Banks'. It won't help make Mom happy."

"It's okay, Benny," Jeanine said. "Sometimes we just need something so bad, we do desperate things."

"Where's the ring now, Ben?" Peri asked.

"At home."

"Maybe we should go get it."

Peri felt sorry for him, but she knew he'd have to be prosecuted for receiving stolen goods. *Maybe I should wait until he's handed over the ring before I tell him that.*

To absolve her own guilt, Peri picked up the check. They all left and said their good-nights to Jeanine, wishing her a safe trip back to Palm Springs. Peri walked Jeanine over to her car.

"Thanks for all your help, Jeanine. You were perfect. I especially loved the sentence about your memories," Peri said. "You're a good actress."

"As Mum would have said, I knew it was the 'money shot'," Jeanine told her, with a wink.

Peri got in her car and followed Benny to his house. On the way, she called Skip. He didn't answer his phone, so she left a message telling him to meet her at Benny's house. He's probably still mad at me, she thought, and screening his calls.

"Not a good time to be avoiding me, Skip," she said, and threw the phone in her tote.

CHAPTER 38

Lights from the parking lot of the church threw odd shadows across Benny's lawn. Peri pulled up at the curb as Benny drove his Cadillac into his driveway. She got out of her car and watched him stop, open the old, wooden door of the one-car garage and ease the black, finned beauty into the space. Benny closed the door and walked to the front porch, where Peri joined him.

"Wait here, Miss Peri, I'll go get it," he told her, and turned to unlock his door. "Sorry about the darkness. My porch light doesn't seem to be working."

Peri looked up at the wall lantern, a whimsical iron and textured glass in the shape of a pineapple, covered in dust and cobwebs. "Have you tried changing the bulb?"

She saw a light go on in the back of the house, and thought about what Benny might be doing, wondering if he stored the ring in the freezer where they'd first found it. He seemed to be taking a long time, so she turned and looked toward the yard, gazing at the gnomes in the shadows.

Suddenly, Peri caught a glimpse of movement against the fence. Her curiosity aroused, she walked into the yard, peering into the darkness. A familiar figure stepped out from the corner.

"Mr. Cheavers," Peri said. "What are you doing here?"

He appeared haggard, rumpled, from his hair to his clothes. "You ruined my life." His voice was soft. "You ruined my marriage. You ruined everything."

"You ruined your own life. If you hadn't—"

She stopped talking when she saw the gun. Even from ten feet away, the barrel looked huge, especially pointing toward her. The air momentarily left her lungs as she considered what might happen in the next few seconds.

"Let's talk this out, Mr. Cheavers," she said at last, trying to keep her voice from trembling. "Maybe, if you offered to go to counseling or something, you could keep your marriage."

"My *wife* suggested counseling." He spat the words. "I don't want counseling. I don't want 'or something.' I want my old life back."

He shook the gun at her. "I want you to give me my old life back."

"Mr. Cheavers, I don't know how to do that. Your wife has seen the pictures. Even if I told her I made a mistake, I can't explain away the photos. She'd always have doubts."

He stopped shaking and became very still. Lowering the gun, he stared at Peri for a long time. His eyes looked sad, his entire face sagging with the weight of his problem.

"I don't understand why you women can't just let us alone," he said. He raised his gun again and pointed it at Peri.

"Miss Peri, who is that?" Benny asked from the porch, holding his trusty umbrella high.

Surprised, Cheavers turned and stepped toward Benny. His foot slipped in the wet grass, putting him off-balance. Peri took a chance and leaped forward, grabbing his wrist and knocking him to the ground. They struggled against each other, Peri trying to wrest the gun from his hand and Cheavers trying to turn the gun toward her and pull the trigger. As her left hand squeezed his right wrist, she brought her fist around to hit him in the face. He caught her hand in his and wrenched it aside, causing her to fall against him. Grabbing her hair, he yanked her head back, trying to get her off him.

The pain of him pulling her hair was searing. She felt as though her scalp would come off in his hand. In addition, he had grabbed strands from her temple, a tender region causing tears to blind her. She felt her grasp slipping from him, and then he was kneeling over her. Swinging her legs wildly, Peri managed to throw Cheavers off balance. A shadow passed by her and she heard the sound of a thwack and a single shot, exploding in the dark, lighting the night with a brief flash.

Cheavers collapsed backward, hitting his head against the picket fence. He landed, unconscious, in the overgrown flowerbed.

"Miss Peri, are you all right?" Benny stood over her, looking down.

"It's okay, Benny," she told him as she stood up and felt around in the grass with her foot. She finally located the gun in the darkness, and kicked it over to her bag on the sidewalk. Then, she picked up her tote and dug inside for her phone.

"Miss Peri, you're bleeding." Benny pointed to her right shoulder, which had begun to drip blood down her sleeve, to her bag.

She looked at her arm. Her white blouse, torn at the top of the sleeve, looked black in the night, shining a faint burgundy in the soft streetlight. She suddenly felt a stinging pain in her shoulder, and noticed the acrid smell from the gunshot, hanging in the heavy night air.

"Aw, it's ruining my bag," she said. "I love this tote."

Benny took the phone from her hand, and made her sit down on the sidewalk. "Leave this to me, Toots," he told her, and called the police.

Cheavers began to moan as Peri sat and waited for reinforcement. He sat up, holding the back of his head, also bleeding from where he struck it on the edge of the pickets. Looking around, dazed, he saw Peri and scowled.

"Stupid bitch," he said, and struggled to his feet.

Peri didn't want to touch the gun, but she didn't want him to get away. "Benny, stop him," she ordered.

"You bet," he told her and ran over to Cheavers.

"What do you think you're gonna do," Cheavers asked him, pointing to the umbrella. "Hit me with that?"

Benny didn't answer. He simply raised the umbrella and smacked the handle across Cheavers' forehead with a thwacking sound. The angry husband collapsed, holding his head.

"Yeah, smart guy," Benny told him. "It's what Dino would do."

Two cars screeched to a stop in front of the house, one a patrol car and one a dark SUV. Skip jumped out and ran to Peri.

"Are you all right? What happened?"

"Next time, pick up the damn phone," she told him. "That's Larry Cheavers, cheating husband of my client. The Reader's Digest version is that he hates me for ruining his good time and wants me dead."

While Officer Chou led Cheavers away in handcuffs, an ambulance and the paramedic truck showed up at the scene.

"Ah, Skip, I can't afford another ambulance ride," Peri said. "I might as well rent a limo for the cost."

"Shut up, and let them take care of you," he told her. "God, Peri, you scared me. I admit I didn't rush right over to Needles' house, but when I heard the dispatch call come through about shots fired, I just thought—"

"You thought, geez, I should've answered my phone. I'll feel guilty if she's dead."

"Oh, Doll, I'm sorry."

Tom Flores was busy cutting her sleeve away and dressing her wound. "It's not deep, Peri, but you should go past the hospital and let a doctor look at it. When was your last tetanus shot?"

"I don't know, Tom. I think about a year ago." She winced and pulled away, "What are you rubbing in there, salt?"

"Antiseptic. We don't want an infection."

"Crap, that hurts more than getting shot." She looked down at her arm. "Goddammit, this was a new blouse, too."

Larry Cheavers sat at the side of the ambulance while another paramedic worked on his head wound.

"How's he?" Peri nodded toward her assailant.

"He'll live," Tom told her. "Head wounds bleed a lot, so they usually look worse than they are."

Peri looked around for Benny, called out to him. He came over to her, his eyes darting away from all the blood. "Thank you, Benny. You saved my life."

"You've been good to me, Miss Peri. I had to do something."

She smiled. "Now you've got to do one more thing, Ben. You've got to hand the ring over to Detective Carlton and tell him what happened."

His shoulders sagging, he looked at the sidewalk and frowned. "I know."

Slowly, he turned and walked toward Skip, as if taking a trip to the gallows. Peri watched the two. Skip stood sideways, his tall frame bent to hear Benny's whispers. The little man alternately lifted his chin to say something, then dropped it down again to mumble. At last, she saw him dig into his pocket and hand an object to the detective. His entire body sighed. Skip reached for his phone.

Peri saw Benny stand up and whisper one more thing to the detective. Skip shook his head, smiling, and answered him.

"There you go," Tom said as he taped the bandage securely. "If you don't want to ride in the ambulance, at least have someone drive you to the hospital. It's not a deep wound, but I had to butterfly it together. A doctor might want to put a stitch or two in to reduce the size of the scar."

"I don't think a scar will hurt my modeling career," Peri told him. "I promise to call my doctor first thing in the morning."

Another patrol car arrived, with two more policemen. Benny began to cry a little. Skip walked him over to the car and spoke with the officers. They opened the back door and Benny looked at Peri, his eyes so cheerless, she thought her heart might break for him. He got into the patrol car, along with the officers, and they drove off.

"Will he have to serve time?" she asked Skip when he returned.

"Receiving stolen goods is a felony," he replied. "But it's his first offense, and he voluntarily gave the ring back. It's possible to get time served plus probation."

"How about Officer Monroe?"

Skip shook his head. "That's going to be a harder case. Benny's fueled by his obsessive-compulsive needs, but Tony has no excuse."

"Did he confess?"

"Not yet, but I'm working on it."

"By the way, what did Benny ask you?"

Skip smiled. "He wanted to know if we ever found any of Dean Martin's DNA on that damn ashtray."

Peri laughed, then winced and held her side.

"That does it, Doll, you're going to the hospital now for some x-rays. It's just possible you actually cracked those ribs in that wrestling match."

Skip helped her into his SUV and drove to Placentia Linda Hospital. The same doctor on duty the last time she came in was on duty again.

"I'm going to get Benny checked in, see if he's okay," Skip told her. "The faster we can get him processed, the sooner he can be home again. I'll come back for you as soon as I'm done."

"Miss Minneopa, it's nice to see you again, but not under these circumstances," the doctor said. "Let's look at your pictures, shall we?"

He examined the black and white photos of Peri's rib cage, while Peri looked over his shoulder and tried to read them as well. They seemed pretty fuzzy to her.

"Here it is, do you see?" he asked, pointing to a blurred darkness with white lines. "The first time you were lucky. You only bruised your ribs. This time is not so good. They are not broken, but they have small cracks."

The doctor read her chart, his eyebrows folding in a frown. "I see last time you checked yourself out AMA. I won't waste a bed trying to make you stay the night, but I do want you to rest in your own bed, at least tomorrow, to allow your ribs to mend."

He wrote on a pad. "Here's a prescription for pain killers. Do not take these with alcohol, do not take them while driving, and do not exceed the dosage. Do you understand?"

"Aye, aye, Captain," Peri told him.

She heard Blanche's voice outside, trying to ask for her. "Min-nee-o-pa," the husky voice enunciated. "Em eye en en—"

"Beebs," Peri called to her. "I'm back here."

"Good God, woman, what now?" Blanche said, rushing into the room. "This is just the last straw. You're going back to housecleaning tomorrow."

"Can't, Beebs, the doctor's making me stay in bed tomorrow."

Blanche turned to the doctor and introduced herself. "How bad is it?"

He pointed to the x-ray. "She fractured the fifth and sixth ribs on the left side, about midway. Some bruises here and there, but the GSW looks clean. Sutures would diminish the size of the scar, but she doesn't want them."

"Gun shot wound?" Blanche looked at Peri, who just shrugged.

"Skip called to see if I could take you home. Is she ready to go, Doctor?"

He nodded. "You may go ahead and get dressed," he told Peri. "Stop by the desk at the front to be checked out."

Blanche helped Peri into the sleeve of her torn, stained shirt. "Skip also wanted me to see if I could talk you out of the P.I. business."

"Trust me, Beebs, if I thought all my cases would involve men trying to beat me up and shoot me, I'd turn in my license right now. I'm sore all over, I feel shaky, and my shoulder hurts in the weirdest way, like it's traumatized over getting shot."

She buttoned her shirt carefully. "But I also feel exhilarated, validated, like I've just answered a million-dollar question. I don't think I can go back to scrubbing toilets."

They walked outside into the night air. Peri felt chilled, but good.

Blanche wrapped her arm gently around her friend. "Come on, Sherlock, let's get you home."

She took charge of Peri, filled her prescription, drove her home, fixed tea, and made her comfortable. Along the way, Peri told Blanche about her adventure and tried not to protest about being treated like a child. Eventually, the best friends curled up on opposite ends of the sofa with hot mugs of herbal tea. They were still talking about Benny's explanation for his collection when Skip arrived.

"How's Benny?" Peri asked.

"He should be home before too long," he said. "I got him a lawyer and worked with the D.A. to put the preliminary charges together so he could be released on bail."

"Poor thing. He must be sick that he's spending money on a lawyer, instead of on Dino stuff."

Skip shrugged. "He's got to pay the price for his crime. Thanks, by the way. Monroe refused to admit any wrongdoing until you got Benny to give up the ring. Turns out he was just greedy. And stupid. You'll love his reasoning: he wanted to apply to the FBI, but he was too deeply in debt. So he took Benny's money to steal the ring so he could pay off his debt and get into the FBI."

Peri laughed, then winced.

Blanche gave Peri a light hug. "I'm off, Girlfriend. It's late and I've got to make certain Danielle makes her curfew."

"Is she still with Chad?"

"Yes, although I get the feeling he's on probation with her. I think he genuinely likes her, but anytime he mentions my work or suggests I might give him a tour of the morgue, she threatens to break up with him. Don't look for the relationship to last the summer."

"August first, like I said," Peri told her, yawning.

"Come on, Sleepy," Skip said as Blanche left. "Time to hit the hay."

"Sleepy," she replied, the pain killers doing their work. "Are you sure I'm not Dopey?"

He helped her into bed. "Grumpy's more like it. I'll sack out on the couch, in case you need me."

"No, Skipper, stay here. I'd like to know you're, um, here, nice people here, um, good in the world tonight." Her mumbling stopped as she fell asleep.

Skip retrieved a beer from the fridge, wandered back into the living room and turned on the news. He sat and sipped the cold drink while he decompressed. Goddamn woman, he thought, she was just supposed to do background checks, insurance fraud. None of it was supposed to end in gunplay, not when she refused to carry a gun.

Cheavers' Glock 17 could have torn her apart if his aim had been better. Skip had seen what guns could do. If it didn't kill her, it could have maimed her, paralyzed her. He agreed with Blanche, she should go back to housecleaning.

Of course, his job entailed those risks, too. Chasing a perpetrator could always result in injury or worse. The scariest times were sometimes the quietest. Occasionally, as he walked up to a tract house to interview a subject, the hair on the back of his neck stood up, and he'd wonder if he'd be greeted with a shotgun.

One thing he knew was that Peri would not be persuaded to do anything she didn't want to do, like give up her new career. He would have to either learn to accept it, or move on.

Slipping out of his jeans and shirt, he crawled into bed beside her. For now, he'd accept it.

At six o'clock in the morning, he felt a jostling motion, hands against his bicep.

"Skip, Skip," Peri said.

"Hmm, wha—?"

"Are you awake?"

"Are you kidding?" He opened one eye to see her sitting up, her hand on her rib cage. "What's wrong? Can't you sleep?"

"Picket fences, Skip," she told him. "I bet that's what Marnie fell against. That's the weird depression in her skull."

He stared at her. "Picket fences. You woke me for picket fences."

"We need to go to Benny's place with the mold of her injury, and the Luminol."

Skip raised up on one elbow and kissed her. "Yes, that's a great idea," he said. "My shift starts at nine, and Jason won't be in much before that, so let's get a little more sleep first."

"You can sleep, Skipper," she said, easing her body out of bed. "I'm going to read the paper, then get cleaned up."

He watched her walk out of the room, close the door behind her so he could sleep. No, he thought, there was no talking her out of her new line of work.

CHAPTER 39

"Ow-ow-ow." Peri tried not to squeal as she slipped into the hot, bubbly water. She wanted a shower, but knew she should keep her shoulder dry, so she opted for the tub. The water felt good once she got used to the heat.

As she soaked, she thought about Marnie's murder. The solution felt so close. If Marnie had fallen against Benny's fence, that would establish how she was killed. Maybe she fell accidentally, and someone moved her body to keep Benny from getting into trouble, but who would do that?

The doctor had told her to rest today. She knew Skip had promised to carry out his orders. After her bath, he had helped Peri back to bed and brought her breakfast and a book. She looked down at the cornucopia of eggs, bacon, toast, and potatoes.

"You know, there is only one of me in this bed."

"I figure this will fill you up until I get back for dinner." He kissed her nose, then added, "You absolutely must rest."

Peri stuck her tongue out at his back as he walked out the door.

Her car was still parked back at Benny's, so in theory, she couldn't go anywhere, anyway. Except she still had two good legs and a pair of walking shoes. Benny's house wasn't close, but she could probably walk there in thirty minutes. After all, she ran past his street all the time.

After breakfast, Peri dressed, in shorts and a tank top. She picked up her tote from the table. It still had bits of dried blood on the side, the streaks standing out against the leopard print.

"Crap," she said, and rummaged through her closet for another bag. Finally, she found a canvas tote, white and navy with a palm tree on the side. Peri loaded her camera, notebook, cell phone, and wallet. *It looks like I'm headed for a day at the beach.* She tied her tennis shoes, put in her earpieces, and picked up the tote. She could carry it if she held it in her left hand, away from her rib cage.

Halfway to Benny's, Peri's pace slowed. She felt exhausted. Her left arm ached from carrying her beach tote, but she knew her right shoulder wouldn't support the weight or the straps.

Well, maybe I can make it there in forty minutes. She flipped through her MP3 player, looking for a song that would motivate her. Aerosmith's *Janie's Got a Gun* perked her up.

Peri arrived at Benny's in time to see Jason Bonham meticulously working on the picket fence. Two boxes sat beside him, one holding unused swabs and envelopes, and the other holding tests that had been taken. It looked as though he had traveled almost halfway around the fence line.

"Hey, Jason," Peri said.

He lifted his chin to see her. A black ball cap with the words *Be Afraid* sat low on his forehead, tufts of golden-brown hair sticking out the sides. Peri thought he looked like he might be twelve years old.

"Peri, what are you doing here? I heard you had some excitement last night."

"A little." She looked past him to the yard, the scene of the crime. A chill ran through her veins. The overgrown grass still showed where they had trampled it in their fight. Dark stains splattered the sidewalk, from her blood.

Jason interrupted her reverie. "You okay?"

"Sure, Jason, I'm fine. How about you? Have you found anything yet?"

He shook his head. "Not yet, but the impression of the wound has been a close match with some of these pickets, so it looks promising."

"Great. I just came for my car."

Peri knew she should drive home and rest, but she couldn't. Turning left onto Chapman, she wound her way down to Esmy's house. Just as she thought, Benny's Cadillac sat in the driveway. His lawyer must have helped him make bail. Walking past the geraniums, she stepped up to the door and rang the bell.

Benny answered the door. "Miss Peri, are you okay?"

"Sure, I'm fine. How about you? Skip said he got you a lawyer."

He ushered her inside, past all of the wildlife, to the kitchen. "Yeah, Detective Carlton's an okay guy." Benny looked at her bag. "You going to the beach?"

"My other tote got," she looked for a word that wouldn't ignite any sudden emotions. "Stained."

"Oh." Benny's eyes went wide. "Sure."

"I was wondering if we could talk for awhile." Peri sat down at the kitchen table, feeling very tired.

Benny got them both cups of coffee and joined her.

"Remember when you told me Marnie had been looking through your trash cans? Can you tell me more about that?"

Peri watched him pour spoon after spoon of sugar into his mug. She wanted to wring the information out of him, but knew she had to wait until he had something to say.

"I was putting out my trash cans on the curb. I put out the green one for recycle, then I went for the black can. When I walked back to the curb, she was there."

"Marnie?"

He nodded. "I didn't know her name, I just knew she was in my trash can, digging around. I said, 'hey, what are you doing in my trash cans?' and she said, 'none of your business' and I said, 'I'm calling the cops' and she said, 'bite me, loser' and I got mad." He hung his head.

Peri put her hand on his arm. "Ben, how mad did you get?"

He mumbled something unintelligible.

"Benny, dear, I didn't quite hear you."

She leaned in to hear him whisper, "I hit her."

"How hard did you hit her?"

"Not hard, not hard," he said, his head popping up and eyes wide.

"With your hand?"

"No." He paused. "The thing is, I get a little nervous at night, so I bring my umbrella with me when I have to go out."

"So you hit her with your umbrella," Peri said with a smile. "That explains the dent on her forehead."

"I swear I didn't hit her that hard. She still talked, okay? She said, 'ow, that hurt' and walked away. Or, ran. She kind of ran away."

"Benny, that's the best news ever." Peri rose, wrapping her arm around her ribs as she did. "I've got to go rest now, but I want you to know I'd be happy to be a witness for your defense."

On the way home, Peri dialed Skip's number, then canceled the call. He'll be plenty mad to know I didn't stay home and rest. Instead, she put her car in the garage, and went into the house and took her pills.

Twenty minutes later, Peri dozed on the sofa while Cary Grant spoke elegant words to Grace Kelly on her TV. The phone startled her awake. Skip wanted to know how she was feeling.

"Hmm, I was feeling pretty good until you woke me."

"Sorry. Jason processed Benny's fence today. He got all of the evidence that proves your case against Cheavers, but nothing on Marnie Russell. The pickets were a good idea, though. Funny, I couldn't see what the wound looked like until you mentioned the pickets. Now I can't see it as anything else."

Knowing Skip would be mad eventually, Peri decided to take the direct route to the argument. She told him where she'd gone and what she'd done.

"Peri," Skip said, his voice on the edge of disapproval. "How did you get to Esmy's house?"

"I walked over to Benny's and picked up my car. Jason was there, I figured he told you."

"I guess Jason thought I'd be upset."

"It's not like I ran, Skip. I walked, I took my time." She yawned. "Let's fight later, Skipper. The pills are making me sleepy."

"Okay, Doll. I've got class to teach tonight, so why don't you come in tomorrow and give your statement? We can go to lunch, if you want."

"You bet."

Peri slept a little more, then awoke to the rumble of her empty stomach. She would be due to take another pill soon, so she hunted for food in her kitchen. The selections were meager. There was peanut butter in the pantry, but no bread, three beers and an apple in the refrigerator, and nothing but ice in the freezer. Running a brush through her blonde hair, she pulled it back in a ponytail, then drove to the grocery store.

She wandered the aisles in Albertson's, trying to make smart choices, even though she wanted to stuff her cart with gooey pastries, fried chicken, ice cream and other indulgences. If brownies make you happy, why aren't they good for you? After all, they're good for your emotional health.

Lost in thought, Peri stared at a can of green beans, trying to figure out whether to buy the unsalted, the organic, or the regular, salty ones with taste. She started thinking about organic vegetables, wondering if they were free range veggies.

"Hello, Peri."

She turned to see Karen Anderson standing behind her.

"You get around to quite a few grocery stores," Peri smiled.

"No," she replied, her face solemn. "I just live in Sunny Hills, so I shop at the Albertson's in Fullerton, but I work over here."

"Of course," Peri said, making a mental note to avoid joking with this woman.

"Have you found out who killed Marnie yet?"

"No, but the police are getting closer every day. They have a lot on their hands. Two murders in our little town is a lot to investigate."

"Two?" Karen asked. "Oh, yes, that David person. I thought that was probably just a fight over drugs. Those people stab each other all the time."

Peri took her purchases home and slowly unloaded the food. She had gotten some fruits and vegetables, but after putting everything away, she reached for the ice cream. A healthy diet could wait until tomorrow. Today called for Ben & Jerry's Pistachio Pistachio and a good movie.

Tucking herself into the pillows on the sofa, she watched *The Big Sleep* for the millionth time. She could always watch that movie, even though she knew every scene, every line. She loved moving along with Philip Marlowe through rainy Los Angeles. His wisecracks still made her laugh, especially when spoken in dire circumstances, and she admired his astute reasoning.

"Cases are easy to solve if they exist in a writer's mind," she said to the TV, putting another spoonful of nutty richness in her mouth.

At last, Philip Marlowe confronted Eddie Mars. Peri watched, cheering her hero as he trapped Mars into admitting he didn't know Carmen Sternwood, a pivotal story point. Marlowe gave Peri an idea.

Who knows what they shouldn't know here in Placentia, she wondered, *or vice versa?*

After getting out her notes and laptop, Peri wrote down all of the facts, then checked all of the news articles online to see how many of the facts didn't make the papers. After that, she started reviewing her notes. An hour later, she sat up and gasped. She opened her folder of pictures on the computer and skimmed through the photos. Then she called Skip.

"Give me a call when you get off work," she told his voicemail. "I may know who killed Marnie and David."

Another pill later, she woke to being kissed on the forehead.

"Hey, there, Doll," Skip said. "How are you feeling?"

Peri sat up. "Skipper, let me show you what I did."

Step by step, she explained her logic. He nodded, looking at her notes and pictures. At one point, he took his notepad out and verified her information.

"We need a couple more pieces of the puzzle," she said.

"And we have to be careful about how we collect them. We don't want to tip our hand too soon."

He picked up the phone to call Jason Bonham. "Hey, youngster, what's on your schedule tomorrow? Cause, I've got a job for you."

CHAPTER 40

By nine A.M., HIS House already seemed to burst at the seams with activity. Peri sat in the parking lot, watching the children running around the yard, and up the front porch. She waited in her car and watched Skip and Jason. They stood at the door, giving Karen Anderson pieces of paper while it appeared she gave them a hard time. Peri couldn't quite hear what they were saying, but their expressions said it all, Karen's face red and angry, Skip and Jason staying calm but squaring their bodies, standing firm. A stranger stood on the porch with them. Peri thought he might be a representative from the church next door, that funded the shelter.

Skip and Karen argued back and forth before the stranger intervened. At last, Karen opened her mouth and Jason inserted a swab. *Here we go*, Peri thought.

Jason moved over to Karen's car, a white Ford Mustang from the 90s. He opened the trunk and nodded to Skip.

"Red carpet," he said, and took out his toolkit.

Peri wanted to go out and be part of the action, but she had promised Skip she wouldn't. Still, she fairly vibrated in her seat from the curiosity. Finally, she took out her binoculars to get a better look.

Jason sprayed Luminol on the trunk, then took out a swab and a knife, telling Skip he found blood. After labeling the envelopes, he nodded to a tow truck waiting on the street. Then he turned his attention to the fence.

Like Benny's house, the homeless shelter had a white picket fence around the front yard. Board by board, Jason compared each picket to the impression from Marnie's wound, swabbing and testing as he went. He didn't get far. The fourth picket from the sidewalk tested positive for blood. Photos were taken, and then the picket was pried from the fence and put in a bag.

Mrs. Anderson, her face now crimson in rage, said, "Don't tear up the fence. You're defacing the property."

The stranger reached out to Mrs. Anderson, put his arm around her shoulder and whispered something to her. Karen burst into tears and buried her face in the gentleman's chest. After speaking with Jason, Skip returned to Karen and the man. Peri thought he was telling them what to do next.

Peri followed them back to the station. "Why didn't you arrest Karen Anderson?" she asked as they walked in the door.

"Because we have to confirm the blood is Marnie's first," Skip replied. "And we still don't have anything to tie her to David Waters."

"But I told you," she said. "That day I saw her in Fullerton, she called David Waters by his full name, even though she told us she didn't know his last name. And she said she bet he 'bashed Marnie's head.' But the news never revealed how Marnie died, just like they never revealed how Waters died. She knew he'd been stabbed."

"I know, Doll. When we get the DNA results back, we'll have her for Marnie's murder, but I don't know how she'd even know Waters, much less want to kill him."

"Maybe she left evidence on him. Trace said they found a hair."

Skip nodded. "We'll definitely test it against Karen's DNA. Maybe we'll get lucky."

"It still doesn't explain why Waters was in Benny's yard." Peri said. "Although, if he was in business with Maria Castillo, she might know why he was in that neighborhood."

"That's an idea." Skip looked at his watch. "Let's go ask her. She's out on bail."

He glanced at Peri's beach bag. "Nice bag, Doll. You hitting Newport after this?"

"I'm afraid the leopard tote has some spots I don't want on it."

"Sorry," he said. "It's just hard to take you seriously when you look like you're headed on a cruise."

"Wait till I have another hot flash, you'll take me seriously."

The Castillo home was nestled back from Palm Drive, near the Alta Vista golf course. Tall and narrow, the builder had tried to affect the look of English Tudor architecture, a style Peri found distasteful.

It's southern California, for Pete's sake, she thought, *it's so far from England it's stupid.*

Maria opened the door, her large eyes round and expression sad. She let them in without saying anything, resigned to her fate.

"Maria, we need to talk to you about David Waters," Skip said.

"I didn't kill him, I tell you, I didn't kill him." She opened her front door again. "I think you should leave and talk to my lawyer."

"We don't think you killed him, Maria," Peri told her. "In fact, we think we know who did. We're just trying to figure out why he was in Benny's yard."

She looked confused. "I don't know. Where does Benny live?"

When Skip gave her the street name, she smiled and nodded.

"He was probably at the church," she told them. "Sometimes I dropped some of our residents at the church for services and prayer groups. I've seen him there before. I think he was waiting for someone."

"The married woman?" Peri said.

Maria nodded. "Maybe."

"When was the last time you and he did business?" Skip asked.

Her chin lowered to her chest, eyes downcast. "Earlier that day. It was when I told him we could not do this anymore."

"There was no money found on him that night," Skip said.

"He should have had three hundred dollars."

Skip and Peri stood up.

"Thank you, Ms. Castillo," Peri said. "And, good luck with everything."

Back at the station, Skip stopped by Jason's office. "Test any unknown trace on Marnie Russell or David Waters' clothes against Anderson's DNA. We want to make our case as tight as possible."

Trying to keep busy while the tests were being run, Peri decided to visit Benny's house. Back at home, he smiled when he saw her at the door.

"I just thought I'd stop by and see how you were doing," Peri said. "And to give you an update on the case."

She filled him in on the discoveries at HIS House, and why David Waters had been in his neighborhood.

"But, Miss Peri, why was he in my yard?"

"That we don't know, Ben. Maybe he was taking a shortcut." She looked out the living room window. "Why don't we go look around your yard and see what might have made him come here?"

The tall blonde and short man walked the width and length of the unmown lawn. Peri went over to where Waters' body had been lying, on the opposite side of the yard from her attack. The ground where Waters fell still showed signs of depression. Wild flowers lay broken on the trampled dirt, the gnomes around them turned around, their backs to the scene.

Peri noted one of the gnomes looked a little cleaner than the others. Staring down at him, she could see a separate depression, showing he had been moved. She dug her camera out of her bag and took a few pictures. Then, she put on a pair of gloves and lifted the gnome.

Underneath the jolly little man, Peri found an envelope, already decomposing from the moisture and heat. She took more pictures, then picked up the envelope and looked inside.

"Here's what Waters was doing, Ben. Hiding his three hundred bucks."

CHAPTER 41

In all of Placentia, the most happening place on Monday morning had to be the Interview room of the Placentia Police Department. Sitting around the table were Karen Anderson, her attorney, a representative from the church, Detective Skip Carlton, and Officer Jason Bonham. Watching in the viewing room were Chief of Police Dale Fletcher, District Attorney Anne McGavin, and Peri, who had taken a vow of silence in order to be in the room with the big dogs.

"So, Karen, we wanted you and your attorney to see the evidence before the District Attorney takes this to court," Skip said. He laid a series of pictures and reports on the table. "We have Marnie Russell's blood in the trunk of your car, and on the picket we took from the fence of HIS House. We also have this report showing the fibers on the trash bag she was wrapped in match those in your trunk, in color and consistency."

"Fibers aren't unique," her attorney replied.

"True," Skip said. "But, with Marnie's DNA on the bag, her blood in the trunk and comparable fibers on the bag, we can make the case that Karen wrapped her up and deposited her in the park."

He pointed to another report. "Here we have a list of witnesses who will testify they often saw Karen and Marnie arguing, which contradicts what she told me in our initial interview. Also, we have a statement from private investigator Peri Minneopa, detailing the fact that Karen volunteered information only the killer would know."

Peri felt the D.A. and the chief glance her way, and tried not to smile.

"Going on to David Waters," Skip said. "We recovered a hair from his clothes that matches Karen's DNA, fingerprints on the murder weapon that match Karen's, and we found a blouse in Karen's home with Waters' blood on it. Of course, we have a report from Miss Minneopa's interview with Karen, where she described the manner of Waters' death, a fact that was hidden from the public."

Skip sat back in his chair. "All we don't know is the why, but we don't care, as long as we've got the other four W's answered."

Karen and her attorney leaned their heads together, whispering. The man from the church didn't join in.

"Why is the church rep here?" Peri asked aloud, then shut her mouth, looking at the chief with wide eyes.

He glared at her and turned back to the window. The D.A. told her, "The church wants to make certain there won't be any charges filed against them. It's call CYA."

Peri smiled. "Cover Your Ass," the motto of any corporation, apparently included churches, too.

"This is all very interesting," the attorney told Skip. "But I don't see where you have proof my client cut off Marnie Russell's hands."

"We don't see that as a problem," Skip said. "Since we can prove the hands were cut off post-mortem, we aren't as concerned about whether Mrs. Anderson mutilated the body. If and when we find any proof she did, we can add that to the murder counts."

"I wouldn't cut off hands," Karen told him. "That's just not right."

Her attorney shushed her, but Skip said, "You might want to tell us what happened, Karen. The way we see it, neither of the murders were planned. We think they were crimes of passion. Maybe if you confessed, the D.A. would be willing to consider a lesser plea than the one they would pursue in court."

Peri looked over at the D.A., who nodded in agreement.

Karen appeared unconvinced. "I don't think so. These people were homeless, jobless, useless. What jury is going to care enough about their lives to put me in jail for even a few months? If I was guilty, that is."

"The jury who sits and listens to our D.A. talk about your hatred of Marnie Russell," Skip told her. "The jury who hears a parade of shelter residents talk about how much you picked on her, and who hears my testimony of how you lied to me and said you liked her. The jury who hears you took the life of a young, pregnant woman and dumped her like trash in the park."

"Pregnant?" Karen's eyes opened in surprise.

"And wait until they hear Carlos Lopez, the father of that baby, talk about how heartbroken he is that you ended his child's life. Or David Waters' mother, talking about losing her only child. You'll be lucky to serve less than twenty-five years."

Skip sweetened the pot. "You have two children, five and seven. You might want to think about what's the least amount of time you can afford to spend behind bars."

Damn, he's good, Peri thought, smiling.

Karen and her lawyer bent their heads together again. They sat up and stared at one another, the attorney holding her hand and nodding to her.

"I didn't mean to hurt anyone," Karen said. "I was hard on Marnie, it's true. Single people just don't fit into HIS House. The shelter is for families, not for wayward tramps. I never believed for a moment that Marnie had turned her life around. Once a grifter, always a grifter, I say.

"When I saw her wearing that beautiful coat, I knew she had to have stolen it. She came home late that night, from catting around, no doubt. I was taking the late shift as a favor to Ellen, the night manager. I confronted Marnie in the yard. Do you know what she told me? That soon she would be rich and out of this dump. HIS House is not a dump."

She pounded her hand on the table. "I resented that, and told her so. She laughed at me, so I pushed her." Karen's head bowed. "I just pushed her, and she fell against the fence. I was so mad, I left her there and went in to do the dishes. 'Get up' I told her. When I went back—"

Karen stopped, as if waiting for tears that never came. "When I went back outside, much later, she was cold. I didn't want her found on our property. Think of the scandal. So I took her to the park."

She looked up at Skip. "And I didn't cut her hands off."

"And Waters?" Skip said.

"He should have been nicer to me," Karen said, in a matter of fact tone. "I helped him, got him a job at the drugstore, paid the deposit for his apartment, and he thanked me by traipsing around with that little whore."

She stopped. "Sorry, I mean, with Marnie Russell."

"Why did you care?" Skip asked. "Were you involved with him?"

Karen blushed, but kept her eyes on the detective. "Yes. I love my husband, but David was, exciting, dangerous. I was bored. I felt neglected."

"But you didn't want to share him."

"I know I had no right," she said. "But if he had other girlfriends, I didn't want to know about them. I certainly didn't want him to be trolling at the shelter. When I saw him with Marnie, I blew up."

"What happened?"

"He met me at the church. We'd usually go for 'coffee' after my Bible study. I was mad, so I told him to leave. Then I had second thoughts. I ran after him, down the street. I thought I saw him on Mr. Needles' porch, so I went up the stairs, but no one was there. I saw a shadow along the fence. It scared me."

"Why would it have scared you?" Skip asked. "You thought he was on the porch."

"But he didn't say anything," she said. "I called out to him, but he didn't answer. My hand found a knife on the table, so I picked it up and started back down the sidewalk. When someone jumped out of the bushes at me, I held my hands out to stop them. The knife was in my hand...it went, it went into his chest."

Her face reddened. "Why didn't he say something? All he had to do was tell me it was him. I wouldn't have been afraid, wouldn't have picked up the knife, wouldn't have…"

Skip turned and looked at the two-way mirror. He nodded, then stood up, along with Jason. "Thank you, Karen," he said. "The D.A. will be in to discuss the charges with you."

He and Jason left, so Peri turned to join them.

"Thank you for your help, Miss Minneopa," the D.A. said.

"Does this mean I'm no longer a suspect in Waters' murder?"

The D.A. smiled at her. "We'll be in touch if we need anything."

Peri walked down the hall, and found Skip behind his desk, typing at the computer. "You were quite magnificent, Skipper."

He smiled and shrugged. "All in a day's work, Ma'am."

"We should go out and celebrate tonight."

"As long as it's not too expensive, I'm in."

"You mean all that superb detective work didn't earn you the big bucks?"

He laughed. "It's not like I work on commission, Doll."

"Well, how about Capone's? I'll see if Blanche and Paul can meet us."

"Sure, see if you can get reservations for eight o'clock."

CHAPTER 42

Peri sat in the foyer of Capone's, waiting for the rest of the party. It had been a thrill to dress up for tonight, in a Michael Kors skirt and top, bright, beaded, and bought on the sale rack at Steinmart. Her blonde hair curled gently around her shoulders, her make-up and nails done, she felt like a dream girl.

"Hey, girlfriend." Blanche's husky voice announced her arrival. "Paul's on his way. Got stuck in a meeting."

The women hugged and took a place at the bar.

"Congratulations on solving the case." Blanche held out a package. "I got you a little something as a reward."

"Thank you." Peri ripped off the paper. She pulled a tote out of the box, a roomy bag in a pink snakeskin pattern. "I love it."

"Thought you could use a new one."

Peri reached over and hugged her friend. "It's perfect, Beebs."

"How are you feeling," Blanche asked. "About everything?"

"Better. The doctor's diagnosis threw me for a loop, I think. I was so focused on my nausea instead of the heat that I kept thinking pregnancy, not hot flashes."

"Well, you're not alone, dear," Blanche said. "Are you still sad about it?"

"I thought I was, but not because I secretly wanted children. It just represented failure. All my life, I've been little Miss Straight A's. Everything I've tried to do in life, I've done."

"Even cleaning houses?"

"Yes, Beebs, even cleaning houses. I know I haven't used my degree, but housecleaning turned out to be a very lucrative business that gave me plenty of time to do what I wanted. And, I got to be my own boss, which was good, since not many employers would have put up with me."

Peri gestured toward the room. "All around me, I see women of all levels of intelligence and education, getting pregnant without a second thought. And here I sit, a smart cookie, who can't have a baby."

"That's just biology. You can't pee standing up, either, but are you going to beat yourself up for not being a man?"

"I can so pee standing up. It's just really messy."

Blanche laughed.

"Menopause," Peri said. "Damn. I didn't just feel old, I felt like an old failure."

"Who's an old failure?" Skip asked as he walked up. He kissed her.

"No one I know," Peri replied.

Skip greeted Blanche. "Where's Paul?"

"He should be here in about ten minutes."

Paul arrived on schedule and the foursome sat down to a big meal and a lot of conversation.

"Dani and Chad still dating?" Peri asked.

"I haven't a clue," Blanche said. "Apparently, he's busy playing gigs and she's busy applying to colleges. I don't know if they really are just too busy or if it's a ruse. Have you heard anything, Paul?"

"I never hear anything, Dear. I'm just the dad."

"How are your daughters, Skip?" Blanche asked.

"Maxie's still in New York, climbing up the ladder of a law firm there. Daria graduates this January so she can marry Alec in June. She and her mom have everything planned, so all I have to do is write the check."

"And walk her down the aisle," Peri said.

He smiled and nodded. "All I care about is that Alec treats her well. Otherwise, I'll have to break out my Scary Cop Dad routine."

"How many boys did you chase away with that?" Paul asked. "Can you teach it to me?"

Skip laughed. "I could try."

"You should teach a class in it," Peri told him.

"I hear you guys solved a case together," Paul said. "That must have been interesting, working with each other."

"Yeah," Skip replied. "Interesting is a great word for it. What is that ancient Chinese curse? 'May you have an interesting life'?"

"Oh, it was fun, wasn't it, Skipper?" Peri said.

"Sure, Doll." He nudged Paul and said, in a mock whisper, "I'll tell you later."

"Hey, we figured out whodunit," Peri told him. "And we found that ring. Then lost it. Then found it. And now it's the court's problem."

"Who do you think will end up with it?" Blanche asked.

Skip shook his head. "Hard to say. Sylvia's daughter has ample evidence to show her mom has had the ring since at least the 50s, and she is Conway's daughter. But maybe the Conway estate can establish that it was stolen. In the end, it might be a matter of who hires the best legal team."

Blanche took another drink of wine. "So, who cut off the hands?"

Peri and Skip looked at each other. "We never solved that part of the puzzle," Peri said.

"You have the murderer, right?" Paul asked.

"Yes, but nothing that ties her to the mutilation," Skip said.

"All we've got on the hand is unknown prints," Peri said.

"And the blood on the freezer door," Blanche added.

"Oh, yeah," Skip said. "We figured that was Benny's mom. It had thirteen alleles in common with his."

Peri put her fork down. "Skip, I cleaned Mrs. Needles' house all the time, and right before her death, she hired me for an entire week to do a massive spring cleaning. Shelves, closets, refrigerator, all cleaned out. That freezer didn't have any ice while she was alive."

"So?" Paul asked.

"So it means that the blood had to be from another of Benny's relatives," Blanche replied.

"Benny has an aunt," Skip said suddenly.

Peri grasped his arm. "Not just an aunt. His mom's twin sister—"

Skip finished the thought. "Who has an interesting hobby."

Blanche and Paul looked at Peri, who told them, "Taxidermy."

"Ew," Paul said.

"Not just a hobby, a passion." Peri smiled and shook her head. "If it wasn't so creepy, it'd be funny."

CHAPTER 43

"Miss Peri, Detective, what a nice surprise." Esmy greeted them at her front door. "What is that patrol car doing outside? You haven't come to arrest Benny again, have you? He's not here."

"No, Esmy," Peri said. "We're here to talk about your hobby."

"Oh, do come in and see the coyote. I think I've truly captured his essence."

As they walked in, Peri felt the glass-eyed creatures looked a little menacing today.

"You told me you like to find things around town to stuff," Peri said. "Is that right, Esmy?"

"My, yes, birds, squirrels, rabbits, even the coyote."

"Do you ever find things in Kraemer Park?" Skip asked.

Esmy lowered her eyes. "I knew I shouldn't have, but I can't stand to see beautiful things waste away."

"Marnie had beautiful hands, didn't she?" Peri said.

Esmy nodded. "When Mr. Whiskers died, I couldn't stand the thought of putting him in the ground, letting the earth and the bugs have something so pretty. It was the same way with Marnie. Her hands were always so perfect."

"Why did you put the hand in Benny's freezer?" Skip asked.

"Well, I was on my way to the church, and I didn't want the hand to ruin, so I stuck it in his freezer to keep it fresh. I planned to get it from him the next day, but when I went back, it was gone. I have to say, I was a little put out."

"I understand, Esmy," Peri said. "But there are rules about that."

"I don't see why. Marnie didn't have any family. No one else wanted them."

Peri looked at Skip for help.

"It's called mutilation," he told her. "We have laws against it, I'm afraid."

"Oh." Esmy was quiet for a moment. "Will I have to pay a fine?"

"Here's the thing, Esmy," Peri said. "You'll have to go with the officers. I'll call Benny's lawyer and he'll take care of you."

Esmy got her purse and followed Skip and Peri outside. As she locked her front door, Skip asked, "Esmy, where's the other hand?"

"Oh, I had to throw it away," she said. "When I sawed it off, I accidentally broke two of the nails."

Skip helped Esmy into the patrol car, while Peri called the attorney.

"I told him I'd investigate the old *diminished capacity* defense, if I was him," Peri said as they got into Skip's SUV.

"I've got some reports to type up," Skip told her. "But I thought we could get together for drinks later. My treat."

"Grey Goose? Four olives?"

"Just the way you like it, Doll."

THE END

ABOUT THE AUTHOR

Gayle Carline is a typical Californian, meaning that she was born somewhere else. She moved to Orange County from Illinois in 1978, and landed in Placentia a few years later.

Her husband, Dale, bought her a laptop for Christmas in 1999 because she wanted to write. A year after that, he gave her horseback riding lessons. When she bought her first horse, she finally started writing.

Gayle soon became a regular contributor to Riding Magazine, and in March, 2005, she began writing a humor column for her local newspaper, the Placentia News-Times. Every week, she entertains readers with stories of her life with Dale and their son, Marcus.

In her spare time, Gayle likes to sit down with friends and laugh over a glass of wine. And maybe plan a little murder and mayhem.

For more merriment, visit her at **http://gaylecarline.com**.

Want more Peri?

Try **HIT OR MISSUS**, the second in the Peri Minneopa Mystery Series!

COINCIDENCES HAPPEN...
Housecleaner-turned-private investigator Peri Minneopa takes a routine case: a rich husband suspects his wife of infidelity. Coincidentally, bad things start happening to her.
Peri's boyfriend, Detective Skip Carlton, investigates the death of Peri's elderly neighbor. It looks like a heart attack. Coincidentally, her husband died of a heart attack two weeks ago.
The elderly couple left legal papers on the table, involving a year-old real estate purchase. Coincidentally, there is a note attached from Peri's client, a real estate developer.
Except, Peri and Skip don't believe in coincidences. When their cases collide, she begins poking her nose into police business, butting heads with her boyfriend.
Stonewalled by Skip and the police, Peri turns to an unlikely partner for help, an annoying little man who is obsessed with Dean Martin.
If she can keep her sanity and her life -
SHE MIGHT JUST SOLVE THIS CASE.

An excerpt from HIT OR MISSUS

CHAPTER 1

In the end, it was a good thing Mr. Mustard didn't like coffee any more than he liked baths.

"I'm sorry, Mister," Dottie Peters told the large, orange tabby. "But you were stinky."

The elderly woman wrapped a thick towel around her wet, struggling cat and lifted him to the rim of the bathtub. She rested a moment, then hugged the bundle to her chest and rose. Steadying her body against the wall, she finally stood erect, more or less, while the cat fussed in her arms.

"Oof, hold still."

Dottie put her nose to the towel and inhaled the warm, primal scent of feline, mixed with baby shampoo. She moved the morning's newspaper from the old leather recliner and sat down, still gripping her entrapped cat. After fumbling with the remote until the TV clicked to life, she leaned back into the overstuffed chair and began massaging her furry hostage with the towel. The morning news show burbled with happy tones, but Dottie didn't smile.

"Bob used to sit here," she said as she rubbed. It had been two weeks and a day since her husband's heart attack, and in his absence, the cat had become her confidant. "He used to have his coffee here in the morning and watch The Price Is Right, remember?"

Mr. Mustard howled.

"I know, Sweetie." Dottie rubbed at the tears stinging her eyes. "If coffee didn't give me heartburn, I'd turn the channel, but I can't watch The Price Is Right without a cup of coffee. It just wouldn't be the same."

Mr. Mustard gave one last growl and disentangled himself from his terrycloth prison, leaping from his mistress's lap. He marched out of the room without glancing back, his tail twitching.

"Fine, Grumpy." She turned back to the TV and watched a young woman point out the latest traffic snarl, happy she didn't have to navigate southern California freeways anymore. Everything she needed was less than six blocks away from her small bungalow. Bob usually drove their little beige sedan anywhere she needed to go.

"Suppose I'll have to do all the driving now," she said to no one, tears pooling again before they tumbled to her cheeks. She and Bob were no spring chickens—she knew that. Still, the sight of him crumbling, slipping from his chair like a bag of potatoes from a shelf, kept replaying in her mind. *Death was inevitable, but did it have to be such a damned surprise?*

She rose and shuffled into the kitchen. "I think I'll have a little coffee anyway—for Bob. I can always take some Tums later."

The yellow paint on the walls of the small kitchen had faded, and there were grease spots over the stove that could have been wiped away, if Dottie's eyesight was better. An oak table stood in the corner with four matching chairs. Only one of them had a cushion, for Bob. Dottie always joked she brought her own padding to any chair she sat in.

She stretched up to the cabinet above the sink and retrieved a small tin of coffee, decorated in a gay autumnal theme, the orange bow still on the lid. After filling the coffee pot, she made sure it gurgled and sputtered before she walked back into her bedroom.

While the coffee brewed, she changed into a housedress, a shapeless swath of blue cotton with small pink roses decorating the collar. She returned to the kitchen and filled a green mug halfway with dark, aromatic liquid, then went back to the recliner.

A cooking show blared on the TV, the celebrity hostess showing the viewer how to make grilled shrimp escabeche for a family of four.

"Whose child would eat that?" Dottie switched the channel to watch the game show. She sipped her coffee, and puckered.

"This tastes different than I remember." She took another drink and watched Drew Carey invite a screeching young woman on stage. Dottie sighed. *Different host, different coffee, nothing stayed the same.*

She picked up the paper from the table next to the chair and read it while she drank. "Damned vultures. Think just because Bob is gone, I'll sell out."

Her pale brow wrinkled as she pushed her glasses back up on her nose.

An adhesive note was stuck to the paper. She pulled it off and looked at the message scribbled in bold black. *DECIDE NOW*, with a phone number, screamed at her.

"Pushy SOB." She wadded the note in her gnarled fingers.

A feline voice trilled from the hallway and Mr. Mustard trotted into the room, his tail high and vibrating. Dottie smiled and tossed the note across the floor. The cat ran to the paper and batted it with his forepaws, before picking it up in his mouth and carrying it back to his mistress. He leapt to the recliner's arm in one graceful bound and dropped his toy on Dottie's lap.

She threw it again, and, once again, the tabby gave chase. Retrieving scraps of paper was the cat's favorite activity. Bob often joked they couldn't teach the cat to use the scratching post, but he could fetch like a damned dog.

Dottie looked up at the TV. Drew Carey appeared fuzzy, so she took off her glasses and cleaned them on her dress. It didn't help.

A moment later, she clasped her right hand over her breast, just as Bob had done two weeks ago. As she reached out for the telephone, she lost her balance and fell to her knees. She managed to dial *nine* before losing consciousness.

Mr. Mustard returned to the recliner and sniffed the coffee, splashed across the carpet. Sneezing, he walked out to find a warm spot for a nap, taking the crumpled paper with him.

CPSIA information can be obtained
at www.ICGtesting.com
Printed in the USA
LVHW080906200322
713914LV00013B/781

FREEZER BURN

"It's Minn-ee-OH-pa."

Peri Minneopa has heard her name mangled a thousand ways and hates them all. What she likes are clean houses, and dirty martinis.

She recently traded in her housecleaning business for a P.I. license. Her timing seems perfect, when she cleans a former client's freezer and finds a severed hand inside, wearing an expensive ring. The client, Benny Needles, is a Dean Martin fanatic who swears he's innocent. But where there's a hand, there's a body, waiting to be found.

It's a brand new world for Peri, and she has a lot to learn. Her first lesson is that investigating murder can be dangerous. Her boyfriend, Skip, a detective in the Placentia Police Department tries to warn Peri, but she can't stop sticking her nose into the middle of things. In the middle of trying to solve the case, Peri takes on a surveillance job and finds that even surveillance isn't always low risk.

As these two cases collide, will Peri learn the truth behind both of them? And more important, will she ever get that dirty martini?

US $13.99

Dancing Corgi Press

ISBN 9780985506001

90000 >

9 780985 506001